Lainey knew he didn't love her.

She accepted it. But even so, she couldn't stop herself from feeling gloriously, perhaps foolishly happy. For Adam did desire her with a heat she couldn't deny. He wanted to live with her, put down roots with her, raise his son with her help.

But only six weeks ago, Adam had been planning to leave, move on. Was he really ready for this marriage?

On this bright October afternoon, as Lainey stood in a room just off the chapel of the church, she wished she knew the answer....

Dear Reader,

Welcome to Silhouette **Special Edition**…welcome to romance.

Bestselling author Debbie Macomber gets February off to an exciting start with her title for THAT SPECIAL WOMAN! An unforgettable New Year's Eve encounter isn't enough for one couple…and a year later they decide to marry in *Same Time, Next Year*. Don't miss this extraspecial love story!

At the center of Celeste Hamilton's *A Family Home* beats the heart of true love waiting to be discovered. Adam Cutler's son knows that he's found the perfect mom in Lainey Bates— now it's up to his dad to realize it. Then it's back to Glenwood for another of Susan Mallery's HOMETOWN HEARTBREAKERS. Bad boy Austin Lucas tempts his way into the heart of bashful Rebecca Chambers. Find out if he makes an honest woman of her in *Marriage on Demand*. Trisha Alexander has you wondering who *The Real Elizabeth Hollister* is as a woman searches for her true identity—and finds love like she's never known.

Two authors join the **Special Edition** family this month. Veteran Silhouette Romance author Brittany Young brings us the adorable efforts of two young, intrepid matchmakers in *Jenni Finds a Father*. Finally, when old lovers once again cross paths, not even a secret will keep them apart in Kaitlyn Gorton's *Hearth, Home and Hope*.

Look for more excitement, emotion and romance in the coming months from Silhouette **Special Edition.** We hope you enjoy these stories!

Sincerely,

Tara Gavin
Senior Editor

Please address questions and book requests to:
Silhouette Reader Service
U.S.: 3010 Walden Ave., P.O. Box 1325, Buffalo, NY 14269
Canadian: P.O. Box 609, Fort Erie, Ont. L2A 5X3

CELESTE HAMILTON

A FAMILY HOME

Silhouette®

SPECIAL▼EDITION®

Published by Silhouette Books
America's Publisher of Contemporary Romance

For my brother,
Dr. Jeffrey Hamilton,
once upon a time known as "Breeze."
I wish I had appreciated baseball
during your "Glory Days."

And for his wife, Donna Duarte Hamilton,
who is a special part of our family.

 SILHOUETTE BOOKS

ISBN 0-373-09938-X

A FAMILY HOME

Copyright © 1995 by Jan Hamilton Powell

This edition published by arrangement with Harlequin Enterprises B.V.

® and TM are trademarks of Harlequin Enterprises B.V., used under license. Trademarks indicated with ® are registered in the United States Patent and Trademark Office, the Canadian Trade Marks Office and in other countries.

Printed in U.S.A.

Books by Celeste Hamilton

CELESTE HAMILTON

has been writing since she was ten years old, with the encouragement of parents who told her she could do anything she set out to do and teachers who helped her refine her talents.

The broadcast media captured her interest in high school, and she graduated from the University of Tennessee with a B.S. in Communications. From there, she began writing and producing commercials at a Chattanooga, Tennessee, radio station.

Celeste began writing romances in 1985 and now works at her craft full-time. Married to a policeman, she likes nothing better than spending time at home with him and their two much-loved cats, although she and her husband also enjoy traveling when their busy schedules permit. Wherever they go, however, "It's always nice to come home to East Tennessee—one of the most beautiful corners of the world."

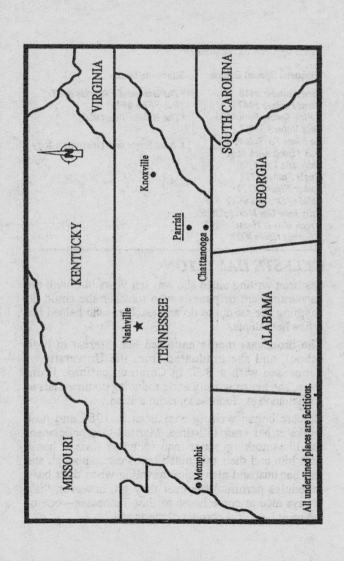

All underlined places are fictitious.

Prologue

"Wake up, dear. We're almost home."

The kind words, softly spoken, roused Lainey from
sleep. For a moment, she clutched her new doll to her
chest, feeling frightened and unsure of where she was.
Then she straightened and remembered she was riding in
a car with a lady she had been told to call Miss Polly. The
summer day was growing dark, and there weren't any
lights on the street. There was nothing that Lainey recognized. Hard as she tried not to, she whimpered.

"There, there," Miss Polly soothed. "I'm taking you
to your aunt and uncle. Remember?"

Lainey remembered, but that didn't help much. Her
aunt Loretta was just a name her mother had mentioned
every once in a while. When she did, there was always a
funny look on her face and sometimes she cried.

"Your aunt and uncle Parrish are really looking forward to having you live with them. They've always wanted a little girl."

"I want my mother," Lainey replied before she could think.

"Oh, honey, I know." Miss Polly sighed as she touched Lainey's arm. "But I believe she wanted you to be with your aunt."

Though Miss Polly had been nice to her, Lainey shrank away. She tried not to listen as the woman said all the things people had been saying to her for a while now. That her mother had gone away and no one could find her. That Lainey was four years old, a big girl, old enough not to cry so much. Lainey knew that, but still she struggled with her tears.

Finally, Miss Polly stopped talking and turned the car down another road. "We're just about there."

Lainey sat up. Just ahead she saw a house. Big and square, with the windows all lit up. It reminded Lainey of the houses she and her mother used to walk by in the fancy part of town. They had walked there often, and her mother had a favorite house, tall and broad with lots of windows and a big porch. "It's perfect," her mother would always whisper, squeezing Lainey's hand. "A perfect family home."

Lainey couldn't imagine a family needing a house that big. But her mother had told her that someday, when Lainey's father came back, they might have a house where Lainey would have her own room and lots of brothers and sisters. Lainey had tried hard to believe that might happen. On the nights when she was left alone or her mother brought men with loud voices and mean eyes to their apartment, her only comfort came from thoughts of the house they would have someday.

But the father she had never seen never came home.

And now her mother was gone, too.

Yet here was the house. The perfect house.

Lainey sat forward, excitement replacing her fear. Maybe it was all a trick. Maybe there was no aunt or uncle. Maybe her mother and father were waiting for her here.

Hope had just unfurled in her chest when Miss Polly guided the car past the house. As they descended a hill, Lainey twisted round in her seat, staring at the lighted windows of the house. She barely noticed when the car stopped. Then a door slammed, and she turned to see a man and a woman come running down the front steps of a small white house. The warm evening air rang with their cries of welcome, sounds that reached out for Lainey.

Her aunt Loretta had Mother's smile. It shone through her tears as she hugged Lainey and exclaimed over her long red hair. Uncle Coy was big, but his eyes were kind and his arms were strong as he carried her from the car to the house. The two of them were so nice that Lainey wasn't even scared when Miss Polly left her.

"Everything's going to be all right," Aunt Loretta whispered when she tucked Lainey in bed later that night.

From the doorway of the bedroom, Uncle Coy added, "You're home now. On Applewood Farm."

But when they were gone, Lainey slipped from bed and went to the window. Lights still blazed in the big house on the hill. "It's perfect," she murmured, mimicking her mother. "A perfect family home."

It was an opinion she never changed.

Chapter One

"Come on, Dad, pitch me a hard one!"

Adam Cutler tucked a baseball into the worn leather of his glove and grinned at his son. "You think you can handle it?"

With solemn determination, Gabe waved his too-large bat over the patch of dirt serving as home plate. "Put it right in here." His cap was pulled down low over his eyes, his jaw was set. Three months shy of his sixth birthday, and he already had the heart of a competitor.

Adam fought to hide another smile, trying to appear just as serious as his son. He could remember being this age. He'd been five when he had fallen in love with baseball. On a hot August afternoon a lot like this one, at one of the many campgrounds where he and his father had lived that particular summer. He didn't know now if that camp was in Arkansas or Texas or Arizona. He just remembered the endless baseball games played by the older kids. Games where he sat off to the side, shy and quiet, but fascinated by what transpired on that dusty make-shift ball field. Finally, an older boy had taken pity on him, placed a ball in his hand and shown him how to throw.

Even now, some thirty Augusts later, Adam remembered the initial burst of pleasure that came from gripping that ball. He could feel the rough stitches of the seam, the rip in the cowhide cover, the way the ball fit his hand. Few things had ever felt so right.

His playing days were now over. Bad knees had reduced his speed. His right shoulder had known three surgeries and could probably stand a fourth. He was unemployed and raising Gabe alone. But none of that mattered when he held a baseball. None of that mattered right now as he stood in his sister's backyard, facing down a small but formidable batter.

"Let's go, Dad," Gabe implored.

The redhead crouched behind the plate played into the boy's seriousness with a loud, "Fire it right in here."

But Adam took his time, adjusting the ball in his hand, savoring the feel the way some men might savor the weight of a lover's breast.

The analogy hit him just as he released the gentlest of pitches. Just as his gaze collided with that of the red-head. The pitch went wide to the left; she had to jump up to haul it in. He took pleasure in the adept way she handled the ball, in her clear enjoyment of the moment, in her laughter, which carried through the hot, humid air of this lazy Sunday afternoon. And he had to admit—reluctantly—that he enjoyed the saucy bounce of her breasts beneath her light blue T-shirt, enjoyed the way her jeans molded to her slim hips.

His interest was sparked. Hell, it was more than interest. It was pure, undiluted lust. And more than sparked, it was fully aroused. And that was just no good.

He had met Lainey Bates two weeks earlier, and had been fighting his attraction to her ever since. Celibate for over a year, since long before his wife's death, he was faced with male radar that had kicked into hyperdrive and focused on Lainey, a most unlikely woman. Unlikely, because she wasn't the sort of woman who usually attracted him. Unlikely, because his reaction was wrong, or at the very least, inappropriate. A cousin by marriage but not related by blood, Lainey was a big part of his sister's family, an important part of the family Adam hadn't known existed until a month ago.

He wasn't about to let his suddenly rampant libido interfere in the pleasant texture of this family reunion. Technically, Lainey wasn't related, so there was no reason why he couldn't be interested. But experience had taught him that romantic or sexual interest created a world of complications. Complications he didn't want and could ill afford.

Beyond that, there was the matter of Lainey's interest in him. It seemed to be zilch. A big, fat zero. She was friendlier with his son than with him. Which, aside from the matter of his pride, was a blessing. But as he focused on her vivid features again, he couldn't help wondering what it would be like if Lainey Bates, with her fresh-scrubbed looks and innocent smile, looked at him with the same interest that stirred in him.

Her voice cut into his contemplation. "Are you in a trance or something out there, Cutler?" The ball she tossed his way went right through his fingers.

Gabe groaned. "What's the matter, Dad?"

"Maybe Lainey ought to be pitching," Adam suggested, glad to retrieve the ball, glad to be doing anything that forced his attention away from her.

"But that won't help me with my hitting," Gabe grumbled. "Lainey's a *girl*."

While Lainey protested that sexist remark, Adam picked up the ball. He walked toward her, took in the long red braid that fell over one shoulder and smiled at the playful way she tugged on the brim of Gabe's cap.

Then she looked up and grinned at Adam, and he felt as if the already scorching sun had been turned up a notch. And instead of agreeing with her positive assessment of female athletic ability as he had intended to do, he said, "You're right, Gabe, Lainey is most *definitely* a girl."

Lainey's eyes widened. A flush deepened beneath the freckles that had popped out on her cheeks. She stared at Adam. He stared at her. He would have given his prized Sandy Koufax-autographed ball to change what he had said and the way he had said it. The tension beaming between them reminded Adam of a laser gun in a sci-fi movie—white-hot and dangerous.

Even Gabe noticed something was amiss. "What's the matter with your face, Dad?"

Lainey took a sudden, intense interest in her baseball glove while Adam forced a light note into his voice. "My face?"

"You look like this." Gabe arranged his features into a cross between horror and dismay.

"Like this?" Adam said, mimicking him.

"Or like this?" Lainey said, following suit.

The face-making diverted Gabe's interest in their adult byplay, diverted their interest in each other. Further distraction came in the form of a shout from the two-story white farmhouse behind them.

"Ice cream's made," Adam's sister, Caroline, called.

Gabe, who hadn't tasted homemade ice cream until a week ago but was now addicted to the stuff, took off toward the house. After only a second's hesitation, Adam followed close on his heels. Besides the fact that he loved running with his son, who was gradually regaining the little-boy buoyancy that had disappeared after his mother's death, Adam eagerly seized the chance to put some space between himself and Lainey.

He and Gabe clambered up the steps and through the door to the screened-in porch, tossing their caps and ball gloves onto a nearby table.

Caroline, whose baby son was drooling on her pink blouse, laughed. "What's this? A stampede?"

With a desperation out of proportion to the moment, Gabe said, "I need ice cream."

Caroline pointed to the kitchen. "In there. Tell Reid to give you a big dish." Reid McClure was her husband and the father of her baby, Christopher.

As the kitchen door banged shut behind Gabe, she looked at Adam. "That was some pretty impressive speed for someone who said bad knees kept him out of the majors."

He was bent over a table, catching his breath. The run had proven he was in worse shape than he thought. When he could talk, he said, "You should have seen me in college. That's when I had the speed that got the pro scouts' attention."

"I wish I had seen you."

The quiet words made Adam straighten.

Regret was shadowing Caroline's dark brown eyes. "I would have been there. If I had known, I would have—"

"Don't," Adam cut in, with a light touch on her arm. "No regrets. That's what we decided when I got here." That was the wisest course of action. But he knew it wasn't easy to remain calm and detached when considering the years he and Caroline had lost. Until a month ago, Adam had believed Caroline was dead. They'd lived thirty-two years without each other.

She attempted a smile that didn't quite work. "I know we agreed not to worry about the past, about what we can't change. But every once in a while, I get so angry."

"What good does anger do?"

"No good at all, of course." But anger still tightened her lips as she turned to place the baby in an infant's swing set up nearby. "I just wish I could forgive our father for taking you away when we were three. Or Mother for allowing him to do it. I know what happened. I know Grandfather forced—"

"You've got to let it go," Adam told her.

Caroline looked up from the swing with a frown. "You're so accepting of it all. Why is that?"

"Maybe it's the Cherokee blood. Our ancestors had to accept a lot. Forgive a lot. Then move on."

"But you and I have the same blood. And I have so much trouble accepting all of this."

Their Cherokee blood, their father's heritage, showed in her high cheekbones and defined nose. Adam recognized his own features, although softened and feminized, in her face. He could see their father strongly in the firm set of her jaw. It was a characteristic Gabe had inherited, and that little Christopher showed signs of, as well. Adam often wondered if Caroline saw anything of their mother in his own features. Even after studying the few photographs Caroline had of her, he still couldn't make their mother's face focus in his mind. The only thing he knew was that his own lean build and height had come from her family, the Parrishes who had founded the nearby town and first farmed this valley.

"If only Grandfather...if he hadn't ruined everything." Caroline's voice broke as she fumbled with the clasp of the security belt that would hold Christopher in his swing. The baby began to fuss.

Adam knelt and pushed Caroline's hands away. Christopher was secured and the swing set in motion before Adam looked up at his sister again. She was standing with shoulders rigid, hands clenched at her sides, obviously battling her emotions.

"He's not worth any more of your tears," Adam murmured, referring to their maternal grandfather, Robert Parrish. "Before I showed up here, you said you had made peace with the past. My coming here stirred it all up for you again."

"There are times when the insanity of what happened to our family hits me all over again."

"Just don't cry."

She blinked the tears away, and an unexpected smile appeared. "You always used to tell me that."

"Did I?"

"Don't you remember? When I'd fall, or we'd get caught doing something we shouldn't, you'd say, 'Just don't cry.'"

Adam frowned, trying to remember. Caroline had the amazing ability to recall many things about their first few years together. For him, that time from early childhood was nearly a blank, as he supposed it was for most people. Caroline had kept those memories intact, had kept him alive in her mind. But no amount of concentration brought anything back for Adam. And as he confronted that void, he gave in to the sadness and regret he had just advised Caroline to ignore.

She must have read that in his face, for her smile dimmed. "I wish you could remember."

"Me, too."

Before they could say anything more, Lainey came onto the porch. Caroline turned to greet her. Adam gave the redhead a brief smile as she set down the balls and bats they had left in the yard. Though it could have been his imagination, he thought she hesitated just a moment before going into the kitchen. Adam volunteered to stay out on the porch with the baby while Caroline went inside, as well.

When the women were gone, Adam took a seat and smiled down at Christopher, who had already nodded off. The baby reminded him a lot of Gabe at the same age—chubby cheeks and lots of the black hair he and Caroline shared, as well.

From the kitchen Adam could hear Gabe's giggle mingling with the others' laughter. It was good to hear his little boy laugh. For too long after Debbie died, Gabe had been unnaturally solemn. The two weeks here with Caroline and her family had been good for the child, better than the months they had spent with Debbie's parents. Adam was now certain he had done the right thing in leaving his in-laws. He would never deprive Debbie's parents of Gabe, but living with them wasn't the best situation for his son. His mother-in-law tended toward the overprotective side. And besides, he and Gabe needed to be together. Adam could handle his son on his own, just as his father had handled him.

But his father had walked away from Caroline.

Adam frowned, trying to reconcile the man who had raised him with the man who had left his daughter behind. It was something that, as a father himself, Adam was struggling to understand.

How could his father have done it?

His knew the obvious reasons. His Grandfather Parrish had hated Adam and Caroline's father, John Cutler. An embittered, prejudiced man, Robert Parrish had been unable to accept that his only child, Linda, had married someone he labeled a "dirty Indian." Robert had done everything he could to destroy the marriage. When he succeeded, John left with Adam while Caroline remained with their mother and grandfather.

Thoughts of that leave-taking brought Adam to his feet again. He wandered restlessly to the end of the porch, finally settling on the edge of a picnic table as he contemplated the rich green fields of Reid and Caroline's farm. A breeze stirred the leaves of the trees and blew through the porch, carrying the scents of new-mown hay and rich earth. To the east the farm stretched to the lower slopes of a gently rolling ridge. To the south was a creek that formed the boundary between this place and Applewood Farm, the farm that had once belonged to his grandfather and was now Lainey's.

Adam knew he and Caroline had come to live on Applewood Farm with their parents when they were almost a year old. It took nearly two years for Robert Parrish to rip their family apart. Were they ever happy? Adam liked to think so. It wasn't difficult to imagine children being happy in this fertile little valley slipped between the Tennessee hills. Perhaps he and Caroline had gotten lost in a rustling field of corn as Gabe had done yesterday. Maybe they had lain awake in their room at night, listening to the frogs sing in the creek. Or played hide-and-seek in the cool shadows of the big house at Applewood, the house where Lainey lived now. He wanted to recall just one of those happy memories.

But Adam had only one early memory. He remembered standing on the seat of Dad's rusty, old truck, his face pressed against the rear window as he waved to someone. Even now, he could taste the dust that had boiled inside as the truck raced away. He could hear his father telling him to hush. He could see his tears smearing the dirt on the glass beneath his cheek.

Was it Caroline he had waved to? His mother? Adam supposed he must have asked his father about his sister and mother a lot right after they left. But Adam wasn't sure when his father had first lied and said Caroline and his mother were dead. But he must have said it enough for Adam to believe him. There had been a time when he had actually doubted that Caroline ever really existed.

Why tell such a destructive lie? Adam wondered, as he had ever since learning that Caroline was alive. Robert Parrish had duplicated the lie, telling Caroline and their mother that Adam and John had drowned soon after leaving here. Two similarly monstrous lies from two such different men. Adam supposed Robert could have found John and lied to him about Linda and Caroline's death. But in his gut, Adam didn't think there had been any contact between the men after John and Adam left Applewood.

His father hadn't lied to him about everything. For as long as Adam could remember, he had known about Robert Parrish and about this valley just outside of tiny Parrish, Tennessee. His father had talked of this place often, usually with a peculiar mixture of longing and hatred. For the rest of his life, which lasted only until Adam was sixteen, John Cutler hadn't lived anywhere as long as he had lived on Applewood Farm. Neither had Adam.

One spring when Adam was playing baseball with a minor-league team in Birmingham, he had toyed with the notion of driving up and finding this valley. But he had worried about what he would find. His father had told him his grandfather hated him and that even before she died, his mother hadn't wanted him around. So Adam had stayed away and had been traded before the temptation to visit became too great.

It was just as well, he supposed. That spring he was in Birmingham, he wouldn't have found Caroline here. Their mother had died in a car accident when Caroline was seventeen. Caroline had been in the car, as well, but had retained no memory of how or why she came to be there. Soon after, she had run away from Grandfather Parrish. She had made a life for herself in California. She married and divorced, and eventually became the author of a popular series of fantasy novels, all written using her first husband's surname. Novels about a twin brother and sister, a prince and princess forced to survive in a fantastic, dangerous world.

Adam's wife, Debbie, had read and loved Caroline's books. Adam had looked at the covers, held them in his hands, and yet never dreamed the author was the sister he had lost.

Last summer, Caroline had come back to this valley. She had fallen in love with Reid, and she had remembered what happened the night her and Adam's mother died. That night, now nearly eighteen years ago, Robert Parrish had revealed his lie about Adam and his father's death. Afterward, Caroline and their mother had a car accident while trying to leave the farm. Then Robert had murdered their mother. Her death had looked accidental, and Caroline had blocked the horrible truth out of her mind. What she had been unable to block was her fear that his murderous anger would turn on her, as well. So she had run. For years, she had been crippled by what she couldn't remember.

Caroline now said that remembering had set her free, and that loving Reid made up for any pain in her life, that the memory had led her to look for Adam.

She had found him this summer. Her story had a happy ending. But Adam wished Robert Parrish was alive to answer for what he had done to her, to his mother, to them all.

"Adam?"

He glanced over his shoulder. Lainey stood on the other side of the table, holding a bowl of homemade ice cream in each hand. It was clear she had said his name more than once.

"Sorry," he said, standing up to accept the bowl she offered.

She nodded in the direction of the kitchen. "Reid and Gabe are about to start a checkers marathon, if you're interested."

"I think I'll stay out here and gather some more wool."

Her smile flashed. "I haven't heard that expression for a while."

"My father frequently accused me of wool-gathering."

"My aunt Loretta did the same with me."

"You?" From what Adam had seen of Lainey, she wasn't the dreamy type. Most of the time she was a study in constant motion. She ran her dairy farm and her home with little assistance. She was always doing for others— bringing dinner over here to Caroline's, sewing a blouse for Reid's teenage daughter, going to check on a sick neighbor.

"Aunt Loretta didn't put up with idleness or foolishness of any sort," Lainey said matter-of-factly. "She had no patience with what she interpreted as laziness. To her, reading a book was the same as daydreaming.''

Adam took a bite of ice cream, savoring the cool vanilla flavor. "She sounds like quite a taskmaster."

Lainey ate a spoonful of ice cream, an emotion Adam couldn't guess at dimming the sparkle in her emerald eyes. "Aunt Loretta was a fine woman. She and Uncle Coy were very good to me."

"I didn't mean to sound as if I was criticizing her—"

"Oh, don't worry." Lainey's gaze swung to meet his. "I didn't take it that way. It's true Aunt Loretta was strict. Real strict. I think she thought she had to be or I would turn out like my mother." With a sudden frown, she dipped her spoon in her ice cream again.

"And what was your mother like?"

"I don't remember much about her."

Adam read the evasive note in Lainey's voice quite well. She didn't want to talk about her mother. He was a private person himself and could respect that in another. But he had noticed Lainey didn't often talk about herself or her life. He knew she was twenty-nine, six years younger than he and Caroline. That she had come to live at Applewood Farm after her mother had disappeared, leaving her alone. Her father was never in the picture. Her mother's sister, Loretta, had been married to Robert Parrish's younger half brother, Coy. Caroline said Coy was a gentle man, content to run the family farm while Robert drove the rest of the family holdings into bankruptcy. Coy was the one Parrish relative Adam wished he had known.

Lainey set her half-finished bowl of ice cream on the table beside them. "Adam, there's something I want to talk to you about."

Her nervousness put him on alert. He thought of the sexual energy that had been arcing between them out in the yard, the interest he had been feeling since the moment he met her. He set down his ice cream, prepared for her to say almost anything to him.

"I want you to have part of Applewood Farm."

The words didn't compute for a moment. When they did, Adam stared at her.

A flush crept into her cheeks. "Well?"

"I don't know what you're saying."

Lainey spoke quickly, as if she was giving a rehearsed speech. "Your mother, yours and Caroline's, would have inherited part of the farm along with Uncle Coy when your grandfather died. But she was gone, and everyone thought you and your father were dead, and Caroline had run away, so everything was willed to Uncle Coy. That wasn't right. Uncle Coy knew that. For years, he saved part of the profits for Caroline, in case she came back." She hesitated, biting her bottom lip. "Of course, for a lot of years, there weren't any profits, but Uncle Coy and I tried—"

Adam held up a hand to stop her. "You don't have to explain."

"I made Caroline use part of that money to hire the private investigator who found you. But there's some left. Caroline won't take it, won't take any of the farm. But you—"

"I don't want the farm."

"Legally, it should be yours."

"It's your home."

"But you...you and Gabe need..." The words trailed off into a miserable silence.

Adam could fill in the blanks. He was an unemployed, washed-up ball player. Lainey thought he and

Gabe needed the farm, needed what she could give them. And maybe she was right. But he wasn't taking it. "I don't want the farm."

"I don't see why—"

"Robert Parrish wouldn't have wanted me to have it."

Lainey's eyebrows arched in surprise. "What does he have to do with it?"

"Everything."

"He's been dead for nearly seventeen years."

"Praise God."

"So it doesn't matter what he would want."

Adam glanced toward Applewood. In his mind's eye he could see the big redbrick house built on a rise, the ancient apple orchards that spread out below the sloping front lawn. The beauty of the place had reached out to him the first day he had driven up to the house. But he didn't want to respond to the place. He wanted to remember that it was that curving gravel driveway that his father's truck had fishtailed down so many hot summer days ago. He could pretend to Caroline that they needed to put the past behind them, but in reality, there were pieces of that past that Adam clung to. Those pieces, those memories, clogged his chest with anger he fought to keep out of his voice. "Robert Parrish threw me and my father off that land."

"All the more reason for you to take it back. It's rightfully yours."

"No, thank you."

A stubbornness Adam hadn't suspected she possessed showed in the set line of Lainey's mouth. "You and Caroline are both determined to make me feel bad."

Her logic escaped him. "Because we don't want to take away what's yours?"

"I'm proposing we share it."

"I'm not a farmer."

"You don't have to be."

"Then what would I do with my part of the farm? Sell it?"

Horror, too raw to hide, momentarily filled her eyes. She covered that, but her voice was strained. "If that's what you wanted—"

Anger flared inside Adam again. Irrational anger that had nothing to do with this woman or what she was offering. His voice rose. "I don't want your damn farm, okay?"

On the other side of the porch, Christopher stirred and whimpered in his sleep. Lainey sent Adam a confused look, then went to the baby, soothing him by setting the swing in motion again.

Adam took a deep breath to steady himself. He didn't know what in the hell was wrong with him, barking at her this way.

When he looked up, Lainey was coming across the porch toward him. "I'm sorry," he told her.

Muscles worked in her slender throat before she spoke. "I was only trying to be fair."

"Of course you were."

"I certainly wasn't trying to upset you. I believe you and Caroline should both have what your mother would have left you."

He was careful to keep his tone as even as possible. "That's very generous of you, but I can't accept. I can't even remember my mother. I don't want anything from her. And besides, from what I can see, and what Caroline and Reid have told me, you've turned the farm into what it is, you and your uncle—"

"He was your uncle, too."

"I know."

"I think Uncle Coy would have wanted you to share Applewood with me. That should count for a lot, since he loved the place for the right reasons. He wasn't greedy or full of self-importance like your grandfather."

"If he was the sort of man you all say he was, I think Coy would understand why I can't accept what you're offering."

He saw Lainey bite back a protest. He supposed that to her, to someone who was as rooted in this Tennessee soil as the corn growing in the fields, his refusal to accept part of the farm was hard to grasp. She had offered him something she loved. He struggled to find an explanation for turning it down.

"It's because of my father," he began after a long pause. "I believe he really wanted to live here. He came here initially because he was out of work and felt he had no choice in order to support his family, but I believe he made an honest effort with my mother, with Robert Parrish. But they turned him away. And I . . . I don't really want to take what he couldn't have." He frowned. The words didn't really express his tangled emotions. "Does that make any sense?"

"No."

Adam looked at her in frustration. She cocked her head to the side. A unexpected smile hovered at the corners of her mouth. He threw up his hands in mock exasperation, the last of his anger erased by that smile. "You think I'm crazy, right?"

She nodded. "I think anyone who wouldn't want part of Applewood is nuts."

"Don't take this the wrong way, but for me it's hard to imagine getting so attached to any one place."

"But how can you *not* love it here?" She gestured to the view beyond the porch. "I haven't seen much of the world. Not the way you have. But surely this valley is the most beautiful place in it.''

Adam saw the same landscape that she did. And something did quicken inside him as he surveyed the land. He fought it, however. A lifetime of leaving had taught him not to care too much about where he was at any particular moment. Change was always right around the corner.

So instead of admiring the countryside, he just looked at Lainey. Wayward strands of hair had escaped the constraints of her long braid and gleamed red and gold in the late afternoon sunlight that stole across the porch. The vivid color, combined with deep green eyes set in coal-dark lashes, was particularly pleasing. Adam forgot about what he was trying to explain to her. He let himself just look at her. It wasn't that she was beautiful, he thought. Some people might even think her plain. But in this light, with her head turned that way, with that smile on her lips, she was . . . unique. That was the only word that seemed to fit.

Maybe she sensed the direction his thoughts were taking. She glanced at him, then looked quickly away. The light shifted. The moment was gone. Adam was left wishing he had reached out, touched her in some way.

He let that thought dissolve into a nervous laugh. "I guess I should mark this down. It's not every day that a guy gets offered a farm."

"No, it's not," Lainey replied.

"I might even regret it when I'm gone."

"Gone?" Caroline's voice made Lainey and Adam turn around. She came across the porch from the kitchen doorway, worry knitting her brow. "What do you mean, gone? You can't be going anywhere. Not yet."

He shifted his weight from foot to foot, surprised. "Caroline—"

"You've only been here two weeks. That's not long enough."

Darting a look from brother to sister and back again, Lainey started to edge away.

Adam looked confused. "I didn't come to stay."

"But you could."

He regarded his sister in silence.

"I want you to stay, and..." Caroline's gaze locked with Lainey's, her expression changing to triumph as she seemed to seize upon an idea. "Lainey wants you to stay, as well."

Startled, Lainey looked at Caroline, trying to interpret the silent message she was attempting to convey with her eyes.

"Lainey needs your help on the farm," Caroline continued.

Adam chuckled. "I have a feeling Lainey could run two farms without my help."

"That's not true," Caroline claimed with another urgent look at Lainey. "Just this morning at church she told me how hard the work has been on her this summer. It's been so hot. And one of her hands, a high-school boy who works part-time, has skipped out on her."

The summer hadn't been any hotter or harder than most and the hand who had let her down was no real surprise. But Lainey had picked up on what Caroline was trying to do. So she turned to Adam and said, "I really could use some help, if you want to stay."

He regarded both women with suspicion. "Caroline, I just told Lainey I didn't want any part of the farm."

"I told her you'd say that," Caroline said. "I understand your feelings. I've never wanted the farm, either. But that doesn't mean you couldn't stay around and help her out. Lainey's been so good to me."

The subtle coercion made Lainey flinch. Though she could feel Adam's gaze on her, she fixed her own on a point just over his shoulder.

Caroline was tightening the screws of her argument for Adam to stay. "Reid could use you around this place, too." She took a step back toward the kitchen. "I'll go get him. He'll tell you."

"That's not necessary." Adam halted her with an upraised hand. "Of course I want to help, but—"

"You can stay and we'll enroll Gabe in kindergarten."

"Now, wait—"

Caroline interrupted him. "But it makes sense for you to stay, Adam. I mean, what else have you..." She caught the last words, but it was already too late. Her meaning was clear. *What else did he have to do?*

Darting a glance at Adam, Lainey could see dull red color creeping up his neck. Caroline had assaulted his pride. But in doing so, she had merely voiced the same thoughts Lainey had been having.

"I have plans," Adam said, his words very distinct, his tone controlled.

Caroline clasped her hands together in front of her. "I'm sure you do," she replied evenly. "But if you can put those plans off, I'd really like you and Gabe to stay here." She swallowed, hard. "After all...all these years, Adam, I'd just like you to be here. With me. With us."

The faint tremble in Caroline's voice made Lainey realize how fragile she still was. A year had passed since Caroline had put the horrifying pieces of her broken memory back together. She had faced the fact that her grandfather had killed her mother and might have eventually killed her. Reid's love had helped her deal with the truth of her past and grow strong. Christopher's birth had fulfilled a deep need. Adam's arrival had been the culmination of a lifetime dream. But faced with the prospect of his leaving, she seemed suddenly delicate.

Please don't hurt her. Lainey tried to communicate those words to Adam as she went to Caroline and slipped an arm around her waist. Earlier, when Adam had turned down her offer of the farm, Lainey had been secretly relieved. Not only did she have some strong proprietary feelings about the place, but having Adam Cutler around all the time, having to deal with her reactions to him, had been an unsettling prospect. But for Caroline's sake, she guessed she could handle it.

With all the sincerity she could muster, she said, "I really would appreciate it if you could give me a hand over at my place for a little while, at least."

She was sure he knew exactly how she really felt. But after giving her a long, searching look, he turned his attention to his sister once again. His tone was gentle. "I would really like to stay, if I could. You know what it's meant to me to be here, to find you again. But Gabe and I are crowding you guys out of your house."

"That's nonsense," Caroline protested. "It's a big house."

"You and Reid haven't even been married a year. You've got Christopher and Reid's daughter—"

"Sammi loves having you and Gabe here, too."

"And I like Sammi just fine, too. She's been a good sport." Adam ran a hand through his hair, looking completely perplexed. "But I really think most any seventeen-year-old girl would prefer not having to share her bathroom with so many other people."

"That's easy to fix."

"Don't tell me you're going to add on another bath."

"No. You're moving to Applewood."

Lainey swallowed a startled protest. Her gaze flew to meet Adam's. He looked as distressed as she felt.

Caroline paid no attention to the undercurrents. "I think you should move to the little house where I lived last summer over at Lainey's place. It's just down the hill from the big house. Lainey used to live there with Uncle Coy and Aunt Loretta before Grandfather died. I stored part of the furniture and household things from my place in California there. Lainey said, not long ago, that it was too bad the place was empty. You and Gabe should have everything you need."

Lainey struggled to hide her dismay. She wanted Caroline to be happy, but this was asking a lot. Though she had been seeing Adam nearly every day while he and Gabe had been at Caroline's, if he were living just down the hill from her they would see even more of one another. She would have more time to watch him, more reason to react to him, to think about him. More reason to torture herself.

"I don't think—"

"Do you really—"

Their hasty protests, spoken together, were quashed under Caroline's enthusiastic, "I don't know why I didn't think of this earlier." Turning before any further arguments could be made, she headed for the kitchen, calling her husband's name.

Lainey and Adam continued to look at each other.

"She's like a dog with a bone about this," he finally ventured.

Knowing Caroline as she did, Lainey thought his description was mild. But she also understood what was behind Caroline's scheme. "She just doesn't want you to go. Not yet. And after all she's been through. All you've both been through."

Adam sighed heavily. "Is this really all right with you? I don't want to make you uncomfortable or... or anything." The last word hung in the air between them.

Well-developed pride took over for Lainey before he could continue. She wasn't about to let him see exactly how much his living so close would disturb her. Though there were moments when she thought something was at work between them, she couldn't imagine that this man was really attracted to her. And she didn't want him to know how attracted she was to him. At all costs, she didn't want to look like a fool. Not to him. Not to any man. Not ever again.

So she pretended an unconcern she didn't feel. "Why not move in? Caroline's right. You and Gabe will enjoy having your own space. You won't bother me. We probably won't see much of each other."

Adam cocked one eyebrow in her direction. "You think so?"

"Yeah." She thrust suddenly sweaty palms into the pockets of her jeans and faced him with as blank an expression as she could muster. "Most of the time I probably won't even notice that you're on the place."

But she did.

Lainey knew it was over a quarter of a mile from the big house at Applewood to the white-frame cottage down the hill. She had memorized the distance years earlier, when she spent a fair amount of time "wool-gathering" about moving up that hill. But with Adam and Gabe ensconced on her property, the distance shrank to a minuscule measure.

The cottage was at the bottom of the driveway that ran past the big house. The farm buildings, a cluster of barns and sheds, were also well below the main house, separated from the cottage by a broad expanse of yard that Lainey kept as manicured as the lawns that surrounded her home. Flowers bloomed along the fencerows and in patches near the cottage. She and her farmhands worked hard at keeping the entire farm showplace perfect. She figured the habits of hard work would stand her in good stead while Adam was here. Work would keep her mind off the distraction he presented.

Monday afternoon, she braced a ladder against the side of the pump house and tried to stop herself from glancing toward the cottage. Gabe was in the side yard, enticing her collie, Goldie, with a big red ball. Lainey didn't see Adam. She didn't want to see him, she told herself, as she checked the hammer in her work belt and climbed up the ladder. On the roof, she tried her best to concentrate on repairing loose shingles. It was a struggle to keep from glancing toward the cottage again.

Adam and Gabe had moved in this morning. Caroline had put everyone to work last night and earlier today, airing the place out, arranging and rearranging furniture, putting linens on the beds and stocking the small kitchen with groceries. Lainey had helped, but hadn't said much. Adam had been pretty silent, as well. Caroline was in a fever pitch to keep her brother and nephew nearby for as long as possible and couldn't see beyond that. Lainey didn't think she was acknowledging that Adam had only promised to stay another week or so, although he was evasive about his future plans.

Lainey didn't think he had any real plans. And that seemed odd to her. He was such a loving father. She had no doubt he wanted the best for his son. But what was he doing to ensure that? He said he had taught and coached at the high school level some years ago, before making his final attempt at pro ball. His baseball career had stalled and then ended forever in the accident that had claimed his wife's life. He had spent the past year working in his in-laws' building-supply business. Perhaps he was going back to that.

Or perhaps he would change his mind and stay here.

The thrill that thought gave her made Lainey pound her hammer a little harder than necessary. For a woman who prided herself on her good sense, she had been having far too many fanciful thoughts since Adam Cutler came up the driveway in his battered old truck.

She supposed he was the sort of man lots of women daydreamed about. Long and lean and darkly handsome. Carelessly styled straight black hair that invited the touch. A ready, charming smile. Dark eyes that hinted at more than a passing acquaintance with pain. He was the hero of most heartbreak country songs. He was the stranger in town, the box of troubles you can't resist opening. And he certainly wasn't her type.

Her type. The words almost made her laugh. Since when did she have a type? If she ever became involved with a man, and she was beginning to doubt she ever would, it would be someone nice and steady. Some unassuming guy who wanted a family just as she did. Should romance and marriage ever enter her life, it would all be very practical. There wouldn't be a lot of pulse pounding or funny little tingles in her belly.

"Need some help?"

Lainey jerked up, saw Adam's face peeking over the edge of the roof and dropped the fistful of roofing nails she held. Most eluded her grab, rolling down the shingles and over the edge. A flush heated her cheeks as she looked at Adam again.

His smile was weak. "Sorry." He climbed the rest of the way up the ladder. She had to squint up at where he stood above her, his partially buttoned, loose cotton shirt flapping in the hot breeze. Sitting at this angle below him, Lainey was in a perfect position to catch a glimpse of his washboard-defined flat stomach above jeans that rode low on his hips. She stopped her perusal at his belt buckle. She didn't need to go any farther.

Because her pulse was pounding.

And her belly was tingling.

"Lainey?" Adam was giving her a puzzled look.

And the only thing she could think to say was one short, expressive word. Yet it fit, she decided. For she definitely knew more about cow manure than managing her reactions to this man.

Chapter Two

As Lainey fumbled for composure, Adam continued to stare at her. "I didn't mean to startle you. I called your name, but I guess you didn't hear me."

She finally tore her gaze away and concentrated on keeping hold of the nails that hadn't rolled off the edge of the roof. "No, I didn't," she mumbled.

"I thought you might need some help."

"I don't."

"I could go get some more nails for you."

"Don't bother."

"But I—"

"I've got enough." Lainey didn't intend to sound so irritated, but she also didn't want to encourage him to stay. Without glancing up, she pounded the last two loose shingles into place. The exertion allowed her to school her expression and get herself under control. When she finished, Adam was still standing on the edge of the roof, hands on his hips, looking down at her.

"I could have done this for you," he said. "I thought you were needing my help."

"You just moved in."

"No, I was moved in. There's a slight difference."

She pushed herself to her feet. Standing on the slanted roof was awkward, but she felt at more of a disadvantage with him looming over her. She raked a forearm across her face to clear away the perspiration that streamed from beneath her thick hair. "If you didn't want to move over here, you shouldn't have."

"Yesterday you were all for the idea."

"I still am, if it's what you want."

"What I want? What about helping you out around here? That was just a ruse, wasn't it? Something you and Caroline cooked up?"

Lainey felt a prick of conscience but ignored it. "There's always plenty to do around here. I'll be glad for your help."

A frown drew Adam's eyebrows together. "Then why are you acting like I've pissed you off?"

"I'm just hot and tired."

"Then let's get off this roof and talk about this where it's cooler."

"Talk about what?"

He blew out a breath and looked at her as if she were simpleminded. "I want to know what I'm supposed to do to help you."

"When you're settled—"

"I'm not living here for free, Lainey. Not even for a day."

"Oh, for heaven's sake, it's not as if I moved a paying tenant out for you to live in the house."

"I don't need anyone's charity."

There was such rigid determination in his posture that Lainey didn't argue further. She motioned toward the ladder. He went down first. She hooked her hammer in her work belt and followed.

She supposed it was just good manners that made Adam reach to help her down the final few rungs. She should have accepted the gesture with the casualness with which it was offered. But the moment his hands fastened on her arm and her waist, she went still.

She felt the heat shimmering off his body. She heard his breath catch in an odd little hitch that matched the sudden flutter in her chest. Her back was to his torso, almost touching. If she turned, she would look right into his face. Their lips would be only inches apart. But then what? Did she really think he might kiss her? No, that was stupid. Kissing her would never occur to this man, just as it had rarely occurred to any other man. And she didn't want him to kiss her, either. She didn't need that kind of foolish impulse in her life.

Breaking free of her temporary paralysis, she cleared the bottom rungs of the ladder and Adam stepped away. But instead of relief, she felt an unexpected stab of disappointment.

Leaving one hand on the ladder to steady herself, she watched him thrust a hand through his shaggy dark hair and peer at her with a strange expression on his face. He looked about as puzzled as she felt.

But he broke the uncomfortable silence. "Tell me what you need me to do."

Her problem was that she didn't want him doing anything that might bring the two of them into close contact all the time. She wanted to keep her distance. So she seized the first idea that came to mind. "Painting. You do know how to paint, don't you?"

He frowned. "Of course I know how to paint."

"The back porch of my house needs a coat of white."

He glanced toward the house on the hill, then looked at her, one eyebrow quirked. "That'll take maybe a day, tops."

"You can mow the lawn."

"All right."

"And trim the bushes and hedges."

"No problem."

"Every week."

The beginning of a smile teased the corners of his mouth. "Caroline told me I could mow her lawn every week, too. I guess the two of you figure to keep me so occupied with yard work that I don't notice the passage of time. And before I know it, of course, Gabe and I will have been here months and months. We'll be so settled that I won't want to go."

That idea made her muscles tense, but Lainey knew Caroline would be thrilled, so she said, "Would being near your sister be so bad?"

His smile faded. "Of course not. But staying here..." He shook his head. "It's just not what I'd planned." Before Lainey could make a reply, he dug in the pocket of his jeans for a moment and brought out a couple of folded bills which he offered to her. "Here."

She stared at the money but didn't take it. "What's that?"

"I made a couple of long-distance phone calls after you and Caroline left the cottage after lunch. I got the charges from the operator. This will pay for them."

"Don't be silly."

Firmly, he grasped her hand, put the money in her palm and folded her fingers around it. "Just take the money, all right?"

Lainey could see that arguing would only make him angry. Goodness, but she had never met a man so full of pride. So she pocketed the money and tried to think of a tactful way to find out who he had called.

As if he had read her mind, he said, "I had to call some friends of mine in Florida. Some people I used to work with."

"Former teammates?"

"That's right." He squinted at her, hesitating before he continued, "There are a couple of people who might—"

The blare of a horn cut into his next few words. He and Lainey both looked up as a dusty blue compact pickup barreled down the driveway and swung to a halt just yards from them, spraying gravel onto the grass. A teenage boy spilled from the passenger side, a cocky grin on his face, while a tall, leggy blonde slid out from under the steering wheel.

Muttering under her breath, Lainey stalked toward the truck. "Neal Scroggins, you've got a lot of nerve showing up looking happy as a cow with a brand new block of salt to lick. Where have you been for the past two weeks?"

The boy's smile didn't dim, though he darted a quick look behind her. Adam was left with an impression of blond hair and sky blue eyes before the boy suddenly fell to his knees in front of Lainey.

Adam started forward as Lainey stepped back with a startled, "Neal, what in the world—"

"Oh, Miss Bates," the boy pleaded in mocking tones. "Please tell me you haven't replaced me in your affections. Tell me you haven't taken up with this gentleman." He gestured toward Adam.

The woman who had driven the truck put her hands on her hips. "Neal, get up and quit acting the fool."

"But Mama—"

Startled, Adam looked at the blonde again. Could she be this boy's mother? She was slim as a girl in her jeans and cotton shirt. Her hair was done up in a ponytail. But on second glance Adam could see there was a careworn look around her eyes and mouth.

Lainey introduced Adam. "This is Marnie Scroggins. And this character is her son, Neal. They own a farm down the valley."

"It used to be a farm," Marnie said with a tired sigh as she nodded to Adam.

Lainey went on to explain Adam's relationship to Caroline and that he and Gabe would be staying at the farm for a while. "Neal here used to work for me. But I haven't seen him in a while."

Ignoring the hand Adam offered, Neal got to his feet and busied himself dusting off the knees of his worn and tattered jeans. He was a tall boy, with a rangy build, although the arms revealed by his cutoff T-shirt sleeves were muscular.

"So when did this hellion here show up?" Lainey asked Marnie.

"His father finally brought him home yesterday."

Lainey looked at the boy. "You want your job back?"

Neal shrugged. His mother answered for him, "Of course he wants the job, Lainey."

But Neal didn't look happy. "No offense, but I really don't—"

"Just hush," his mother cut in. "Don't start that nonsense about getting a job in town. After all the trouble you and your buddies got into last year, I'm not going to have you working in town every day."

Adam saw real anger kindle in the boy's eyes. "Maybe I won't work at all."

"And have more time to just hang around with those losers?" His mother shook her head. "No way. If Lainey will have you..."

Lainey turned to Neal. "I need to depend on you."

Anger faded as Neal faced Lainey. Adam was glad to see he had the grace to duck his head in shame. "I'm sorry, Lainey. I didn't mean to let you down. But Dad showed up and wanted me to go off with him for a while, and...well, he kinda loses track of time, you know."

Though Adam could see the softening in Lainey's expression, she kept her voice stern. "I need you here early every morning to help with the milking and all day Saturday to do other chores, just like before. How's that going to work out with football practice?"

The boy dug the toe of one tennis shoe into the ground. "Since I missed two weeks of preseason practice, Coach Medford might not let me play."

"We just saw Coach Medford," Marnie said. "I'm hoping he'll take the situation into consideration and let Neal on the team."

Lainey nodded. "It does seem a shame for the Cougars to lose one of last year's best players."

Neal looked up, his wide grin back in place. "Maybe Dad's finally gonna get to see me play—"

"Your dad?" Lainey lifted an eyebrow in Marnie's direction.

"He's moved back in," Neal said, darting a look at his mother.

"Oh." Lainey's thoughtful one-word reply spoke volumes. Marnie was silent. And Adam wondered what the deal was with the Scroggins family.

"You want to get to work now?" Lainey asked Neal. The boy shrugged. She nodded toward the largest of the dairy barns, where her full-time farmhand, an older man, was just rounding the corner. "I bet Fred could use your help. And I'm sure he'll run you home later."

With a resigned air about him, Neal started toward the barn. His mother let out a sigh and rubbed a hand across her chin as she gazed after him.

Lainey took hold of her arm. "Let's go up to the house, Marnie. You look like you need a glass of iced tea." She glanced over her shoulder at Adam. "Care to join us?"

He shook his head. "I think I'm going to take a look at that porch you want me to paint."

"Don't forget about Gabe."

Adam glanced toward the cottage, where Gabe and Goldie had settled on the front porch. "He looks pretty content."

"But you keep an eye on him," Lainey ordered in tones Adam thought taskmaster Aunt Loretta would have approved. "I don't want him wandering off. He's not used to the farm and there's plenty of equipment around here that can be dangerous to a kid. Don't you forget."

The sharp warning made Adam flush. Who did she think she was, ordering him around about his own son? Did she think he didn't know how to look after him? He bit his lip to keep from snapping at her. Not that she would have heard any reply. She was already climbing into the truck with Marnie to drive up to the big house.

Adam took a good, deep breath. Lainey Bates was one confusing woman. Or maybe the confusion was his fault. Perhaps he had imagined all the interest sparking back and forth between them yesterday afternoon and just a while ago when he helped her down from the ladder. To her, he was just an unemployed almost-relative, just Caroline's brother, whom Lainey was giving a place to live. As he had suspected yesterday, she had him staying here out of pity. And it was pity, not some sense of rightness, that had motivated her to offer him part of this place yesterday.

Well, by damn, he didn't need pity. He and his father might not have ever owned a patch of dirt, but Adam had been taught how to earn what he needed and how to provide for the people depending on him. He was going to stick around only long enough to ease the blow to Caroline, then he was getting out of here. Before then, however, he was going to show Miss Lainey Bates that he knew something about responsibility and hard work.

He called for Gabe, who came running with the collie at his heels. They walked up the hill to take a look at the porch on the big house.

The wooden structure attached to the back of the red-brick house wasn't technically a porch. Adam supposed it had started out that way. But from earlier visits to the house, he knew half the space had been enclosed into a mudroom/utility area containing a washer and dryer and a half bath. The rest of the porch was screened in, and though the positioning didn't allow for the wonderful cross ventilation Caroline and Reid got on the porch over at their place, it was still a pleasant space. White wooden furniture was covered in yellow cushions and ferns hung from the ceiling.

A close inspection revealed peeling paint and signs of rot near the gutters. Adam was surveying the damage when Lainey and Marnie came out on the porch with their iced teas in hand. He frowned and backed away, grateful that neither woman appeared to notice him.

While Gabe and the dog gamboled around the tidy backyard, Adam decided to take a quick tour of the rest of the house's exterior. Everything was as neat as he would expect from someone as efficient as Lainey. But it was an old house, and the foundation was crumbling in spots. The eaves and shutters on the west side were as in need of paint as the back porch. Bricks were loose on the periphery of the front steps. If Lainey didn't need him anywhere else—and he doubted she would—there was plenty to keep him busy here for the next week. He would enjoy the work, he decided, thinking back to the times he had helped his father with the odd carpentry jobs he had picked up.

In front of the house, Adam stepped back to admire a mass of yellow-and-white petunias blooming against the dark green boxwoods. The symmetrical beauty of the old house struck him anew. Over a century old, this house had been built to celebrate the success of a family who had come to this valley with nothing. The Parrishes had amassed a fortune, at one point owning several of the businesses in town and a textile mill that provided employment for a large segment of the population. But the family had gradually died off. The fortune began to crumble. Robert Parrish lost everything but this farm and this house before his death. But somehow Coy, aided by his wife and Lainey, had held on to this place.

What irony, Adam thought. Coy Parrish had been the offspring of Robert's father's second marriage. According to Caroline, Robert had always insisted that Coy wasn't really his brother, that they didn't share the same father. But it was Coy, whom Robert didn't think had Parrish blood in his veins, who had saved the family house. And Lainey, who wasn't a Parrish, now resided in the house Robert had once refused to share with Coy and Loretta. Adam couldn't help but feel satisfied at the way it had all turned out.

He folded his arms, his gaze again following the expansive lines of the house. Probably considered a mansion by most people when it was built, this was still an impressive structure. Yet he would bet the big, empty rooms could be lonely for someone living alone.

Ever since meeting Lainey, he had wondered why she wasn't married with a family of her own. True, she was a rather reserved woman, and she couldn't meet many people living way out here. But she attended church. She had neighbors, friends. There must have been someone, sometime. Caroline could probably tell him why Lainey was alone.

But that thought drew him up short. Lainey's romantic past was none of his business. He wasn't about to go asking Caroline a bunch of questions about her.

With a grunt, Adam retraced his steps around the house. A scan of the yard revealed Gabe and the dog sprawled in the shade of an oak tree to the side of the porch. Lainey was still with her visitor. The murmur of the women's voices could be heard in the background as Adam ambled over to sit next to his son on the grass.

The boy looked up with a smile. "Goldie's a great dog, isn't she, Dad?"

"She seems to like you." Adam patted the collie's tawny coat and got a lick on his hand in return.

Gabe sat up and looped his arms around his bent knees in imitation of Adam's posture. "I've always wanted a dog."

Adam grinned at the seriousness of the boy's expression. "You have?"

"Grandmother said she didn't like dogs."

No, Adam could imagine that his mother-in-law wouldn't like any kind of animal scarring her polished floors or shedding hair on her prized antiques. Adam knew Debbie's mother loved Gabe with all her heart, but she would draw the line at some indulgences. She had tried to draw the line when Debbie wanted to marry a baseball player with limited prospects and boundless dreams. To her credit, however, once Adam had married her daughter, she and Mr. Larson had respected their union. When Debbie had grown sick of chasing Adam's dreams, it was Mrs. Larson who had urged her to try one more time.

Adam wondered if his mother-in-law ever regretted that advice. For if Debbie hadn't gotten into the car with Adam that early February morning, she wouldn't have died.

"Dad, do you like dogs?"

Focusing on his son instead of melancholy memories, Adam smiled. "Sure I like 'em."

"Did you ever have one?"

"No...well..." Adam hesitated because Caroline had told him they'd had a dog when they lived here together, a beagle pup Coy had given them. "I think your aunt Caroline and I had a dog once," he told Gabe. "I don't remember him, though."

"Since we're not going to live with Grandmother and Grandfather any more, can I have a dog? Maybe one like Goldie?"

Adam rarely made promises to Gabe which he couldn't keep. That was the way he had been raised, and that was the way he and Debbie had agreed to deal with their son. But the wistful look in Gabe's brown eyes made him waver. "Maybe," he said finally. "When you're older."

Gabe hung his head. "Ah, Dad. I'm old enough now."

"We'll talk about it when we're settled somewhere."

His son regarded him thoughtfully for a moment, then looked away, rather astutely changing the subject. "Did you and Aunt Caroline really live here once?"

"Yep."

"I like it here," Gabe pronounced.

"You just like this dog," Adam retorted, laughing.

Gabe tipped his head back, his voice slow and dreamy, befitting a hot summer afternoon. "I like Aunt Caroline, too. And Christopher and Sammi. And I like the cows and the way Uncle Reid lets me ride the tractor with him. And I like Lainey." He looked at Adam again. "I think I like Lainey best of all."

Adam wasn't surprised. From the moment Gabe and Lainey had met there had been a bond. She had this way of getting right down on the boy's level, of looking him straight in the eye. She had done that on their first day here, when emotions had been running thick between Adam and Caroline, and Gabe had been confused, trying to sort out the new relationships. She had taken Gabe's hand, and Adam had been surprised to see the boy's response. Gabe had clung to Adam and to his grandparents since Debbie died, but with one, simple touch, Lainey had earned his trust. Adam had noticed Lainey really listened to what Gabe said. It was a rare quality. Most adults didn't pay close attention to children who weren't their own.

Once again, he began to wonder why Lainey wasn't married with a houseful of babies.

"Can we stay here, Dad?"

The question caught Adam's full attention. Gabe was so solemn, sitting there, waiting with round eyes and little-boy expectations. Adam had asked his own father this question many, many times. Until he learned not to ask. Would Gabe learn the same lessons?

Guilt tore at Adam's gut as he reached out and tousled his son's hair. "We're going to Florida," he told the boy.

Gabe's brows drew together in a frown. "Where's that?"

Adam explained in terms the boy could understand, adding, "I've got some friends who live down there. Guys I used to play ball with. They're looking around for a job for me. We'll get you started in school. Then, in February, when spring training starts—"

"You gonna play again, Dad?" Gabe's eyes lit up.

"Not play," Adam said. "But there just might be a job with one of the teams."

"What kind of job?"

Adam wasn't sure. His plans were anything but concrete at this point. But the friends he had called today had always been stand-up guys. Both had seemed pleased to hear from him, and eager to help him and Gabe get settled when they made it on down. They were family men, themselves. One guy now owned his own car dealership and promised Adam a job with no questions asked.

Adam didn't know if selling cars was what he wanted. After all these years and all his struggles, it was still difficult to let go of baseball. But he figured if he got down to Florida, was there when spring training started next February, he could end up with a job with a team. He still knew a lot of people in the game, and if he was right there . . . well, Adam liked the thought of working into a manager's position some day.

Of course, what he should really do was try to get a job managing a team in the South American leagues where he had been playing a couple of years ago. He had been into his second season down there when Debbie had asked for a divorce. At that point, fighting for his marriage had been more important than anything else—even baseball. But lots of today's big-league managers started coaching in that league. And he would go, except that Gabe wasn't old enough for South America just yet. And there was no way he was leaving his son. Even without the promises he had made Debbie before she died, he didn't think he could bear being separated from Gabe.

"What kind of job do you want, Dad?"

Adam shrugged, tousling Gabe's hair again. "We'll see."

Skepticism crept into the boy's expression. Adam was reminded almost painfully of Debbie, but again he shunted those memories to the side. "No matter what, you and me will be together," he promised.

"You won't send me back to Grandmother's?"

"Why would I do that?" Adam asked, surprised.

"She said I could come back."

"You can visit, of course. Your grandfather and grandmother Larson would be sad if you never visited."

"But the night before we left, they said I could come back and live with them, if you needed me to. I mean, me and Mom had to go live there when you had to go play ball a long way away. Grandma said something like that could happen again, and that I could live with them."

Adam did a slow burn, but held his anger in check. As supportive as Debbie's parents had been through the years, he shouldn't begrudge them a few doubts about him. Of course they wanted Gabe to know they were there for him. But that was all the more incentive for Adam to show them he could take care of Gabe on his own.

He leaned over, touching his forehead to Gabe's. "You and me are a team. You go where I go."

The boy's arms slipped around Adam's neck. "All right, Dad." He was silent, submitting to a good, long, hard hug. Then he drew away, his eyes solemn once more. "But..."

"Yeah?" Adam prompted.

Gabe settled back on his heels. "I was thinking that if you did have to leave me somewhere, maybe I could stay here. I like it here."

So they were back to that—Gabe liked it here. Adam sighed, unsure of how to reply. Was the boy afraid Adam was going to leave him behind? Was he steeling himself for the inevitable separation? That knocked Adam down several notches. While he was pondering the situation, the screen door on the porch slapped shut. A row of boxwoods shielded the gravel walkway from where Adam and Gabe were sitting. Only the top of Marnie's blond hair was visible, but her voice and Lainey's carried well.

"So you think I'm a fool for letting Glenn move back in," Marnie said.

Lainey protested, "I didn't say that."

The crunch of gravel and opening of a truck door were the only sounds for a moment. Then Lainey spoke. "I just want to say one thing, Marnie, and only because you've asked for my advice."

"Yes?"

"Glenn has never been able to settle down. Do you really think that at this point in his life he's going to change?"

Marnie made a reply Adam couldn't hear.

Lainey's voice rose. "Maybe it's my own background showing, but I just don't have any use for a man who puts his own needs before those of his children. All these years, you've been raising Neal and Jilly alone, always waiting for Glenn to come home, to settle down, to grow up and stick with a job. He's forty years old...."

Adam missed the rest of what she said. He could only think how glad he was that Marnie and Neal had appeared down at the barns before he told Lainey about his plans to go to Florida. No doubt she would lump him into the same category as this Glenn Scroggins. Adam didn't like the thought of trying to defend his decisions and his life-style choices to her.

He started to tell Gabe not to mention their plans for Florida to anyone. But the collie suddenly barked at a squirrel and leapt up, and the boy followed her across the yard. Just as well, Adam decided, reconsidering his impulse. He didn't like the idea of asking Gabe to keep secrets. There was, after all, nothing wrong with him taking his son to Florida. Whether he took the job his friend offered or not, whether a job in baseball ever came through, he could provide for his family. He had some money saved, and there was Debbie's life insurance money tucked away to look after Gabe. He wasn't worried. Whatever happened, he knew he would land on his feet.

That was one advantage of a childhood like his; he had learned at a young age to adapt to change, to be self-reliant. His early experiences had shaped his entire life. In a positive way, he thought. If he and his father hadn't moved so often, he might not have developed his athletic abilities. Being good at sports had provided an entrée into each new school, every new set of friends. Sports had paid for his college, had earned him a living for a lot of years now.

While Adam was deep in thought, Marnie Scroggins's pickup pulled away, and Gabe and the collie came around the boxwoods with Lainey in pursuit. Adam got to his feet. Lainey drew to a quick stop, looking surprised to see him.

He felt awkward, like a kid caught loafing in school. He gestured toward the house. "I'll start on the porch in the morning if you've got the paint."

"There's paint and everything else you'll need in the supply shed."

"Which shed is that?"

"I'll show you."

"You could just point it out."

She flipped her braid over her shoulder. "I'm headed that way, anyway, to see if I can help Fred and Neal with the late milking."

"I could do that for you, too."

Chuckling, she walked toward the gravel drive that led down to the barns. Gabe fell in step beside her.

Adam caught up to them. "What was that for?" he asked Lainey.

"What?"

"That little laugh. I assure you I could help with the milking. I've helped Reid several times these last few weeks."

She turned wide eyes toward him. "I didn't mean you couldn't."

"Then why did you chuckle?"

"I was just trying to imagine Fred's reaction if you showed up down there. He doesn't much cotton to strangers around his cows."

Adam frowned, summoning her farmhand's paunchy, gruff countenance to mind. "But I've met Fred, haven't I?"

"You're still a stranger."

The truth of that statement went far beyond the obvious, Adam realized with sudden insight. He was a stranger to more than just Fred. Even though he felt an undeniable tie to his sister, he was an alien here, just as he had been an outsider in the nine-to-five world his in-laws had wanted him to live in. He had never lived the way these people lived. He probably never would.

Gabe piped up, "I thought me and Dad were family. Aunt Caroline said so."

Lainey hesitated, so Adam supplied the answer. "We are family, son. To Aunt Caroline. And Lainey is...well, almost an aunt, too."

"Then why are you a stranger?"

Lainey explained. "Honey, all I meant was that Mr. Fred, who helps me run the farm, doesn't know your dad."

"Then make 'em get to know each other," Gabe said, looking as if the adults should realize the solution was simple.

"I will—"

"And then Dad can help milk your cows," Gabe said. "He might like it. And we might stay here."

Adam began a startled protest, but Gabe was already running ahead, his sturdy brown legs pumping hard, his arms outstretched from his sides as he rushed down the last slope of the hill. There was an abandon in his movements, a pure, unspoiled joy that filled Adam's heart. At the same time he admired the little guy's persistence. Even after their long talk about Florida, Gabe wasn't giving up on the idea of staying here. There was Parrish blood in him, and this land of his ancestors had laid some kind of claim on him.

Lainey was watching the boy with an odd expression. She turned to Adam, no doubt ready to fire some questions his way.

He started to tell her his plans for Florida. He started to explain his reasons. Then he stopped. He was a stranger, remember? He owed her no explanations. He shouldn't even care what she thought of him.

So why did it seem to matter so damn much? Why did he look into her eyes and feel compelled to bare his soul?

She drew herself up to what he guessed was her full five-foot-two height and instead of asking questions, started making demands, "Now Adam Cutler, you just can't take that boy away from here—"

He cut her off, rather gruffly changing the subject. "Let's go find the paint I'll need tomorrow. Then maybe I can *observe* the milking."

His sarcastic emphasis wasn't lost on Lainey. Neither was his refusal to discuss Gabe's little bombshell about wanting to stay here. But Lordy, how could the man even consider leaving when that boy looked up at him with those melted-chocolate eyes? As Adam continued down the hill, Lainey stared after him, her lips pursed in disapproval.

When she didn't follow, he turned to look at her. "Well? Let's shake the lead out, all right? The afternoon is fading fast."

His tone rocked Lainey back on her heels. Glaring at him, she didn't move.

He surprised her by chuckling. "What's the matter? Not used to being ordered around?"

She gaped at him for a moment, shocked that he had so accurately read her mind. No one had bossed her since Uncle Coy died three years ago.

His chuckle turned into outright laughter. "The next time you start issuing orders about my son, just remember how you feel right now." The laughter robbed the words of out-and-out venom, but his message came through just fine.

So she snapped her mouth shut and caught up with him. For the rest of the day and well into the night she told herself that, Gabe or no Gabe, it would be a good thing when Adam Cutler left.

After having dinner with Caroline and her family, Adam went to bed early with one of Caroline's books. He was tired, so he drifted off quickly, but awoke about eleven-thirty. It took a moment for him to remember he was in the back bedroom of the cottage, a moment more for him to make out that Gabe was calling for him from the other bedroom.

A night-light was burning near Gabe's bed, so Adam could easily see him thrashing about under the sheets. Quickly he gathered him close to his chest, murmuring words of comfort. Right after Debbie died, Gabe had had nightmares every night. Their frequency had diminished, but they still happened once or twice a week.

Finally the boy stopped struggling and cried for a few minutes in Adam's arms. And when he lay back down, he was wide-awake.

"You feel okay?" Adam asked, touching the boy's forehead for signs of a fever.

"I was scared."

"Of what?"

"He was here."

"Who?"

"Grandpa."

Adam smiled, drawing the sheet up Gabe's chest. "You must have been dreaming about Grandfather Larson."

"Not him. Grand*pa*."

Realizing the distinction the boy made, Adam said, "You mean Grandpa Cutler? But Gabe, you never met him."

"I've seen his picture."

"You were just dreaming. Don't worry."

"I saw him."

"You need to close your eyes and go to sleep. Even if you dream about Grandpa Cutler, you shouldn't be afraid. He was a great guy, and he would have loved you."

"But Dad—"

"Close your eyes," Adam said firmly. "I promise I'll stay with you until you go back to sleep. There's no reason to be afraid."

He sat with Gabe for about fifteen minutes. By then Adam was too awake to return to bed. Back in his room, he pulled on jeans and then wandered through the darkened living room. Despite the two window air conditioners that were working overtime, the house was stuffy. He moved restlessly out onto the front porch. Thunder was rumbling in the distance. The wind was picking up, as well, blowing around the eaves of the small house. It looked as if the heat of the day was going to culminate in a storm.

It was there on the front porch, with the hot wind moving over his bare chest, that Adam felt his father.

Felt? His very choice of words gave Adam pause. But they applied. He could feel his father as strongly as if the man were standing right beside him. He turned around, suddenly eager. But there was no one on the porch. A dull ache spread through him, the familiar throb of missing someone who has been gone for a long time. Adam told himself he was being affected by Gabe's dream. And yet...

Drawing in a deep breath, he thought about his father. And what came sharply to mind was their last day together. Adam had been sixteen. He spent that day sitting beside his father's bed, trying to comprehend everything the doctors had tried to explain about his father's sudden, massive heart attack. John Cutler had drifted in and out of consciousness all that day. But for one, brief, lucid moment, he had looked right into Adam's eyes and said, "We'll walk the same path."

Through the years those words had made little sense and brought little comfort.

Until now.

At this moment, Adam felt his father was there, beside him.

But why now? Why here?

No answer came to him. There was only the wind, and gradually the feeling, which Adam knew all too well, of being alone.

He stood for several moments, watching lightning flicker over the hills to the west. Sightlessly, he stared toward the farm buildings. Some time must have passed before he realized one of the barn doors was open and banging in the wind, an event strangely out of place on Lainey's neat and tidy farm.

Frowning, Adam slipped into the house and checked to make sure Gabe was sound asleep once again. He put on shoes, went outside and crossed the yard separating the cottage from the barns.

Outdoor lights burned overhead, but the interior of the barn was dim as Adam peered around the edge of the door. Thunder cracked, closer than before. In the stillness that followed, he heard the crooning voice. The hairs stood up on his arms, but he shook off an eerie feeling of déjà vu and took another step forward. His eyes adjusted to the light, and he could just make out a figure at the far end of the corridor that ran between the barn's stalls. His unease abated somewhat when he recognized the voice as Lainey's.

"Now, just hush," she murmured as he stepped farther into the barn. "It's okay. It'll be okay." The words and the tone echoed those Adam had used to comfort his son only a short while earlier.

Adam hesitated, wondering who she was talking to, wondering if he might be interrupting some personal moment. The thought of Lainey meeting someone down here brought a unwelcome heaviness to his chest. He told himself to ignore the sensation, to just back up and leave.

As he turned to go, he heard the soft, unmistakable nicker of a horse. His muscles untensed, and he moved forward again. No doubt Lainey was soothing one of her beloved animals. He knew one of the horses was quite old. There might be a problem. Perhaps she could use his help. He was about to call out when he heard another voice and a deep chuckle.

He stepped back quickly, too quickly in the dark of the unfamiliar barn. His foot crashed into a bucket. Figures rushed forward from the darkness at the end of the corridor.

In the darkness, Adam recognized Neal Scroggins. Lainey was right on his heels, calling, "Who's there?"

"It's me. Adam," he said, banging into yet another bucket.

An overhead light switched on. The three of them stood, blinking at one another.

Adam took in Lainey's loose white T-shirt and the shorts that left her slender legs bare. Her hair was undone for once, spilling over her shoulders and down her back in red-gold waves. She looked so different from normal, softer, less contained.

What in the hell had he interrupted?

He stepped away from the stack of buckets that had tripped him up. "I'm sorry," he murmured, darting a puzzled look from Lainey to Neal and back again. "I didn't mean to... umm... *intrude.*" He hadn't intended the last word to sound so suggestive, but it came out that way.

Lainey made a choked response, her hands going to her hips in a pose Adam was getting accustomed to. Neal's brow furrowed.

"I'm going to go," Adam muttered, pointing over his shoulder and backing away awkwardly. "I'm sorry. Just go... go on with whatever... with what you were doing."

Just shut up, Cutler, he told himself. *Shut up, turn around and get out of here fast.*

But he just couldn't seem to keep his mouth shut. Lamely, he said, "You two just... carry on."

"Oh, for God's sake," Lainey began.

Neal's frown disappeared; understanding dawned in his expression. He laughed and shook his head, looking completely amazed. "Since everything's under control, I'm outta here, Lainey. I'll see you tomorrow." He strode toward the door, pausing beside Adam to shake his head and laugh once again. Then he stepped out into the gathering storm.

Adam swung around to face Lainey, who tapped her foot on the concrete floor and demanded, "What in the hell is wrong with you, Adam Cutler?"

Something in her tone set Adam's teeth on edge. "Wrong with me?"

"Yes, you. Sneaking in here like this—"

"Sneaking?"

"Isn't that what you were doing? What in the world—"

"You're a fine one to cop an attitude with me," Adam retorted.

"What does that mean?"

"You're the one down here in the dark with a teenage boy."

In the long, startled moment following that ill-conceived remark, Adam thought Lainey was going to slap him. In fact, he was sure she would have.

If lightning hadn't flashed so close by.

If they hadn't been plunged into darkness.

Chapter Three

Before she could react to the power going off, Lainey heard the first urgent drops of rain hit the roof of the barn. Adam caught her hand in his.

"Come on." He pulled her toward the door.

She drew away. "Why?"

"You don't want to be caught down here in the storm, do you?"

She had waited out innumerable storms in this barn, but Adam gave her no time for argument. He grasped her hand again and pulled her outside. Together, they secured the barn door, then sprinted through the beginnings of a downpour to the cottage. Inside it was darker than outdoors, but Adam moved with surefooted ease to Gabe's bedroom. Lainey hung back by the front door. The flashes of lightning came often but weren't long enough to illuminate the living room.

She jumped when Adam's voice came through the darkness. "Gabe's still asleep."

Lainey heard him moving around, then the rasp of a match being struck. The brief flare sent flickering light over his face as he turned and lit the candles his sister had placed on the fireplace mantel just this morning.

"Are you okay?" Adam asked. Lainey nodded, but Adam must not have been able to see her clearly, for he took both candlesticks and stepped toward her. "Lainey?"

"I'm fine."

"You need a towel or something?"

"I didn't get very wet."

"But it's really raining now."

Rain beat against the roof and the windows and across the porch. Water was even splattering through the screen door and onto the back of Lainey's legs. But she wasn't about to close that door. She didn't care to be locked inside this small, dark house with this man.

Besides, the rain and the run from the barn hadn't cooled her irritation with him. "What was it you thought I was doing with Neal?"

Adam placed one candle on the old trunk that served as the room's coffee table and moved toward her with the other one. "Don't you want to sit down?"

"I want you to answer my question."

His sigh was heavy. "I assumed from your and Neal's reaction that I misinterpreted the whole thing, so let's not get into what I first thought when I realized who you were with."

"What were you doing in my barn at this time of night, anyway?"

"I noticed the open door."

"Did it occur to you to speak up and let someone know you were there?"

"Yes...well..." He cleared his throat. "To be honest, I thought that if you were down there with...with a man—"

"A man?"

"A lover...or something," Adam explained sheepishly.

"What?"

"Hey, it seemed possible to me."

That set her back on her heels. No one she knew would expect sensible, practical and plain Lainey Bates to be meeting a lover in the barn. She wouldn't even expect it of herself.

"Neal seemed pretty young, but it's been done," Adam continued.

"Well, I haven't done it."

He peered at her for a moment, one eyebrow lifted.

"What I mean," Lainey amended hastily, "is that I'm not into seducing teenagers in my barn."

"Where do you seduce them?"

"Adam—"

"All right, all right, poor joke."

"No kidding."

"But what were you doing down there with Neal?" Almost the moment the question left his mouth, Adam held up a hand to stop her answer. "Wait a minute, wait a minute, I know that's none of my business."

Lainey impatiently pushed her hair back from her face. "I don't mind telling you we were checking on Neal's horse. I would have told you before if you hadn't acted so...so—"

"Stupid?" Adam supplied. "Dumb? Dim-witted? Awkward?"

She couldn't help but smile. "I guess that about covers it."

Thunder cracked overhead, followed by a particularly violent bolt of lightning. The candles' flames wavered in the wind that blew through the screen door. Lainey shivered.

Adam was immediately at her side, closing the door, urging her toward the couch. "I think there are more candles around here. And an afghan."

Within minutes, the room was lit by several more candles and Lainey was seated on the couch with one of Aunt Loretta's old crocheted afghans tucked around her.

"This probably won't last much longer," she said as thunder boomed again. The lightning that followed wasn't as immediate as before. "See, there was time between the thunder and lightning. The storm's beginning to move away. I can go home soon, so you can get to bed."

"To tell you the truth, I think I could use the company." Adam darted a quick look around the room before he eased down into the chair opposite her.

That's when Lainey looked, *really* looked at him. She supposed she had noticed he wasn't wearing a shirt, but she'd been so angry over the way he had reacted to finding her and Neal together that she hadn't taken time to notice Adam's state of undress. But now she did. Apparently unconcerned with what he wasn't wearing, he settled back in his chair. She let her gaze roam over his firm muscles, lingering on smooth coppery skin burnished by the soft candlelight. It was a chore to wrench her attention away. But he looked at her in such an unsettling way, as if he knew exactly the direction her thoughts had taken her.

"Why is Neal's horse in your barn?" he asked.

She was grateful for such a safe subject. "Their barn burned last year."

"That's awful. Did they lose any animals?"

She shook her head. "Neal's horse was the only one there, and he barely got her out before the whole place went up in flames. I've been keeping Blackie for him ever since. He took her out for a ride this evening after he finished helping Fred, and Blackie was favoring one of her legs afterward. Neal didn't say anything to me when he got back from his ride, but he had thought about her ever since leaving. He finally called, then came over, and we checked her out together."

"Should you call a vet?"

"I don't believe it's anything serious. Vets cost money."

"And money's in short supply at the Scroggins house, isn't it?"

Lainey hesitated. She knew more than most about the Scroggins's business, but that didn't mean she should share the details with anyone else. A victim of gossip herself, she had learned at an early age to avoid it at all costs.

"Is money the reason Marnie Scroggins wants Neal working over here?"

"Heavens, no," Lainey retorted. "Marnie just wants him to stay out of trouble. I think she figures that between working here and his sports, he'll stay too busy to get in with the wrong crowd."

"Is that what he did last year?"

"Yeah." Lainey bit her lip because she had so quickly reversed her decision not to talk about the Scroggins's problems. She steered the conversation to more positive aspects of Neal's personality. "He's a wonderful athlete."

"Football, right?"

"And basketball and baseball and track. Marnie's hoping there'll be a scholarship in his future, if he can keep his grades up."

"You think his coach will let him back on the team?"

"Coach Medford's been around since long before I went to that high school," Lainey murmured. "So he's from the old school of coaching. He's known as a hard-nosed disciplinarian."

"Then Neal may be out of luck. Getting that many teenagers to work together as a team isn't easy."

"Did you ever coach football?"

"One year I coached at a little high school where I had a hand in just about every sport. I've played them all at one time or another."

"Did you like coaching them all?"

He looked away. "Baseball is definitely my favorite."

"Once Neal finds out you were a big-league player, he's going to be impressed."

"I didn't spend that much time in the majors."

"But still, you were a pro."

Adam merely shrugged. Lainey decided his career ups and downs must be something of a sore point.

She quickly changed the subject. "I hope Coach Medford realizes how much letting Neal play will go toward keeping him out of trouble."

A line appeared between Adam's eyebrows. "If he's a troublemaker, why do you want him around here?"

"He isn't really a troublemaker," Lainey said, leaping to Neal's defense. "He just got into some scrapes in town last year. Schoolboy pranks, mostly. Neal's just a high-spirited kid with a lot of anger about the problems in his parents' marriage." There she went again, talking out of turn about Marnie and Neal Scroggins's business.

"So the father's not around much?"

"Who told you that?" she asked, surprised.

"I overheard you and Marnie talking. I didn't mean to, of course," he added when she made a soft protest. "But I gathered Neal's father is gone most of the time."

Lainey pushed aside the afghan that had grown too warm and stood. "I try not to gossip about my neighbors."

"I'm not asking you to gossip." There was an edge of irritation in Adam's voice, but he didn't move from his chair. "I was just wondering about Neal, which I believe is natural since I assume he's going to be around here a lot. Around Gabe, probably. This afternoon, even Neal's mother said he had been in trouble. I'm just a little surprised that you'd hire a kid like that."

She stiffened at the implied criticism, drawing herself up and expecting to do battle. "Well, since you're so worried, I can assure you Neal has never caused a problem for me, aside from taking off with his father this summer. And I don't blame him for that."

"All right."

The unexpectedly mild response made Lainey settle back on her heels. She dropped to the edge of the couch, frowning at Adam in confusion.

"There's no need to get yourself in a snit."

"I'm not in a snit."

"I wasn't questioning your judgment," he said. "I was just wondering about the boy. It was just idle curiosity."

"Aunt Loretta always said idle curiosity was just a highfalutin way of trying to know somebody else's business."

Adam chuckled. "I sure do wish I could remember Aunt Loretta."

"She was a feisty lady. I'm really surprised that any-one would forget her."

"Is she who you get your feistiness from?"

Lainey shrugged, uncomfortable with the steadiness of his regard. She pushed a hand through her heavy, un-bound hair and tugged at the hem of her misshapen T-shirt. She knew she looked a mess. That was probably why he was looking at her with such a strange expres-sion.

"Are you like her?" Adam pressed.

"I suppose you could say that. She was a pretty straightforward sort of woman. She taught me to be honest and hardworking."

"And what did Uncle Coy teach you?"

"To love this farm." Lainey smiled at her own quick answer. "He knew every inch of this place like the back of his own hand. He taught me how to run it."

"You loved him a lot, didn't you?"

She started to toss off a casual sort of answer, but standing here in this room where she had first become acquainted with Coy Parrish, she wasn't inclined to be casual. Instead, she said, "He was the first decent man I ever knew."

Adam was intrigued by that statement, and by the tenderness of her expression. *She* intrigued him, if he admitted the truth. Her decision to stay in this valley and run this farm was at odds with the ambitions of the modern women he knew. But perhaps that was what set her apart from those other females. She wasn't modern. She had an old-fashioned quality about her. That didn't mean she wasn't strong. The very way she ran this farm, the way she had fired orders at him about Gabe this af-ternoon, proved she was far from a shrinking violet about many things. But when she talked about her troubled neighbors or about her uncle, there was a softness, a gentleness about her that had appealed to him from the very first time they met.

He thought it would be damn nice to sit here talking with her all night. To watch her smile come and go. To find out how her thick, fiery hair would feel to his touch...

With some effort, he pulled his thoughts away from that dangerous direction. He didn't understand why his reactions to Lainey ran such a wide gamut. This afternoon he had been eager to put a couple of states between the two of them. Now he was wondering how he could bring them as close as a man and woman could get. And unfortunately it was the second reaction that was exerting more power right now.

And that was damn stupid.

He stood, clearing his throat, feeling unaccountably nervous.

Lainey looked as if she had picked up on his feelings. Her movements were awkward as she pushed herself to her feet. "I should go."

"It's still raining."

"Just barely."

"But you'll get wet."

"It won't kill me."

"Let me walk you up to your house."

She made an impatient gesture. "I've been splashing around in the rain on this farm since I was four years old. And besides, you shouldn't leave Gabe."

"He's dead to world. Let me walk you home."

But Lainey would have none of that. Only under duress would she accept a waterproof Windbreaker of Adam's to keep off the worst of the continuing drizzle.

It took him a few minutes to locate the jacket in the bedroom closet he had filled just that afternoon. "Sorry I don't have an umbrella," he said, after he returned to the living room and followed Lainey onto the front porch.

"This will be fine." She reached for the jacket.

Instead of handing it to her, Adam drew it round her shoulders.

And that was his first mistake.

Because it brought them closer together, face-to-face, closer even than they'd been this afternoon when he'd helped her down the ladder and stood like an idiot wondering if she could feel how she affected him. Right now, he knew she could see how he was affected. The farm's electricity had come back on. Light was beaming from the powerful outdoor lights that stood on poles outside the barns and at intervals beside the driveway down from the house. Adam had no trouble at all seeing the expression on Lainey's face. Half confusion, half expectation, her look was probably the same as the one he was giving her.

He told himself to back away, drop the jacket, stop the impulse that was hammering inside him. But he didn't do any of those things.

That was his second mistake.

He paused, considered all his options, stepped closer, murmuring, "Three strikes and I'm out." Then he kissed her.

No matter how she had been looking at him, she was startled. He felt the jerk of her body. He expected her to pull back. But she didn't. She stood there, her mouth soft and pliant beneath his. She kissed him sweetly, with the questing innocence of a girl, an unstudied openness that took him by surprise. But his body wasn't responding like an inexperienced boy's. He was tightening, hardening, with a man's desires, a man's knowledge of what could come next.

He dropped the jacket and let his hands come to rest on her arms. He let the kiss deepen, his lips opening just slightly. Lainey clung to him, responding, her hands slipping up his bare torso. She made a sound deep in her throat—half sigh, half groan. Then she stiffened and pulled away with a gasp of dismay. She looked up at him, and in the moment that followed Adam could hear only the dripping of the rain from the edge of the porch roof and the shallow breaths she took. He was struck by her fear. She was afraid. Of him?

He murmured her name and touched her cheek, hoping to reassure her, to take the apprehension from those wide, dark-lashed eyes.

She wasn't comforted, however. Ignoring the jacket that had fallen to the porch floor, she turned and hurried down the steps and into the rain, her slim back straight and stiff.

Adam picked up the jacket and started after her, calling her name. But she started to run, and he stopped. Clearly, he had screwed up, big time. To pursue her would no doubt cause only embarrassment.

Cursing himself, he splashed back to the cottage. He paused in the doorway, however, staring up toward Lainey's house, watching until the lights on the porch went out, then those in the kitchen and upstairs. Soon, the whole house was dark. Dark and empty looking.

He felt terrible. Ashamed, because he should have known how she would react. He wasn't very experienced in the way of first kisses. There had been some women in his life, girls mostly, but he had never considered himself a big-deal ladies' man. He had met Debbie in college and remained faithful to her ever since. But it didn't take a stud to recognize the difference between a woman you could kiss on impulse and a woman who required all the preliminaries. Lainey was definitely of the second variety. Hadn't he just decided what an old-fashioned woman she was? So why in the hell had he kissed her?

It didn't matter that signals had been flashing between the two of them from the moment they met. Adam should have been strong, should have ignored the invisible force drawing them together. For even if Lainey had wanted to kiss him—and he was sure she had—she probably knew what a dumb, rotten mistake it would be. She was very practical. Without a doubt, she knew the old adage about oil and vinegar. Her aunt Loretta likely had some other colorful saying that conveyed the same meaning. But Adam had forgotten the truth of that cliché. Caught up in his own desires, he hadn't stopped to consider that Lainey was a permanent sort of woman, and he was a man who was just passing through. She wasn't a woman you kissed just for the sake of a kiss.

Now, instead of the possibility that they might ignore their attraction and settle into an almost-family sort of friendship, this kiss and the awkwardness it had caused would always be there. He had ruined everything.

Sighing, Adam went into the cottage. But even as he moved toward his bedroom, filled with regret for how badly things had ended, he realized something else. He didn't regret the kiss itself.

The way he had handled it all, yes, he hated that. The way Lainey would probably act when they saw each other again, yes, all of that he was truly sorry for. But not the kiss. Not that moment when his lips had laid claim to hers. Certainly not the way she had stirred him to sharp, undeniable arousal.

Those were feelings a man just couldn't regret, no matter what the consequences.

The hour just before dawn found Lainey awake the next morning, just as usual. She moved with heavy, tired steps around her room. She had spent the better part of the night replaying the way she had run away from Adam.

Now she could think of a dozen witty remarks she might have made. Now, when it was too late, lots of lighthearted ways to defuse the situation occurred to her. Adam, of course, hadn't meant anything by that kiss. It had been an impulse. He was a worldly, well-traveled person, to whom kisses meant very little. If she had reacted the way most halfway intelligent women would have, the two of them could have just laughed it off. But no, she had to run away like a child.

As Aunt Loretta might say, she had behaved like a newborn fool.

Lainey showered and pulled on work clothes, trying not to feel so humiliated. In the mirror over her dresser, she faced herself and began braiding her hair. But she could barely meet her own gaze. She certainly didn't like the image the mirror threw back at her. Skin freckled by too many hours in the sun. Green eyes too big for her small heart-shaped face. Hair too wavy and thick to do much more than just control. She couldn't imagine why Adam had been moved to kiss her in the first place. But whatever his reasons, they didn't excuse her silly reaction.

"Oh, God." Leaning her elbows on the edge of the dresser, Lainey dropped her face to her hands.

She hadn't felt quite so dumb in years. Maybe not since her sophomore year in high school, when she had been certain Bobby Maxwell was going to ask her to the Valentine dance. For weeks he had talked to her every afternoon on the bus. He was so nice, so attentive. She spent all day, every day, looking forward to that half-hour ride. He was the first boy to make her forget she was a homely tomboy. Aunt Loretta had noticed the extra care she had taken with her clothes and hair. Uncle Coy had teased her a little. She had finally told them about Bobby, about her hopes for the dance. They knew Bobby's folks, so Aunt Loretta had approved.

But the Monday before the dance Bobby told Lainey he was taking Holly Gaston. He even asked Lainey's opinion on the sort of flowers he ought to order to match Holly's dress.

Lainey remembered how she had felt that day. How she had been sure Bobby was secretly laughing at her. Him, and half of the people on the bus. She had held back her tears until her eyes had felt raw. When she got home she had run all the way up the driveway, past the house, to the barn. In the stall with the little mare Uncle Coy had given her for her birthday, she had cried, her face pressed tight to the horse's smooth coat.

Uncle Coy had found her there, got the story out of her, patted her back in his awkward but kind way. He told her some boys were just naturally blind. That night, Aunt Loretta came to her room and brushed her hair for a long, long time, something she hadn't done since Lainey was small. But she didn't reassure Lainey about her future with boys. In fact, Lainey got the feeling her aunt was secretly relieved that boys left Lainey alone. Loretta always said too many admirers was what had caused Lainey's mother's downfall.

From that point on, Lainey had been careful not to think any boy wanted more than friendship with her. She had probably worked a little too hard at being just pals with everyone; she cultivated her tomboy image. Later, when she did take another stab at romance, the result had been disastrous.

And now she was twenty-nine. In November, she'd be thirty. She was sure people didn't think the idea of that birthday bothered her. After all, she was good, old Lainey Bates. She could work like a man. She was independent and maybe a little eccentric. When times were good, she helped folks celebrate; when they were bad, she was there to lend a helping hand. Her life was busy, full, content.

But the things she really wanted—a man's love, his touch, their children to fill this house, a family—those things were slipping further and further from her grasp.

Nobody, *nobody* knew how Lainey ached for what she didn't, couldn't have.

But she was afraid Adam might guess.

Adam. An impossible man. Quite beyond the realm of a twenty-nine-year-old virgin. What a disaster if he were to figure out all the secret yearnings Lainey tried so hard to keep hidden from the world. Since he had arrived, she'd been having a hard time containing her dreams. But if he figured them out, he would pity her. Last night's kiss might well have been pity. And what had she done? She had kissed him back, given in to the moment. She could still feel his smooth skin beneath her fingers, his firm, warm mouth moving across hers. And she could still remember running away.

Lord, would she never stop reliving it?

A rooster crowed in the distance. The rising sun glinted through her ruffled curtains. A glance at the clock showed Lainey she was late. Resolutely she went downstairs, grabbing an apple for breakfast before heading to the barn for the morning milking. Fred and Neal were already at work. They paused to stare at her when Lainey stepped inside.

"What's the matter?" she asked gruffly. "Can't a person be late every once in a while?"

Fred grunted, Neal nodded, and they all set to work putting the milking machinery in place.

Lainey buried herself in the morning's chores, the arrival of the truck from the dairy company that bought their product, the mucking out of the barns. She tried her best not to look toward the white-frame cottage beyond the farmyard. If Adam and Gabe were out and about, she didn't want to know.

Before noon she headed toward the house to prepare lunch. During the week, she supplied Fred with his midday meals. He worked hard for minimum pay, and she tried to make sure his lunches were hot and filling. Today, however, she was already so tired, she thought she would reheat last night's supper. Her steps were dragging and shoulders slumping as she walked up the hill.

Gabe was playing with Goldie in her yard. The boy raced over, calling her name. Lainey glanced up at the screened porch, where the eaves and wooden posts bore a new coat of white. Farther along the back of the house, Adam was up on a ladder, wearing a white T-shirt and jeans, with a baseball cap tipped back on his head, whistling as he scraped the woodwork around the windows of the utility porch.

"Look at all Dad did this morning," Gabe said. "He even let me paint some."

Grinning, Lainey stroked the smudge of white paint on the boy's cheek. "So I see."

"Yeah, he made me stop cause he said I was wasting paint." He flashed a smile that made him look more like his father than ever, then dashed away again, the dog who had become his constant companion in hot pursuit. Lainey could see she had been replaced in that canine's affections, but she didn't care. The boy would keep the aging collie active, and it was good to hear a child's laughter on the place.

The boisterous pair disappeared around a corner of the house, and Lainey glanced toward Adam again. She might as well get this over. So she straightened her shoulders and started forward. As she approached, Adam didn't even turn around, yet he acknowledged her presence with, "How's the porch look?"

She drew to a stop. "Good."

He still didn't look at her. "I thought I'd tackle all the windows, up and down, on this western side. Should only take me a couple of days. And the rest of the house looks pretty good, I think."

"All right."

He tucked his scraper in the back pocket of his jeans and wiped the perspiration off his forehead before adjusting the baseball cap on his head. Then he squinted in her direction. "It's a hot morning, isn't it? I thought last night's rain would cool things off a little more."

Lainey tried her best to act as casual as he. "The last weeks of August are sometimes the hottest part of the year."

"Figures." He took two steps down the ladder and held out his hand. "Can you hand me that bucket of paint?"

As she handed it up, their gazes met and briefly clung. She looked away before he did. "I'm fixing lunch for me and Fred, if you and Gabe want to join us." She could have slapped herself for the invitation. She didn't know why in the world she had had to absorb such good manners from Aunt Loretta.

But Adam was already busy uncorking the lid of the paint can, and didn't even glance at her. "We'll head down to our place for a sandwich later. Caroline filled our refrigerator yesterday."

"Whatever." Lainey turned on her heel and left. Once inside the kitchen she allowed herself to take a deep, steadying breath. So... this first, post-kiss meeting was over. Adam was evidently going to be decent enough to let the whole incident die a natural death. Thank goodness for that much. If he had brought it up, she would have been humiliated all over again. But now, if she could just be around him and not let him see how affected she had been, things would be fine.

It was a big if. Particularly since the farm's proportions seemed to shrink more and more with the passage of every hour of the next few days. With everything she had to do and as busy as Adam stayed, avoiding each other should have been easy. But Adam seemed to wait around every corner.

She would look out a window and find him just outside, painting or repairing something. They ran into one another down at the supply shed, they collided in the largest of the barns, their trucks passed several times on the narrow drive. Gabe kept drawing them together, too. Every discovery the boy made about the farm—the mother cat and her kittens in the hayloft, a giant-size frog down by the creek, the watermelons ripening in the garden—all of it he wanted to share with his father and with Lainey, preferably both of them at the same time.

Lainey did her level best to keep her equilibrium. It wasn't easy, when every glance she sent Adam's way made her remember that kiss. She knew she was overreacting. It was clear he had already forgotten all about it. But she just couldn't. There hadn't been many kisses in her life. Not any from men as dynamic or attractive as Adam. She just couldn't be cool around him. She was so afraid he would be able to see the yearnings that he had awakened inside her. Then he would feel awkward, and she would be mortified.

Her continued skittishness surprised Adam. He had expected a coolness, a reserve, a hint of disapproval and a definite distancing. But he had hoped to dilute the fall-out by maintaining a calm friendliness. As he had told himself on the morning after it happened, it was only a kiss. A very chaste kiss between two unattached adults. Even if it was a mistake, it shouldn't be fodder for a tragedy. But Lainey jumped whenever he approached her. What was going on with her?

He toyed with trying to talk to her about it, but something told him that would make matters worse. So he just waited, knowing he and Gabe would be leaving soon and that Lainey would be happy to see him go.

But Gabe wouldn't be happy to leave. That became more and more apparent with each passing day. Adam was determined to leave before the situation got out of control.

Friday afternoon, having finished painting and mow-ing the lawn, he was trimming the boxwoods that edged Lainey's house near the screened porch. Just within his view, Gabe and Lainey were sitting together on the porch, stringing beans. Lainey hadn't acknowledged Adam's presence with more than a nod, and that had him irri-tated as all get out. He thought it served her right that Gabe was in his question-a-second mode.

"Lainey, why do green beans have strings?"

"God made them that way."

"But why did He give 'em strings that we just have to pull off?"

"He just did."

"It would have been easier to leave off the strings."

"But the strings hold the two sides of the bean tightly together, see?"

Adam, who had stooped to pull some weeds from the soil beneath one of the shrubs, peeked around the edge and saw Lainey hold up a bean for Gabe's inspection.

She continued, "Now if the string wasn't there to hold the bean so tightly together, it probably wouldn't be so tender inside. And if the beans weren't nice and tender inside, they wouldn't taste so good after we cook them."

Gabe appeared to think about that for a good, long time as he turned a bean round and round in his fingers, studying it intently. Adam could almost predict his next question. "Wouldn't the bean be just as tender if it didn't have two sides and we didn't have to string it?"

"Well, maybe—"

"Then why does it really have two sides?"

There was a long-suffering sigh from Lainey. "It's just because God made the bean that way, okay?"

For a few moments, the quiet of the afternoon was broken only by the snap of the beans. Adam continued pulling weeds, smiling to himself.

Then Gabe said, "Why can't Goldie have babies, Lainey?"

"I decided she shouldn't have any more, and the vet did an operation on her."

"You mean she had some babies before?"

"Yes."

"And you gave them away?"

"To good homes."

"But why did you decide she couldn't have more?"

"Because she's getting old."

There was more breaking of beans.

"I guess that's why my mom didn't have more babies," Gabe said after a long pause.

Adam frowned. The beans stopped snapping.

"What do you mean?" Lainey asked cautiously.

"I guess she got too old. And then she died. But I wish she'd had at least one more baby. Somebody for me to play with when everybody else is busy."

Adam was surprised. Other than the odd passing observation that most kids made, Gabe had never expressed a deep desire for a sibling.

Lainey cleared her throat. She was in profile to Adam, so he couldn't really read her expression. Finally, she said, "I'll bet your mother only wanted another baby if she could be sure he'd be just like you."

"Nah, she probably wanted a girl."

"Why do you think that?"

"My grandmother said most ladies like having one of each. Boys and girls."

"I guess some ladies do."

"Don't you?"

The beans were snapping again—faster than ever. "Maybe."

"If you had some babies, could I play with 'em?"

"Sure."

"Then I hope you have some." Gabe darted a look toward the boxwoods, and Adam was immediately certain his son had known he was listening all along. "I hope I get to live here and play with your babies."

Lainey turned her head just in time to see Adam straightening up from behind the other side of the bushes. She gave him a good, long, hard stare, but she didn't say anything. He didn't have a clue about what she was thinking. She stood rather abruptly. "Come on in the kitchen, Gabe. You can help me make an apple pie for dinner."

Adam sighed. This was great. Now, along with everything else Lainey found objectionable about him, she probably thought he had been hiding in the bushes, spying on her and Gabe. *Great, just great.* He couldn't win with this woman.

Not that he wanted to win.

Not that he wanted anything from her.

On those hastily amended thoughts, he headed out of the yard and nearly collided with Neal Scroggins driving his mother's blue pickup. Adam leapt out of the way while the boy brought the vehicle to a screeching halt.

Neal scrambled out of the truck in his usual haphazard fashion. "Hey, Mr. Cutler, I'm sorry."

"It's okay," Adam replied, wiping some of the dust the truck had raised from his eyes. "I wasn't paying any attention to where I was going."

From the porch, Lainey called out, "Everything okay out there? I heard the brakes squeal."

Yes, her hearing is just as efficient as everything else about her, Adam thought, setting his jaw.

Neal answered, "We're fine."

"Watch where you're going."

"Yes, ma'am."

"That woman can really rag on a man," Adam muttered, only half-aware that he spoke aloud.

Neal darted a look toward the porch.

Adam grunted in disgust. "I doubt her hearing is that good." He was immediately sorry, however, since the boy looked puzzled. "Don't mind me, kid. I'm just blowing off some steam." He doffed his baseball cap, raked back his damp hair and saw Neal's gaze center on the logo emblazoned on the cap. "You a fan?" he asked. Though Lainey had predicted the boy would come around once he knew Adam's sports background, they'd had little contact until now.

Neal's shrug was elaborately casual as he continued to eye the cap. "That team's not my favorite...."

"Mine, either," Adam muttered. "They traded me so fast, all I got out of the deal was the cap."

Forgetting his adolescent pose of disinterest, Neal laughed. "So you really played in the majors?"

"Some. Mostly I had a distinguished minor-league career—eleven years total for four different major-league farm-team organizations."

"I've heard it's getting harder and harder for guys to make it out of the minors these days."

"Because they've got to pay you big money when you make it to the show. Even the guys who aren't stars are pulling down a bundle. They can starve you in the minor leagues."

"That's what my dad says. He thinks football's a better bet."

"So you're back on the football team, are you?"

"I guess Coach Medford's getting kind of soft. He even canceled practice this morning." The boy shrugged. "Do you think pro football is an easier route?"

"It depends." Adam settled his cap back on his head and picked up the clippers he had dropped. "You've got to love what you play. Even when the money is really big, you can't play for money alone. It's just too damn hard for that. You have to go with the sport you love."

"I like both football and baseball."

"But what do you *love?*"

A grin curved the boy's mouth. "Well, mostly I love throwing strikes."

After a lifetime spent pursuing a dream, Adam understood the look on this boy's face. He grinned back. "You a good pitcher?"

"Folks tell me so."

"Why don't you show me?"

"When?"

"Now, if you want."

Blue eyes alight, Neal said a quick, "All right." Then he stopped, frowning as he darted a look down at the dairy barns at the bottom of the hill.

"Make it this evening," Adam invited. "I'll probably be up here." He nodded toward Lainey's house. Much as he'd prefer to avoid her, every Friday night since he and Gabe had arrived, everyone, including Caroline, Reid and their family, had eaten here at Lainey's. Since Adam was living here, it would be rather obvious if he didn't show up.

"I'll see you later," Neal promised before jumping back into the truck and taking off in a cloud of dust and gravel. He didn't even pause to ask Adam if he wanted a ride.

Adam shook his head at the youthful exuberance. But already he was looking forward to seeing what kind of stuff Neal could throw. Though he had been busy this week with painting and yard work, both of them left his mind free to roam. He hadn't been sleeping well, either, even though he'd been physically tired. At night, he kept thinking of his father, kept having those same weird sensations that had hit him Monday night. Baseball, even of an amateur nature, had always been an escape. It would be good to toss the ball around with this youngster, get his thoughts off other troubling matters.

Like Lainey Bates.

Like Gabe, who never asked for much, but wanted to stay here on this farm.

Chapter Four

Lainey served dinner in the dining room. She wasn't sure why. It wasn't a special occasion. Like her, everyone was dressed in shorts or other cool, comfortable attire more suitable to the porch than this formal room. But she wanted a change from the kitchen where she ate day in and day out.

The dining room, with its highly polished mahogany table and china cupboards, was little changed from before Robert Parrish's death. When Aunt Loretta and Uncle Coy were alive, it was a room reserved for Thanksgiving, Christmas, Easter and the Sundays the pastor came to midday dinner. The days of putting on airs and participating in the social life of the area's more affluent citizens were only a memory. The Parrish home at Applewood might be a place of some historic significance in the county, but with Robert gone, this was first and foremost a working farm. During some lean years,

Coy and Loretta had sold some of the antique furnishings from other areas of the house. More prosperous recent years had brought modernizations and redecorating, a lightening and brightening of many rooms.

But as Lainey surveyed the group gathered at the table that evening, she was glad this room had survived just as it was. The rich woodwork and old, slightly yellowed wallpaper provided a fitting backdrop to this big gathering. Besides herself, there were Caroline and Reid, his daughter, Sammi, and her boyfriend, as well as Adam, Gabe, and as a last-minute addition, Neal. Baby Christopher was asleep in a portable seat nearby.

The table was filled with good, simple food. Baked chicken and ham. Fresh beans, corn and okra from the garden. Coleslaw and flaky biscuits. For dessert, apple pies prepared from the pick of last fall's harvest, served warm with vanilla ice cream melting on top.

But it was the plain, ordinary fellowship that filled the real hunger in Lainey. Talk and laughter were what this house was meant for. Tonight, with family and friends gathered under her roof, she could even forget about keeping her guard up around Adam. She laughed with everyone else when he told some anecdotes about sharing an apartment with spiders and an occasional snake in South America. She met his eyes without imagining he was reading something into her glance. She sat back, watching him interact with his sister and the others, watching him enjoy himself, thinking how he had managed to become a part of the family and their lives in three short weeks.

Gabe had made a place for himself here, as well. The shy, quiet child who had emerged from his father's pickup the day they arrived was now at ease with everyone here. He sat beside Caroline, smiling up at her as she brushed his hair back from his forehead. He wanted to stay here. He had made that clear the first day he and Adam moved in. And today, beneath the comment the boy had slyly directed at his eavesdropping father, Lainey had sensed a genuine plea.

But what if they stayed? She had spent most of the week hoping they'd go.

After dinner, as she scraped plates at the kitchen sink, she told herself if they stayed, she would just have to adjust. Soon, Adam would seem like just any man. Like Fred, whose gender mattered to her not at all. Like Reid, who had been a friend long before he married Caroline. She would forget her foolish attraction. Life would go on in exactly the same calm direction it had been moving before Adam arrived and blew it off course.

While she told herself that, he strolled into the backyard just outside the window. Baseball glove in hand, he turned, called something to someone she couldn't see, then leapt up to catch a ball. His long, lean muscles moved in fluid concert. His easy smile brought a frustratingly familiar flutter to her pulse. Sighing, she fought that feeling.

"Something interesting in the backyard?"

Lainey glanced at Caroline, who was rinsing the plates she scraped. Adam's sister was sharp, and she knew Lainey better than most. Lainey didn't want her to guess how attracted she was to Adam. With an offhand shrug, she said, "I think Neal's showing his pitching off to Adam."

Sammi straightened away from the dishwasher she was loading. "I hope you guys realize that while the males in this group—all the males, including Christopher, who isn't quite three months old—are out enjoying themselves, we're still in here working away like slaves."

Caroline and Lainey exchanged a look, set down their plates and shut off the water. "Come on," they said in unison to Sammi, who slammed the dishwasher with a snap.

Outside, Neal's pitching exhibition went on for a while, with Adam seeming suitably impressed. Soon, everyone got in the act. Even Caroline, who said she hadn't picked up a baseball bat since grammar school, took a few turns at the plate. It wasn't a game, really. Just hitting and running. Laughing in the muggy summer evening air, taking advantage of skies that would stay bright until late. It was simple, innocent fun. Surrounded by friends and family, Lainey remained at ease around Adam.

She supposed everything would have been fine if she hadn't tried to evade the tag Adam attempted as she raced to their makeshift first base. But she did. Their legs got tangled. She fell into him. And somehow they ended up in a heap on the ground. Him on top. Her body half pinned beneath his. Everyone laughed.

Except Lainey.

She stared up at Adam in the rapidly fading twilight, and she was suddenly right back where she had started at the beginning of the evening. No matter what she told herself, he wasn't just another man to her. Not like Reid. Certainly not like Fred. And Adam could see that, she thought. He could see her reaction. She was convinced his dark eyes could see all the fantasies her traitorous mind had woven about him.

She had to get away from him. "Get off me," she muttered, pushing.

"Just a sec." He grunted, shifting his legs. Unfortunately they shifted right between hers.

"Get off me right now!" Panicking, she shoved hard against his chest and scrambled to her feet.

He was still on the ground, blinking up at her, a grim expression on his face. "Just what is your problem, anyway?"

She stalked away. And though everyone else was still laughing, Caroline gave her a peculiar look.

Lainey tried to laugh it off, as well. "I think I'd better call it a night before I hurt someone."

After that, the party disbanded pretty fast. The teenagers left. Reid and Caroline came into the house to collect the baby's things. Gabe appeared, asking for another slice of pie. They were all on the porch when Adam came to the screen door.

Lainey had just taken Christopher from Caroline. She put her cheek to the baby's head, drawing in a few calming breaths of his sweet, powdery scent. He was sleepy, content to snuggle against her, and he provided her with the perfect distraction from Adam's dour features.

But Adam wanted everyone's attention. "If you've got a second, I've got something to tell you all."

Reid let the portable baby seat he held rest on the porch table. Caroline frowned. Gabe paused by his father's side. Adam put his hands on the boy's shoulders.

"We'll be leaving next week," he said.

Caroline murmured a soft protest.

Gabe didn't say anything. His brown-eyed gaze swept from Reid to Caroline and came to rest on Lainey. Then he twisted from his father's grasp and out the door into the newly fallen darkness.

To Lainey's amazement, Adam didn't follow him. He just stood there, calmly explaining the plans he had made to go to Florida, his friends, the promise of a job, his hopes of hooking up with one of the teams in some capacity come spring.

When she realized he wasn't going to move, she handed the baby to Reid and pushed past Adam to the door. "I'm going to find Gabe."

He caught her arm. "Just let him go."

"He's too little to be out there alone in the dark."

"He'll be fine."

But Lainey, whose memories of being a frightened little girl confused by the actions of the adults in her life were still very strong, couldn't stand knowing Gabe was alone. She jerked her arm away. When Adam tried to stop her again, she said, "You don't deserve that boy."

She didn't stop to hear his sputtering reply before she banged out the door, calling for Gabe.

If Lainey's scornful tone weren't enough to make Adam feel like the worst kind of heel, his sister's crestfallen expression completed the job.

"Don't leave," Caroline said, stepping toward him with outstretched hands. Over her shoulder, Adam could see Reid looking at her with concern.

"I need to get moving," Adam insisted, trying not to be swayed by Caroline's distress as he had been last Sunday. They'd all be better off if he had never moved to Lainey's place with Gabe. "School starts next week around here. So that tells me I need to get Gabe enrolled in a school down in Florida before Labor Day."

"But what if you don't go to work for your friend with the car dealership? Maybe the job won't really be there for you."

"This guy wouldn't lie to me."

"But what if you hate it?"

"I'll be okay. I have some money put back."

"Then what happens in February if you do end up with a job with one of the teams? You'll probably have to travel, and there'll be no one to help you with Gabe."

"You don't have to worry. I'll work something out."

She touched his arm, her hands cool against his skin. "You don't really want to sell cars, Adam. At least stay here until spring training starts. I really want you here."

"But what would I do?"

"Help Lainey and Reid, like you're doing now."

Adam laughed. "It's not easy to let people invent things for me to do. I have some pride, Caroline, and I'm used to making my own way."

"But Adam, we're your family—"

"You're not losing me."

"It feels that way." For the second time in less than five minutes a woman pushed past Adam and out the door.

He gave Reid a wry smile. "My luck's not running too well with females, is it?"

"Nope." With his son held expertly against one shoulder, Reid frowned at Adam. "You haven't asked my opinion, but I think you ought to give a lot of good, hard thought to what Caroline has said."

"Reid—"

"I know where you're coming from," Reid interrupted. "I understand about pride and all that. But after my first wife left, I raised Sammi on my own. It's not easy."

"I know that."

"So why do it, when you've got a family who wants to help you?"

"Listen, my in-laws wanted to help the same as you guys do. They gave me a job. I hated it."

"And you're going to love selling cars?"

Adam couldn't answer Reid's skepticism. He merely shrugged. "I just want to make my own way with my son, okay?"

Reid lifted the portable baby seat with his free hand. "If you do decide to stay, keep in mind that I won't have to invent any work for you, no matter what you think. Neither will Lainey. If you stay and want to work, you'll make your own way." He headed toward the door. "Now if you'll excuse me, I think I need to see if Caroline's okay."

"I'm sorry she's so upset." Adam swung the door open so Reid and the baby could pass.

Pausing on the threshold, Reid looked him right in the eye. "I hope you appreciate that I don't care for Caroline being hurt."

"I understand," Adam replied steadily.

"Then give this whole thing a little more thought, why don't you?"

A few moments later, Reid and Caroline's car engine started. Adam walked to the edge of the driveway, watching until he saw their taillights turn onto the county road. Then the evening air was very quiet. Hot and still. Fragrant from the freshly mown grass and the roses that grew over an arbor at the corner of the lawn.

Adam wasn't worried about Gabe. He was sure Lainey would find him. And though it was upsetting to realize how much his son wanted to remain here, Adam was equally sure Gabe would get over it. The boy was young and resilient and would be fine once they made the move.

He wished Caroline would try to look at things from his perspective. He hadn't come here to stay. He had left his in-laws with every intention of moving on. This was just a stop. A good stop, yes, but not a destination. He would be back. Many times. He and Caroline had found one another. That meant a great deal to him. Nothing could change that. Their relationship could continue to grow, even long-distance. That's why telephones, airplanes and automobiles were invented.

But I need to go, Adam told himself as he started down the driveway. He felt the familiar itch to make a change. He supposed that was something few people who hadn't shared his type of upbringing or life could understand.

Lainey certainly couldn't. Adam met her and Gabe beneath one of the big outdoor lights, about midway down the hill to the cottage. His son wouldn't look at him. There was ice in Lainey's gaze.

With her arm laid across the boy's shoulders, she said, "He'd like to spend the night with me."

"No," Adam replied.

"But—"

"No buts." Adam caught Gabe's chin in his hand, forcing him to look up at him. "Getting Lainey to feel sorry for you isn't going to get you anywhere. Now go on and get ready for bed."

Gabe's lips trembled, but his gaze didn't falter from Adam's. Then he walked toward their place with his head up and shoulders back.

"You're heartless," Lainey muttered when the child was out of earshot.

"That's a popular opinion tonight."

"I'm sure Caroline's as devastated as Gabe."

Adam struggled to keep his tone mild. "Caroline and Gabe and the rest of you should stop acting like this is some form of child torture."

"Maybe it is."

Sighing, Adam started to walk away. "I don't have to discuss this with you. I don't know why I'm even trying."

"Perhaps it's your guilty conscience."

He wheeled back to face her. "My conscience is clean. But yours shouldn't be. By running after him, plying him with sympathy, you just made him more miserable."

"I don't think it's wrong to comfort a child."

"Comfort is one thing. But when you try to subvert a parent's authority, that's something else. And I don't appreciate it."

Her laughter was short and mirthless. "Subvert your authority? Good God, is that what I was doing? I found him crying in the hayloft. I just held him and let him cry."

"And did you tell him that maybe, just maybe I might be talked into changing my mind about leaving?"

Lainey opened her mouth, but a denial didn't follow.

Adam grunted. "Gotcha, didn't I?" Again, he took a couple of steps away.

"You should change your mind."

He stopped, silently counted to ten, then turned. He kept his voice low and controlled as he approached her. "I don't understand why you're doing this. We both know you'd love to see me go. I don't see that what I did—what *we* did the other night—was enough to get you so all-fired mad at me, but I can see that you are. Hell, you almost took a swing at me during that stupid ball game. So why are you asking me to stay?"

She sucked in her breath. Adam could see her jaw tighten. But she faced him straight on and didn't address the issue of what had occurred between the two of them. "Gabe's had enough disappointment and heartache. He misses his mother so terribly much."

"You think I don't know that? I miss her, too. And I know exactly what he's feeling, because I grew up without my mother."

"And so did I—"

"Staying here won't lessen his pain over Debbie's death."

"But why cause him more pain? You've already taken him away from his grandparents. Why move him again?"

Adam's hold on his anger finally gave way. "Stop acting like this is something horrible I'm wanting to do! I'm sorry Gabe doesn't want to leave, but hey, he's not the one in charge. Life's about all changes and compromises, and he'd best get used to that now."

"But he's a baby."

"He'll be six in early November. He is *not* a baby. He is old enough to know that he doesn't get his way all the time."

"I guess you found that out early yourself—traveling wherever your father's whims took him."

Wincing at her choice of words, he struggled again to rein in his temper. "We may have moved a lot, but my life wasn't so bad."

She gave him a hard, assessing glance. "Not so bad, but not so good, right?"

"That's not what I said."

"If your life on the road with your father was good, then that's the word you would have used to describe it. But you didn't."

"You're twisting my words. You didn't know my father. You can't know how it was for us, how we took care of each other."

"Is that what you want for Gabe? You want him to take care of you?"

Adam started a protest that died quickly. Because he didn't want Gabe to take care of him. At least not the way Lainey meant, and not the way he had ended up caring for his own father. During the last year of John Cutler's life, the miles had caught up with him. Adam had been young, and he had stood by in confusion as the loss and pain of a past he hadn't understood gradually closed in on his father. They had moved four times during that last twelve months. Whatever John had been running from pursued him to the end.

Then Adam had been alone. Desperately, terribly alone.

No, he didn't want that for Gabe. But staying here wasn't the only solution.

"I'm not staying," he said bluntly.

Lainey raised one clenched fist, then let it fall back to her side. Her voice softened. "Would it hurt to stay here just a while, just six months? Couldn't you do it for Gabe, or for Caroline?"

Raw anger churned inside him again. She was getting to him, and Adam didn't like that one bit. His own arguments for leaving, compelling days ago, only moments ago, felt vague and unconvincing right now. So he snagged hold of the first thought that came to mind. "Six months here sounds like purgatory to me."

Lainey's eyes widened.

He wasn't sure why he wanted to hurt her, but he did. "I'm not much interested in hick towns like this one. I would have stayed with my in-laws, if that's what I wanted. And if I had the slightest interest in this farm, I'd have taken you up on your offer to split the land with me. There's not a thing on the place that I'm interested in."

Lainey felt as if he'd slapped her. For surely the meaning behind his last statement was directed right at her. He wasn't interested in *her*. Though it was no surprise, it hurt to hear him say it.

The ache in her chest was all out of proportion to the situation. She'd been off kilter all week, all month. She should walk calmly away before she did something more to humiliate herself. Her brain told her to move, but she didn't. She couldn't just leave without defending her home, if not herself. And for Gabe's sake, she wanted to make a point to Adam.

Struggling to keep her emotions level, she tipped her head back. Insects were swirling in kamikaze flights around the light above them. She identified with their self-destructive ways, and like them she didn't stop. "There are lots worse places than this town or this farm," she murmured.

"How would you know? Where have you been but here?"

"I've been . . ." Lainey swallowed hard. She rarely thought of the first four years of her life, of the time spent in Memphis and New Orleans with her mother. She never spoke of it. But she felt compelled to do so now. She wanted him to know she wasn't just some dewy-eyed country bumpkin who had never left the farm. She was an innocent in many ways, but not in her view of the world. And she understood Gabe's perspective.

Hands again balling into fists at her sides, she looked at Adam, who was watching her with ill-concealed impatience. "I have been somewhere else," she told him. "I used to live in another world."

"What do you mean?"

"I lived in a room with my mother. A room where she entertained friends, *men* friends, while I pretended to be asleep."

Adam's low sound of dismay interrupted her, but Lainey held up her hand to stop him when he took a step forward. Her voice shook, but she persevered. "I lived in places where I was hungry and cold and scared. Those are the places I call purgatory. And I suppose that's also why I think of this farm as paradise."

The harsh overhead light set Adam's face in lines and shadows as he stared at her for a long, long moment. But his voice was soft when he finally spoke. "I'm sorry, Lainey. I guess I understand a little better why you feel the way you do about this place."

"I'm sorry, too," Lainey replied, suddenly embarrassed by what she had revealed. "Maybe I didn't need to tell you all that about me and my...my mother. It was over and done with a long time ago, and she sent me here to Loretta and Coy before anything happened...before I..." She couldn't bring herself to speculate on the fate that might have been hers if her mother hadn't finally left her at a Memphis police station with Loretta's name and phone number taped to her dress.

"She did the right thing," Adam said.

"You're right. I know that. And that's why I want Gabe—"

Adam interrupted with a fierce, "I hope to God you're not comparing me to your mother."

Her reply was fast and emphatic. "Oh, no. Of course not."

"My son will never be cold, hungry or neglected."

"Of course not, but—"

"Then what does this have to do with him?"

"I'm just saying that like me, he *has* been through a lot, and he's responded so well to being here, and he wants to stay. I understand his feelings, you see, because I felt the very same way when I came here to live. Here, I just felt so safe."

"Gabe's safe wherever I am."

"But..." She bit her lip, afraid to go too far.

"What?"

She took the plunge. "Gabe needs more than you."

There was only silence from Adam.

"He needs a family."

"I'm his family."

"He wants more." Taking another deep breath, she decided to go way out on a limb. "And I think you want more, too. I was watching you tonight, at the table—"

"You don't know what I want."

"But Adam—"

"I think you'd better stop, Lainey." Rather than merely angry, his voice had gone steely cold.

Lainey broke off her next protest.

"I appreciate your concern," Adam said. "I appreciate everyone's concern. But I don't need your help. I don't need a place to live. Or a job any of you can give me. I don't need your charity. Or even your advice. Until three weeks ago, none of you even knew me, so I'd like you all to just shut up and leave me the hell alone."

His tone brooked no argument. She bowed her head in defeat.

And Adam walked away.

That was that.

She went home, too. She retreated to her corner of the farm and thought about the man and the boy alone in the little house where she had once lived. For hours, she thought about the rooms that would be empty when they left.

Empty and lonely.

A lot like her.

In the morning, Lainey went about her business as usual. No one stirred at Adam and Gabe's place. Only the truck parked beside the house gave evidence that they were home. Though Goldie lay on the front steps with a hopeful air about her, the boy didn't come out to play. It was a prelude of things to come, Lainey thought. The dog would miss her playmate.

Lainey drew on her practical nature and told herself it was all for the best.

But late in the afternoon she was looking from her kitchen window down toward the cottage for perhaps the fiftieth time, when Caroline came through the back door calling her name.

Seeing her, Caroline let out an unexpected squeal. "You're not going to believe what's happened."

"You're pregnant again?" Lainey ventured.

Caroline, her face coloring, looked startled. "Well, maybe, but that's not what I'm talking about." She was practically jumping up and down with excitement. "Coach Medford found out yesterday that he's got a serious heart problem."

Lainey blinked. "And that's good news?"

"His doctor has already scheduled a bypass operation, and he told the school board this morning that he's taking a leave of absence. Effective immediately."

Lainey just wasn't following why this would cause Caroline this sort of elation. "Why are you so happy about this?"

Caroline grabbed her hands and squeezed them. "His assistant is taking over as head coach. But they have to replace the assistant, too. Reid has already talked to the school superintendent about Adam taking the job. They want to see him tomorrow afternoon."

"On a Sunday?"

"School starts next week. There's a football jamboree on Friday night. They have to do something fast. Adam is exactly what they need."

Stifling a groan, Lainey sat down at the kitchen table.

"What's the matter?" Caroline demanded.

"What makes you think Adam will even consent to the interview?"

Caroline's jaw squared. "I'll make him."

"You can't do that."

"Yes, I can. He's my twin brother—"

"But you don't really know him."

Blinking in surprise, Caroline placed her hands on her hips. "Why in the world would you say something like that to me?"

Upsetting Caroline was the last thing Lainey would ever intentionally do. But she thought it was time the woman faced up to a few things. "You don't know him," she insisted, thinking of what Adam had said to her last night. "You lived apart all these years. You thought he was dead."

"That doesn't matter." Caroline put her hand over her heart. "Adam was always alive for me right here." Her hand curled into a fist. "Right where it really counts. So I *do* know him. I know he really wants to stay here."

Lainey had to laugh. "I sort of told him the same thing last night."

"And?"

She shook her head. "I think I really made him angry. He's probably more determined than ever to get out of here."

Caroline squared her shoulders. "Then I guess I'd better get busy." She left without a backward glance.

Sighing, Lainey got up and went back to the window to stare down at the cottage where Caroline's car soon drew to a stop. "She just might be able to do it," she mumbled to the empty kitchen.

The idea gradually took hold inside her.

And struck by inspiration, she got out the telephone book. She was a taxpayer, and she knew a couple of people on the school board quite well from church and the farmer's co-op. Reid had already made similar calls, but if Caroline actually managed to talk Adam into going to that interview tomorrow, it wouldn't hurt to try and stack the deck in his favor.

As she dialed the first number, she told herself she was doing this for Caroline. Before the second call, she decided it was for Gabe. After the third call, she gave in and admitted she was doing this for herself.

Quite apart from anything or anyone else, she just wanted Adam to stay. Despite all the confusing emotions he evoked in her, she wanted him here.

Just for a little while.

Just to see what would happen.

She realized that until Adam showed up she hadn't had to wonder about what would happen. Her days rarely deviated from a preset pattern. Sometime long ago, the little girl who used to wool-gather on a frequent basis had turned into a woman afraid to dream, afraid to hope. More than the absence of a man in her life, the absence of hope was eating her alive. She didn't want to end up a shell of a woman. She wanted to live. And Adam made her feel alive.

Of course, Aunt Loretta would have said...

Firmly, Lainey shut her mind to the advice she knew her aunt would have given. Her fears that Lainey would end up like her mother had caused part of this problem. Good, decent, kind Loretta Parrish had done what she thought was right. But she had helped create a woman who ran from possibilities and hid from the world. And that had to change. Lainey wanted to change—with Adam.

She went back to the window and looked to see if Caroline's car was still at the cottage. When she saw that it was, Lainey made herself a promise.

If Adam stayed and if he ever kissed her again, she wasn't going to run away.

Sitting in the conference room of the county schools' administrative offices, facing a panel of interviewers, Adam silently cursed persuasive women.

He thought he had learned about female coercion from his wife. But Debbie was a rank amateur when compared to his twin sister.

He had been watching a ball game on television while Gabe sulked in a bedroom when Caroline appeared at the cottage yesterday. She was full of enthusiasm about this coaching job, and full of arguments for why he should stay—at least until after the first of the year.

Adam, weakened by last night's argument with Lainey, weakened by a day spent indoors with a recalcitrant child, had put up a valiant fight. He sent Gabe outside and dug in his heels. They left skid marks all the way from Applewood Valley to this afternoon's interview.

He now faced the scrutiny of the five-member school board, the school superintendent, the high-school principal and the new acting head football coach. They were seated at a long table in a conference room. Adam sat at one end, facing them, uncomfortable in a sports jacket and tie. But uncomfortable mainly because he was going to get the job.

When he had wearily given in to Caroline yesterday, he had told himself there were no risks involved. He could appease her by at least going for the interview, but he was sure he wouldn't be offered anything. He wasn't really qualified. He had played football in elementary and high school, yes—at a total of nine different schools. Just before and after Gabe was born, he had coached the sport for two seasons at a small high school. His expertise was baseball. Most of his life had been baseball. He figured these good folks would take one look at his work experience and send him packing with a handshake, a smile and a thanks, but no thanks.

He was wrong.

They wanted someone to take over two history classes in addition to the assistant coaching duties for the football team. He had minored in history in college, had taught it for one of the two years he had coached. Besides that, there were the recommendations the board had received from Reid. And it seemed Lainey had been busy, as well, calling everyone with her own testimonial. In addition, there was Adam's status as the son of Linda Parrish. Despite the family history involved, the name still carried some weight.

A blond school-board member who had been eyeing him in a speculative way ever since she came in the room, said, "Mr. Cutler, your arrival here is almost providential."

Perspiration collected at the small of his back and on his forehead. These people were really going to hire him. Their heads were nodding so fast they reminded him of a group of those plastic dogs he used to see in the back windows of cars.

Adam did his best to put the brakes on. "I haven't taught in almost four years, you know."

The principal, who reminded Adam of a crustier version of Santa Claus, peered over his glasses. "You haven't forgotten how, have you?"

Adam was tempted to lie and say yes, but that would mean he had completely wasted their time. Caroline and Reid, who had set this up, would look like fools. So Adam went on to his next protest. "What about my teaching certificate? Will the state allow—"

A gray-haired woman waved her hand in dismissal. "We're in a bind here, needing a coach and a teacher with school set to start this week. We can hire you now, on a temporary basis, and you can take the test to get certified later."

Adam made one last stab at downshifting the process. "I don't want to teach the whole year, you know."

"Good," Santaman shot back. "We probably won't need you all year. There's every reason to think Coach Medford will be back after the first of the year."

"Although," the newly appointed head coach said with a smile as bright as a headlight's beam, "I sure would love to have you around for baseball season. Someone with your experience—"

"Are we almost through here?" another board member asked, looking at his watch. "It is Sunday afternoon. The Braves are playing the Dodgers on TV at four, and I don't want to miss it."

The school superintendent stood and extended his hand to Adam. "We'll have to do just a little checking of your credentials and talk this over. We'll let you know no later than tomorrow night." But his wink told Adam that this was a done deal.

After thanking them all Adam went outside, where a drizzling rain was only exacerbating the heat and humidity. He paused under the overhang of the building, yanked the knot in his tie loose and shrugged out of his jacket. His underarms were damp and his head was spinning. All in all, he felt like a man driving the wrong direction on a Los Angeles highway.

"What in the hell have I done?" he muttered aloud.

Hearing voices in the building behind him, he sprinted for his truck. He peeled out of the parking lot as fast as he could, hoping they'd see him and decide they didn't need to hire someone so reckless.

But he obeyed the speed limit as he drove down the sleepy main street of Parrish. The high school was on the outskirts of town. *Outskirts.* The word made him laugh. What kind of outskirts could a town that was only four or five blocks square have? Shaking his head, he drew to a stop across the street from the school building. It was pretty standard stuff, square and red brick, three stories high. A sign outside read Parrish County High School, Home of the Cougars.

"Support our team," Adam read from the banner stretched beneath the sign. Then he shoved his truck into gear once more and headed for the farm.

He could get out of this job, he told himself. He could turn it down, say he'd changed his mind. Caroline would be hurt, Gabe disappointed, and Lainey...

Thinking of Lainey, he released a frustrated sigh. He hadn't been able to get what she'd told him about her mother out of his mind. She was a private woman, someone who didn't even gossip about her neighbors without qualm, but she had opened up, told him something profoundly disturbing about herself, all in an attempt to get him to stay here with Gabe. Of course, she had made an impact. Most of all, she had made him think about his own childhood.

Though he hadn't suffered as Lainey had as a young child, he certainly hadn't grown up in the ideal "Leave It to Beaver" way. The bond between him and his father had been strong. Moving around made them dependent on each other. Adam had learned to like the sudden changes. When he was young, his father told him they were like two birds, and they could fly whenever they wanted.

But if they had grounded somewhere, would his life have been easier, at the very least, different?

When his father died, they had been living in Northern California. Adam was a junior in high school, but had only been there for a few short weeks. They had no ties to the community, no friends. Though Adam knew his grandfather might be alive in Tennessee, he hadn't told the authorities. He wound up in a foster home, a good one, with a nice couple. He completed high school, went to college on a baseball scholarship, met Debbie, married her and was drafted by his first pro team before his senior year.

Debbie, a small-town girl, had liked the idea of travel. The minor-league teams, with their assortment of bachelors and young couples mostly far from home, had fulfilled the need for family and friends. In the off-season, Adam sometimes played in other leagues, other times they stayed with Debbie's family. Injuries knocked him out of ball for one full year, during which Debbie persuaded him to complete his college degree. He made it to the majors the next year. Then Debbie decided she wanted to have a baby, and everything changed. Her unhappiness began. Their marriage started to unravel.

She had wanted him to settle somewhere and coach. In high school, college, *somewhere* where they could have a home and family. And Adam had tried. But those wings of his, the ones his father had given him, how they had itched. So he had flown. Debbie had issued her final ultimatum. He had come home from South America, and she had died.

He wondered now what might have happened if they hadn't had the accident. Could they have found a compromise? Could he have stayed in one spot long enough to suit her?

At the entrance to Applewood Farm, Adam let his truck idle. Rain continued to fall in a slow, steady rhythm. The smell of damp earth filtered through his half-open window. He had to admit he liked that fresh, natural smell. He liked the green of the ridge in the distance. He liked this land. Friday night, Lainey said he really wanted to stay. Caroline had said the same thing. But they had to be wrong. There was nothing about this life, this *settledness* that he wanted.

And yet . . .

He felt his father here. Not in the supernatural sense that had spooked him so on that first night he had spent in Lainey's cottage. But John Cutler was here, with him, in spirit. Now why should that be, on land that had once belonged to a man John hated?

Maybe it's an Indian thing, Adam thought with a fleeting smile. Not growing up in a community with people of Native American descent, Adam knew little about that half of his heritage. But perhaps he should find out. Perhaps then he could understand if there was something his father was trying to tell him.

And maybe he would discover the answer if he stayed here.

Grumbling to himself, Adam drove to the cottage. Goldie was sleeping on the porch, well out of the rain. But neither Gabe nor Lainey, who had volunteered to keep him while Adam was gone, were anywhere to be seen. Inside the cottage, Adam could hear the phone ringing. It was probably Caroline, calling to see about the interview.

The irritation he had felt Friday night returned. Why couldn't everyone have left him alone? If Caroline hadn't pushed him, hadn't set up the interview. If Reid hadn't recommended him. If Lainey hadn't called everyone she knew and told them to hire him. If all of them had just butted out, he wouldn't be faced with this. Without this job he didn't want, he could probably leave without too many qualms, despite the way Gabe felt.

And do what? his conscience challenged. Go to Florida and work another job you don't want for the next six months? Make your son unhappy because you just don't want to stay put?

Ignoring those questions and the phone, Adam turned on his heel and headed to the barns. He disregarded what the mud might do to his only pair of dress shoes. He just wanted some time alone to think.

The air in the weathered gray barn was pungent with the mingled aromas of horseflesh, dung and hay. Adam paused near the doorway, not put off by the scents but wondering if he wanted to do his thinking here. In one of the stalls down the central corridor, Lainey's aging sorrel mare stuck her head over the door and looked at him. Regarding the horse with a frown, Adam said, "What do you think I should I do?"

"You could come up here."

Lainey's whisper startled Adam. He wheeled around. "Up here."

He backed up until he could see Lainey's face peering down at him from the hayloft. "What are you—"

"Shh." She put a finger to her lips. "Come on up, but be quiet."

The rungs of the ladder leading to the loft were worn smooth with age. One creaked ominously, but Adam made it most of the way up without doing anything dire to his best khaki slacks. When he looked over the edge Lainey cautioned him to be quiet again, and Adam saw why.

Gabe was asleep, his head in her lap. It was the sort of sleep Adam often envied children, a dead-to-the-world sprawl of limbs. But Gabe wasn't alone. A big mother cat was curled at his side, regarding Adam with a sleepy but wary gaze while her five kittens snoozed in contented oblivion at various spots all over Gabe.

With a capable, work-worn hand, Lainey touched Gabe's cheek. He didn't even stir. She looked up at Adam and smiled.

Adam didn't know if it was the sight of Gabe sleeping so happily or the brilliance of Lainey's smile that made him reach a decision. But he knew right away what he had to do.

"I'm staying," he whispered.

And when Lainey smiled again, he wished he had the right, the *nerve,* to kiss her.

Thankfully, however, Gabe woke up before Adam found the courage to override his caution.

Chapter Five

Sunday night, Lainey stood in her kitchen, a knife poised over a triple-layer chocolate fudge cake, trying not to smile. She had no reason to feel so foolishly happy. Yes, Adam was staying, but that wasn't cause for such anticipatory elation. His decision had nothing to do with her. If anything, his stay could turn into nothing but five months of prolonged agony.

Sweet, sweet agony.

She lectured herself as she cut into the cake. Just because she had decided not to run if Adam ever kissed her again wasn't any reason to imagine he might. She needed to maintain the right perspective. She was glad he was staying for Gabe's sake. And for Caroline's. They were a family. That was the most important thing to remember.

So why could she think only of that one misguided kiss?

With a sigh, Lainey lifted a slice of cake onto a plate, then sat down to enjoy it with a large glass of milk. Around her the house was silent, save for the humming of the refrigerator and the air conditioner. It was a quiet, very ordinary evening. She was staring dreamily into space, thinking all the wrong kinds of thoughts about Adam, when she realized he was crossing her back porch. She could see him through the glass in the kitchen door.

Glancing at Goldie, asleep in her favorite corner of the kitchen, Lainey said, "Gee, thanks for the warning." The dog didn't stir even when Adam knocked.

Lainey called out, "Come in," but didn't move from the table as Adam closed the door behind him. She wasn't sure what to expect. Even though he had been pleasant enough this afternoon, she could still remember their argument Friday night. Gabe had been around today, so other than the barest details about his interview there hadn't really been a chance to talk. And then Caroline had driven up, too eager to hear about the interview to wait for Adam to call her. Lainey had slipped away and left them alone to talk. So for all she knew, Adam might still be put out with her for the way she had butted into his business.

He hesitated in the mudroom area, just beyond the kitchen threshold. "I hope I'm not disturbing you."

She shook her head. "I was just having a snack. Where's Gabe?"

"Over at Caroline's. Reid dug out one of Sammi's old bikes for him, so Gabe wanted to go home with Caroline. I'm supposed to be on my way to pick him up now." After pausing to give Goldie a pat on the head, he glanced at the cake that rested under a glass dome on the counter. "That sure looks good."

The pleasant tone of his voice put her at ease. "I'll cut you a piece."

Adam pulled out a chair at the end of the table and eyed the remainder of her slice warily. "Not that big, please."

Lainey laughed. People had always teased her about her appetite.

True to form, Adam asked, "Where do you put all the food you eat, anyway?"

"If I told you how many people have asked me that, you'd be embarrassed for not being more original."

He laughed. "Sorry. But a lot of people would also like to have your kind of metabolism."

"Few of them would probably like to work the way I do."

"I suppose that's so."

She rose, got him a plate and fork and handed him a knife so that he could cut as much cake as he wanted and offered him a glass of milk that he declined.

He took his first taste of the cake and closed his eyes. "This is fabulous."

She resumed her seat. "Aunt Loretta's recipe, of course."

For a few moments they each concentrated on their cake, although Lainey's famous appetite had fled.

Finally, Adam broke the silence with a quiet, "I think I owe you an apology."

She looked up in surprise.

"For the other night."

Flushing, she thought of their kiss.

"I shouldn't have told you to shut up the way I did."

Realizing that he was referring to their argument Friday night and not the kiss, Lainey looked down at her plate and twirled a bit of icing with her fork, feeling oddly disappointed. "I understand why you were angry."

"I flew off the handle, and I shouldn't have. I didn't mean what I said about this being a hick town."

Shrugging, she looked at him again. "Well, it's not exactly a metropolis."

"But it's your home. And this farm is your home, and I shouldn't have said living here would be like hell. That was stupid, and I didn't mean it."

"It's okay, really—"

"No," he said, leaning forward, his intent gaze holding hers. "It's not okay. I may not have the same feelings for this place that you do, but it is beautiful and you've opened it to me and Gabe with no questions asked. You've been incredibly generous, and I shouldn't have said the things I did."

She glanced away. Looking into his eyes was much too mesmerizing for her peace of mind. "I think all of us— me, especially, should probably apologize to you, too. I mean, we did kind of railroad you into this job—"

"Maybe you did, but the bottom line is you and Caroline and Reid, all of you just really care about Gabe, and you really care about . . . about . . . me. . . ."

Lainey looked up. Their gazes met for a moment, then slipped away.

Quickly, Adam said, "What I mean is that all of you have our best interests at heart, and Friday night I shouldn't have been quite so . . . well, *bullheaded* is the word I think your Aunt Loretta might have used to describe me."

"I'm just glad you changed your mind." She darted a look at his face and added a hasty, "For Gabe's sake, of course."

"Yes, for Gabe," Adam agreed just as quickly. He went on to say he had called his late wife's parents and told them about his plans. "I expected them to be upset, you know, jealous that I'm staying here, when I took Gabe away from them. But as usual, they were pretty understanding. Mrs. Larson said she thought it was good that Gabe get to know my family."

"They sound like nice folks."

"They've been better to me than I deserve."

Lainey lifted an eyebrow at his bleak tone.

He let out a long sigh as he sat back in his chair. "Let's just say I didn't always make their daughter very happy."

Not knowing what sort of reply to make to that, Lainey just reached for his empty plate. Silence reigned again as she got up and took their dishes and silverware to the sink.

"So do you forgive me for acting like an ass?"

Adam's question made her shoot a sideways look at him. He was still cocked back in his chair, legs widespread, hands resting easily on his thighs. But his posture was deceptive, she realized. The look in his dark eyes was very intense, almost apprehensive.

She turned, leaning one hip against the cabinet. "There's nothing to forgive."

"You're too nice, Lainey."

"Uh-oh. Another unoriginal observation."

A faint grin teased the corners of his mouth. "Sorry to be so predictable."

He was anything but that, but Lainey wasn't going to tell him so. She switched on the water in the sink and began rinsing the plates. "If I recall correctly, there have been a few moments when you didn't think I was so nice."

"Yeah, but..."

She glanced at him again. "But what?"

He hesitated, then sat forward, resting one elbow on the table as he looked at her. "What I was about to say is...there have been a lot of moments when I thought you were awfully nice."

He was talking about their kiss. Lainey knew it, and she wondered that the plate she was holding didn't slip right out of her hands. She swallowed, staring at him.

That must have gone on for much too long, because he finally got up, came over and turned off the water.

Flustered, Lainey set the plate down in the sink and tried to put up a pretense of misunderstanding. "Adam, I don't know what you're talking—"

"Yes, you do." He took hold of her arm and turned her toward him. "I think we ought to clear the air. Since I'm going to be here for a while, I think we ought to talk about that night that I kissed you."

She took a deep breath. "All right."

But Adam didn't say anything. She looked up at him. He looked down at her. Finally he managed a nervous-sounding laugh and let go of her arm. "I guess I don't know what to say."

But she did. She'd had some experience with let-downs, brush-offs and explanations, probably much more experience than he. Lifting her chin, she said, "I think what you probably want to say is that it was a mistake."

He frowned. "Mistake is maybe too extreme."

"Then perhaps it would be better to say it shouldn't have happened."

"Okay."

"That we shouldn't have that kind of relationship."

His frown reappeared. "Shouldn't?"

"Can't?" She wished he would stop looking at her so intently. His closeness made her jumpy enough without that dark-eyed, steady regard of his to complicate matters.

"So we *can't* have *that* kind of relationship," he murmured. "That's what you're saying."

"It's what you're saying."

"But I didn't know what to say."

"I was helping you out."

"Oh." He looked sort of strange. He kept blinking, staring at her.

"Adam?"

Instead of replying, he lifted a hand to her hair. Remembering her vow to stop running and hiding from the world, she stopped herself before jerking away.

He smoothed back the curly tendrils that always seemed to spring loose at her temples. "So that's how that is," he murmured.

"How what is?"

"Your hair."

"What?"

"I like it."

"It's really... red."

"And gold."

"Gold?"

"Yeah." This time he smoothed his hand over her head, around to her thick braid, following its curve to where the end rested just below her shoulder blade.

Lainey was fighting a losing battle with her runaway pulse when Adam kissed her.

It wasn't like before. There was nothing sweet or tentative about this kiss. It was like a storm, Lainey thought. A rip-roarin' gully washer of a storm. The kind that came in hard and fast and caught you unprepared. When she

was younger, she had liked being caught in those down-
pours, liked allowing the water to beat on her shoulders and her face and wash down her body. It had
been . . . thrilling. And that's what this was. A gosh, al-
mighty thrill.

She went with that emotion, opening her lips to
Adam's questing tongue. He tasted of chocolate. He
smelled like the rain outside. She slipped her arms around
his neck while his arms encircled her, drawing her tight
against him. She was short and he was tall, so she
shouldn't have been so surprised when her feet left the
ground. But all Lainey could think was that she was flying, that in the emotion of the moment, she had somehow defied gravity. Deep in her throat, she gave a startled
protest.

Adam moved back, and that's when she realized he
had pulled her feet off the floor. And he had misinterpreted her protest. "I know, I know," he murmured.
"We shouldn't."

Unable to agree, Lainey just lifted her lips for another
kiss.

He obliged, taking her mouth once more with thorough abandonment. But this time he was the one who
groaned. Again, he pulled away, whispering, "I'm
sorry."

She dug deep into her available pool of courage and
came up with, "I'm not."

"Damn." The astonished word was torn from him before he let her slide back to the floor, her body moving
slowly down his. If his kiss hadn't told her how aroused
he was, if she hadn't known by the roughness of his
voice, the slide down his body told her all she needed to
know. Inexperienced, she might be. Stupid, she wasn't.

But before she could give the obvious bulge in his jeans too much more thought, he pressed her back against the cabinets. His lips nibbled at hers with short, easy kisses. One hand was at the back of her neck, his fingers threading through the hair just where her braid began. The other moved up beneath her loose knit shirt, caressing the bare skin of her back. She was trapped, and she didn't care. She was disintegrating beneath his touch, and she wanted it to go on and on.

Forever was too much to ask for, but it might not have ended so quickly if his hand on her back hadn't shifted to the front, hadn't slipped upward. But when his fingertips brushed over the hardening tip of her small, bare breast, Lainey felt as if all the air was pressed from her lungs. She let it out in one long breath.

This time Adam jerked back. The dazed look was gone from his eyes as he stared down at her. He passed a hand over his face, combed it back through his straight black hair.

"Damn," he said again, although this time the word communicated regret instead of wonder.

Lainey turned, taking hold of the edge of the counter to steady herself. When he touched her shoulder, she flinched.

"I'm sorry." He retreated halfway across the kitchen.

"No." She faced him quickly, not wanting him to think she didn't want him to touch her. Because she did. "I jumped because you startled me. It's not that I don't... what I mean is that I want..." She hesitated. Saying she welcomed his touch was much harder now that they were separated by feet rather than inches.

He lifted his hands in a apologetic gesture, then let them drop back to his sides. "I don't want to keep saying I'm sorry."

She stepped toward him. "You don't have to."

"But I shouldn't have kissed you."

"I let you." She'd done much more than that.

"But..." He rubbed his chin, looking confused. "We agreed this was a mistake."

"Yes, but then...now..." She was so rattled she couldn't find the words she needed to express what she was feeling.

"This won't work," Adam continued. "With me living right here. With the family...with everyone. It just won't do. It's wrong."

Lainey struggled to hide her dismay. It didn't feel wrong to her.

He was shaking his head. "I shouldn't have brought all this up in the first place. I should have left it alone. Because you and I, we're so..."

"We're so what?" she asked, even though she afraid she didn't want to know.

"We're different," he said.

"Different," she repeated, trying to follow him.

"Not alike."

"I understand the word," she said impatiently.

He sighed. "Of course you do. It's what I mean that isn't clear."

"No, it's not."

Hands on his hips, Adam tried explaining again. "It's that I don't believe we're thinking the same things. There's this attraction between us." He darted a quick look at her. "At least I think you've been feeling that, the same as I have."

Nodding, she felt herself flush, which was foolish, considering the man could have had her naked by now if he hadn't stopped kissing her. But it was just as foolish to call the storm of emotion that had just gripped them a mere attraction.

Adam was insisting that's what is was, though. "This is just physical, just because I...well, to be blunt, it's been a while for me, Lainey."

She frowned. "A while?"

Now it was his face that went ruddy with color. "I haven't been with anyone since my wife died."

"Oh." Lainey felt like a squashed bug, an emotion she knew well, but which still took her by surprise.

Adam was rattling on. "What I'm trying to say is that here we are with this thing going on between us, and there's all this energy, and I just...well, I thought with the wrong parts of my anatomy." He managed a weak smile. "Twice."

Physical attraction. It had been a while. He thought with the wrong parts of his anatomy.

Lainey struggled to process the information. What he was saying was that there was nothing special about what had happened just now or the first time he kissed her. For him there was no thrill, other than the purely physical. There was no gravity loss. He was just horny. Your ordinary garden variety of horniness. He had kissed her because there was a minimum of attraction between them and she was available.

Yes, she was so damn available. Just like a big, ripe peach, swinging on a branch right next to him. So accessible. So clearly, clearly eager to fall right into his grasp. As she had feared, Adam had read all her signals, read them very, very well. He knew, or at least sensed, that it wasn't merely the physical that motivated her. And he was right. She should be grateful he was a decent man, or he could have taken her a moment earlier. On the floor, probably. Like a rutting animal. And she would have let him, welcomed him.

While those thoughts raced through her mind, she was busy composing herself. "Okay" was all she said to Adam.

He peered at her, frowning. "Okay?"

"It's all right. I understand what you're trying to tell me now. About the way you feel."

"The way I feel?"

She glanced at her wrist, realized she wasn't wearing her watch and then looked at the kitchen clock. "It's late. Caroline will be wondering if you're coming to get Gabe."

"But Lainey—"

"You'd better go." She smiled somehow.

"You're angry."

"I'm tired."

"But I don't—"

"Stop making it a big deal," she said. "We're grown-ups. This was not some reason to get all bent out of shape." What funny words, she thought, coming from a woman who only days ago had charged away from him as if his kiss were the biggest deal that had ever happened to her.

That seemed to be on Adam's mind as well. He was still looking at her with an expression of concern. "Listen, Lainey, I know that you probably weren't feeling...I mean, I think you weren't coming from the same place that I was."

"Oh, really?" She hated that he had figured out there was much more than a chemical reaction happening to her where he was concerned. She arched an eyebrow at him, doing her best to appear unconcerned.

He looked confused.

"Maybe you don't know everything," Lainey told him.

After a pause, he said, "Maybe I don't."

"So let's forget it. For good, this time."

He gave her another long glance. He looked ready to say something more, but Lainey didn't give him a chance. She went to the door, smiling as she opened it and bid him good-night.

Adam walked to his truck, telling himself what an idiot he had been to stop here in the first place. But having decided to accept the job that would be offered tomorrow, he felt the need to apologize to Lainey for everything that had been said between them Friday night. If he was going to live here, he wanted them to get along, be friends. Clearing the air about that first kiss had been an impulse, and everything that had happened afterward was just as impulsive.

Or was it?

That question drummed in his head all during his trip to and from Caroline's to pick up Gabe. By the time he had settled his son for the night, Adam was able to admit that maybe impulse wasn't the whole story. He had wanted to kiss Lainey earlier, down at the barn. He had thought about it most of the afternoon, though he had cautioned himself not to be a fool. But then he had stopped to see her, had sat down in the cozy intimacy of her kitchen, had made that first provocative comment, had moved close to her, had touched her hair.

So was it impulse or intent? He wasn't sure. He just knew it had been a wild couple of minutes. He had come close, very close to losing control. The kissing was bad enough. But backing her up to the counter and groping her like some awkward boy had been worse. Of course, she had been into it, he remembered. She had responded. His body was still reminding him of how she had responded. But that didn't matter. He was the one who had started it. He was to blame for it ending as badly as it had before.

The explanations he had offered, that it was physical, that abstinence had left him easily aroused, were the only ones that had come to mind, and he thought they were valid. She implied it was all just physical to her, as well. But he wasn't sure he believed her. Lainey wasn't that sort of woman. No doubt he would now be treated to the same sort of skittishness and strain that had permeated the past week.

But Lainey surprised him.

The next time he saw her, which was nearly noon the next day, she greeted him with same offhand casualness she might use with Reid or Neal. Maybe she wasn't particularly warm, but she wasn't cool, either. She asked him if he'd gotten the definite offer from the school board yet. She smiled at him. She acted like nothing was amiss.

He was the one who stood there, looking at her mouth, remembering the sweet, chocolatey taste of her. *He* was the idiot. *He* was the person who got away from her as quickly as he could.

That was the ticket, he told himself, to just stay away. Thankfully, he was busy enough to do so.

He got the job late that afternoon. The next morning, he took Gabe to register for kindergarten and the after-school program the boy would stay in until Adam could pick him up in the evenings. Afterward, Caroline took Gabe home while Adam went to the high school to begin preparations for the onslaught of students. Thursday and Friday would merely be registration days. Classes didn't start until the following Tuesday, after Labor Day. But Adam had to find his way around the school, meet fellow teachers and look over texts and lesson plans left by the ailing Coach Medford. And then there was football practice, with plays to memorize and a host of other responsibilities.

The other coach, Vance Trewhitt, was a nice guy who was eager for Adam's help. He said there was raw talent on the team. Adam could see that only halfway into the practice. They had speed on the kick return and from the ends. The defensive line was big and aggressive. Most importantly, Neal Scroggins's powerful pitching arm was just as effective when wielding a football. Yet his two weeks out of practice had knocked him from the starting-quarterback slot.

Adam thought they were penalizing the whole team to make a point with one player. Even the kid playing quarterback now seemed to want to defer to Neal. In addition, Adam saw a lot of unmotivated youngsters who played like they wished they were someplace else. Maybe it was the heat. But whatever the case, Adam wasn't going to start out by criticizing.

The boys were wary enough of him, as it was. Even Neal kept his distance. Adam had been the new kid in town enough to understand the situation. He would have to earn their trust.

By the end of the first week, Adam was weary. The school was much like the one where he had taught before, long on dedicated teachers, short on cash to update the facilities and resources. His frustrations felt familiar. But he had accepted a job; he would give it all he had. After all, it was only temporary; this wouldn't be his life.

Friday night was the football jamboree, which their school had the honor of hosting this year. Twelve teams from around the region were to square off in six quarters of football—one shortened quarter apiece. The Parrish

County Cougars drew the reigning state championships and got whipped.

By the time Adam and the equipment manager dealt with the last set of pads, he felt as if he had personally played every quarter himself, and it was nearly eleven o'clock.

But his family was waiting for him beside his truck. His *family*. Strange how that word sent a tingle up his spine.

Gabe ran toward him with the sort of energy he shouldn't have at this time of night.

Caroline tossed two purple-and-gold paper shakers into the air, shouting, "Yeah, Coach!" Even Reid and Sammi and her ever-present boyfriend were on hand.

Lainey stood behind the others, a little apart, a lot more reserved.

"How did it feel?" Caroline asked.

Adam laughed. "It felt like every other time I've been on a team that's gotten their butts beat. It was character building." He noticed that while everyone laughed, Lainey managed only a faint grin.

Reid slapped him on the back. "It'll get better."

Glancing around to make sure there were no players lurking in the parking lot nearby, Adam said, "I hope you're right. Because it can't get much worse. I think the guys are suffering from Coach Medford's absence."

"But he's such an old grouch," Sammi protested. "It looks like they'd all be happy to have someone young and nice coaching them."

"Nice doesn't always win football games."

Gabe slipped his hand into Adam's. "You'll win the next one, Dad."

He tousled his son's hair. "Thanks. Right now I'm too tired to think about the next time. And we need to get you home to bed."

"Good idea," Caroline agreed. "Christopher's home with a sitter, and I'm feeling kind of guilty for leaving him."

Reid took Caroline's hand as they started toward their car, and glanced over his shoulder. "Lainey, you want to just hitch a ride home with Adam?"

She hesitated ever so slightly, but then nodded.

Gabe let out a delighted whoop. "Come on, Lainey, you can sit in the middle."

She and Adam exchanged a brief startled look.

"*You* can sit in the middle," he told his son as the rest of the group left them.

"Ah, man, I like to sit by the window," Gabe grumbled, opening the truck door. Lainey followed him inside. The door closed with a rusty-sounding creak and had to be slammed to latch. Adam was suddenly aware of how dusty and dilapidated the truck looked.

The door on his side squeaked ominously. "I need to get that oiled," he observed as he slid under the steering wheel.

Lainey said nothing. And perhaps it was her silence that made the sputtering of the engine's start-up sound so feeble.

"Dad got a real deal on this truck," Gabe announced. Adam recognized the remark as a perfect mimic of what he had said after buying this hunk of junk. He wished the boy paid a little less attention to everything he said.

Though it was much too dark for him to see the expression on Lainey's face, he could imagine she was trying not to laugh. He felt compelled to explain as he pulled out of the school's parking lot. "I'm not much on spending lots of money on cars."

She replied with something that sounded like a cross between "oh" and "umm."

Adam took that as criticism. "Having some brand-new, sparkling car has just never been a priority to me. I've always said that if it runs okay, then—" The truck's engine chose that moment to miss a few beats and shudder, almost dying.

"What's wrong?" Gabe asked.

"Nothing." Adam shifted gears, praying the truck would cooperate, letting out a sigh of relief when the sound of the engine smoothed out.

All the while Lainey sat in her corner, saying nothing. And Adam thought that her silence spoke volumes.

He kept thinking of her truck. A late-model full-size pickup, light green in color. It got dusty, sure, but she washed it every week. She kept her truck as clean and tidy as she did everything on her farm. No doubt, she would rather be just about anywhere but in this beat-up wreck of his. And no doubt she thought the truck suited the man.

Adam's jaw was so tight it was beginning to ache. By God, he wasn't going to inflict himself on her any more than he had to. He had managed to avoid her pretty well most of this week. He was sure he could keep it up.

By the time they turned into the long drive at Applewood Farm Gabe had fallen asleep on Lainey, and she hadn't said a word. But Adam had built up a big head of steam about everything he imagined she was thinking. Most of all, he was mad at himself for worrying so much about what she thought.

He pulled to a stop at the edge of the walkway that ran from the drive to her back porch. The truck's engine idled, a loud, erratic sound. Not trusting himself to speak, Adam just stared straight ahead.

Easing the sleeping boy away from her, Lainey fumbled for the door handle. Adam's unsmiling profile was outlined by the lights she had left burning at the house. "Well..." she said. "Thanks for the lift."

Adam merely grunted.

Frowning, she opened the door and climbed out. She didn't want to wake Gabe, so she tried to close the door quietly. But it wouldn't latch. She tried shutting it a little firmer. No luck.

"Just slam the damn door, all right?" Adam barked at her.

Gabe sat up with a little gasp.

Darting his father an irritated look, Lainey reached in to soothe the child. Adam reached for him, too, but she touched him first, murmuring, "It's okay, honey."

The boy rubbed his eyes. "Mom?"

Lainey heard Adam suck in his breath. Quickly she said, "Gabe, honey, it's Lainey. Your Dad's taking you home to bed." She patted his arm, received his sleepy mumble of a reply. Then she slammed the door.

Adam drove off without another pause. She stared after him, feeling as if she had missed something. What sort of bug had bitten him in the rear all of a sudden?

She went inside and up to her room to get ready for bed, telling herself not to worry about Adam Cutler. The few times they had talked this week, she thought she had done an excellent job of pretending to be unconcerned about what had passed between the two of them in her kitchen Sunday night. In fact, she was unconcerned. She was putting him out of her mind. She was...

A liar.

With those words ringing in her bed, she brushed her teeth, unbraided her hair and put on one of the big cotton T-shirts she liked to sleep in during warm weather.

She was pulling back the covers and willing herself not to waste another minute thinking about Adam when the phone rang. She snatched it up, certain that a call at this time of night could only mean trouble.

"We've got a small problem down here," Adam said without preamble. "There's a flood."

"A what?"

"I don't know if the water heater blew or if a pipe's burst or what, but there's water all over the place. I've got a bad feeling it's been running like this most of the day."

Lainey muttered a short, succinctly expressive word.

"That about sums it up," Adam retorted. "Tell me where I can shut the water off."

She gave him a few quick directions even as she was reaching for the blue jeans she had just discarded. "I'll be right down."

An hour later, the water in the cottage was off. The problem was identified as a corroded pipe that had given way under the kitchen sink. The water had spread from the kitchen to carpet throughout most of the house. It was a mess. So Lainey did the only thing she thought was right. She insisted Adam and Gabe come to her house.

Chapter Six

"This really isn't necessary," Adam muttered as he trailed Lainey up the big house's central staircase with a sleeping Gabe in his arms.

"You can't stay down there in that mess."

"Our beds aren't wet."

"But with the water off, you can't even use the bathrooms." Pausing to turn on a lamp on a low marble-topped table, she hurried across the second-floor landing. "You can put Gabe down in my room." She pushed open her bedroom door, beckoning for Adam to follow.

He hesitated on the threshold. "I don't want to inconvenience you like this, putting you out of your room."

"It's the only one that's made up right now, and he needs to get settled down for good." Lainey swept back the covers on the old iron bed she had slept in since she was a child.

"He could have settled down at the cottage," Adam grumbled, laying Gabe on the lilac-sprigged sheets. The boy barely stirred as his father took off his socks and undid the buckle of his belt. Even getting him out of his jeans didn't cause more than a sigh. He turned on his side and snuggled into Lainey's big feather pillow.

She stood to the side while Adam pulled the covers up. With a tender smile, he bent and kissed his son's cheek, a sweet gesture that caused a funny little flutter in Lainey's chest.

She reached for the bedside lamp, but Adam stopped her. "Sometimes Gabe likes the light on."

"Okay." At the switch beside the door she shut off the overhead light. The room was now pleasantly dim. "Do you think that'll be okay?"

"I guess." But still Adam hesitated by the bed.

"Adam?"

"Sometimes he has nightmares. And in a strange place—"

"You want to stay in here with him?"

Adam turned to look at her, then glanced around. Lainey followed his gaze, through his eyes seeing the white ruffled curtains, the lace-edged comforter and the stack of feminine underwear on the top of the bureau. The room was suddenly much too small.

"I'll put you next door to him," she said, backing out into the corridor.

"That'll be fine."

"I'll just get some sheets and make up your bed."

Adam followed her out to the landing. "I can do that."

"Nonsense." From an old pine cabinet that stood near the top of the stairs, Lainey took out a set of sheets. Then she opened the door next to her room. "This was your mother's room," she said over her shoulder as she snapped on a light.

Adam stopped in the doorway, glancing from corner to corner of the big, square room. The furniture was cherry, he thought. The wood gleamed against the pale yellow walls.

"Aunt Loretta and Uncle Coy took this room when we moved into the house after your grandfather died, but they didn't make many changes." Lainey pulled the cream-colored woven bedspread from the high four-poster. Adam took it from her and folded it over a chair beside the bed. Together, they put on the sheets and pillowcases and a blanket she took from the bottom drawer of the armoire that stood in the corner.

"I hope this doesn't smell musty," she murmured as she tucked the final edge of the blanket under the mattress.

To Adam, the blanket smelled like pressed flowers, just as the rest of the room did. The scent teased at the back of his memory. He kept looking around, thinking that his mother had slept here and wondering why that knowledge caused such a tightness in his gut.

Lainey paused in the doorway. "You saw the bathroom next to my room?" At his nod, she continued, "It opens to the hall, too. There are towels and stuff in the cabinets just inside the door. I think there's even an extra toothbrush."

"It's the only bathroom?"

"Besides the one off the mudroom downstairs, yeah." She grimaced. "Four big bedrooms and only one and a half baths. That's the problem with old houses."

"I guess."

Lainey gestured to her right. "I'm going to go to bed now. I'll be just down the hall at the other end if you

need...that is to say...if there's any problem or anything...."

An awkward silence fell between them. Adam cleared
his throat. After vowing to stay out of Lainey's way, this
turn of events was anything but welcome. He wished he
had resisted a little harder when she insisted they come up
here for the night. He was damn sick and tired of this
woman doing things for him.

"Well...good night," Lainey said finally, drawing the
door halfway closed behind her. The floor squeaked beneath her footsteps as she went to the linen cabinet again.
Then Adam heard a door farther down the hall open and
close.

He sat down on the edge of the bed with a sigh. This
was absolutely the last place he wanted to be tonight. Or
maybe any night, he thought, glancing up at the broad-
planed molding that edged the high ceiling. There were
ghosts in this house, he thought. Memories of his childhood, of his mother and father, lurked in the corners just
beyond his recollection.

A chill overtook him. He told himself it was a draft.
Just as he told himself the deepening scent of pressed
flowers was the smell of the sachet that had been packed
with the blanket. He didn't really believe in ghosts. He
didn't want to acknowledge the eerie feeling that his father was right here with him. He wasn't afraid. Never
once in his life had he feared John Cutler. He didn't think
death could change that.

But he wondered at this feeling he kept having. Why
was it so strong all of a sudden? He glanced around the
room. Had his parents slept together in this room? Had
he and Caroline come in some mornings to wake them,
just as Gabe did with him? And when Adam and his fa-

ther were gone and his mother thought they were dead, had she cried for them here?

Impatient with the unanswerable questions, Adam took off his shirt and shoes. The house was so silent his every sound seemed amplified. The door creaked as he peered out into the hall and the landing, where Lainey had left the lamp burning. As quietly as he could, he went to check on Gabe and then to the bathroom.

When he stepped out in the hall again, he collided with Lainey.

"Whoa, there," he said, catching her upper arms to steady her. For one fleeting moment, her hands rested on his bare torso.

Then she shrugged off his touch and backed away. "I'm sorry. I thought I heard Gabe."

"He's fine."

"Then good night again." She whipped around and retreated to the room at the end of the hall, leaving Adam with only an impression of bare legs and a trim body outlined beneath her thin T-shirt.

In the bedroom, he kept seeing her long, unbound hair and her wide, startled green eyes. He kept remembering how her skin had felt the other night, how firm her breast had been, how the nipple had hardened against the mere skim of his fingers. He kept feeling her small hands flattened against his body.

Again and again he turned over in the unfamiliar bed, punching his pillow, trying to think about anything else. About his mother, his father, about everyone who might have lived in this house, occupied this room and this bed.

But as he stared into the darkness, he knew it was the living, breathing woman in the room down the hall who was haunting him, and not the spirits of those long gone.

* * *

"I told you this might happen."

The smug tone of the plumber who was talking to Lainey on the cottage's porch set Adam's teeth on edge. The man hadn't shown up until late this afternoon and then grumbled about being here on Saturday. Now he was claiming the cottage's plumbing needed a major overhaul.

"This place is older than I am." He punctuated each word by pointing at Lainey with a foul-smelling cigar butt clenched between two stubby fingers. "We're talking some major corrosion. I told you that the last time you called me out. If I patch it up, you're just going to run into more problems down the line."

"All right, all right," Lainey said, thrusting her hands in her pockets. "Just call me with an estimate."

"It ain't gonna be cheap."

"I know."

Muttering to himself, the man ambled off toward his truck.

"When do you think you could start work on it, if I decide I can afford it?" Lainey called after him.

"Late next week." Wally got in his truck, then poked his head out the window to add, "Maybe."

Adam set down the wet/dry vacuum he had been using on the carpet and joined Lainey at the top of the steps. "Is he the only plumber in town?"

"He's the best."

Studying the glum set of her mouth, Adam said, "Listen, I don't want you to go to all this expense for me and Gabe. Just have him patch it up, and we'll make out fine. This probably won't happen again."

"That's what I told myself the last time it happened." She shook her head. "In the past, I've rented this place, or I've let hands and their families live here in lieu of some of their wages. This house has generated income, it's not in bad shape, and I'm just going to have to make an investment to keep it that way."

"But you don't have to do it for us. Not right now."

"It'll be worse when it gets cold. The pipes in the bathroom froze and burst last winter."

Adam could see she had already made up her mind. "I guess Gabe and I need to see about a place to stay in town, at least until this work is done."

Instead of looking at him, she picked up the mop and pail she had brought from her house and started down the steps. "There's plenty of room for the two of you up at the house."

"We can't do that." Staying under the same roof with her was impossible.

"It won't be easy to find a short-term lease in town. There's not too much rental property."

"There's Caroline's—"

"Oh, please." At the bottom of the steps, Lainey faced him. "All the reasons you moved from Caroline's in the first place still apply."

"I know, but—"

"So why not just stay at the house?"

Surely she knew why. He didn't want to have to say it.

But she lifted her chin, as if in challenge. "*I* have absolutely no problem with you staying."

So the problem was all his. He was the horny animal who feared he couldn't control his libido. Like the consummate perfectionist that she was, she was in complete control. Adam had rarely been able to back away from a challenge. "All right. We'll stay."

"Good." She started toward her house.

But something else occurred to him. "Aren't people going to talk?"

She wheeled around, mop and bucket at one side, hand on hip on the other. "What?"

"You hate gossip. Aren't people going to be talking about me staying in your house?"

Lainey arched one eyebrow, a disdainful expression on her face. "As Aunt Loretta would say, a clear conscience is the best defense against malicious gossip."

They exchanged a long, steady look. Adam said, "Then we should be well defended."

"Absolutely." Her smile was fleeting before she walked off.

But a clear conscience wasn't easy to maintain.

If Adam thought he was attracted to her before, co-habitation sent his reactions to a new level. Not that he went out of his way to torture himself. He tried to establish a distance between them during the first few days. Thankfully, he was busy with school and football during the day. At night, he worked at his lesson plans at the big desk in the front parlor while she watched television with Gabe in the paneled den just off the kitchen. Later, they went to sleep at opposite ends of the house. He had insisted he and Gabe take the two rooms on the other side of the house from her bedroom and the room where he had slept the first night.

But there was still only one bathroom, which he and Lainey seemed to need at the same time more often than not. There was only one kitchen, too. Even when Adam did the cooking, which he liked and wanted to do, Lainey was usually nearby, telling him where staples were kept and pans were stored. They ate family style at the kitchen table most nights and on the mornings when Lainey came back to the house after the morning milking. They washed dishes together, discussed menus together.

On the surface, Adam met the challenge of controlling his attraction to her very well. When they touched, it was quite by accident. He never lost his focus as he had the second time he had kissed her. He did his best to keep the conversation on safe topics. Lainey responded in kind.

Beneath the surface, however, Adam could feel the energy between them. Sometimes at night he couldn't stop thinking of her sleeping in her sweet-scented, surprisingly feminine bedroom. Other times, he would covertly watch her, when she was clearing the table or talking with Gabe or doing something altogether mundane, and his reaction would be sudden, sharp desire.

He thought about her at odd moments. At school, when he fell into the instinctive, easy rhythm that had earned him high praise during his last tenure in the classroom. Or when he could see by the light in a student's eyes that he was getting through to him. Or at football practice, when Neal hung a perfectly thrown touchdown pass in the air. After practice, when Adam gave the boy a ride home and tried to break through the wall of anger and frustration he sensed building in him.

Adam realized the best parts of his days were coming home to tell Lainey about what had happened. He liked hearing her response. He liked being with her. More and more and he wanted to *be* with her.

One week faded to the next. Work began on replacing the plumbing at the cottage, but the plumber worked at his own pace. A slower-than-necessary pace to Adam's way of thinking. Yet he didn't protest.

He realized he and Gabe and Lainey were slipping into a close family-like unit. Intimacy was inevitable when people shared the everyday, ordinary moments of life. Meals, wet towels, grocery lists. Those commonplace things forged bonds. But that didn't really surprise Adam. What was surprising was how nice those bonds felt. What troubled him was how easily he adapted to the give-and-take of sharing Lainey's day-to-day existence.

Particularly where his son was concerned, it was nice to share. When Gabe gave the details of his first full day at a new school, it felt natural to share a warm, lingering smile with Lainey. When Gabe wanted Lainey to kiss him good-night after Adam read him a bedtime story, it seemed normal for the two of them to stand together looking down at him with affection. And when Gabe had one of his nightmares at the end of the second week, it seemed instinctive that Lainey and Adam both responded.

She let Adam take over. Gabe wanted his dad, who knew just what to say. Lainey waited in the hallway, listening as Adam patiently reassured Gabe that there weren't monsters in the corner, that the face on the wall was just the shadow of a tree branch, that nothing could hurt him. She knew she should just go back to bed, but Gabe's screams had jolted her wide-awake. She wanted to make sure he was okay.

"He's already asleep," Adam murmured when he finally emerged from the boy's room.

Lainey sighed in relief. "He was crying so hard I was worried there was really something wrong."

"He's just unsettled. He was out too late tonight at the game. He probably had one too many of those chili hot dogs from the concession stand." In the dim light of the hall, Adam looked tired. It had been a long week at school, and tonight the football team had lost their second game of the season. She knew he was frustrated and thought they could win.

"We all need to get back to sleep," Lainey told him, moving toward her room.

"Actually..."

She turned, and Adam's winning smile appeared.

"I was thinking about that banana-cream pie you made last night. There's still some left, isn't there?"

She hesitated, knowing she should decline. The last thing she needed was to share a piece of pie with Adam at one in the morning, especially since he was clad only in jogging pants and looked so sleepily, completely sexy. She had managed her attraction to him quite well for the past couple of weeks. Inviting him to stay here had been a challenge to herself, to prove she could handle it. She had done it. Now she shouldn't tempt fate. And yet...

"Banana cream is usually only good for two days," she said, drawing the belt of her robe tighter at the waist.

Adam's smile flashed again. "Then let's not let it go to waste."

They were soon in the kitchen sharing the last of the pie.

Groaning, Adam pushed his empty plate away. "If Gabe and I keep eating all this good stuff you bake, we're going to have to go on a diet."

Eyeing his lean but muscular frame, Lainey laughed. "Yeah, right."

"It's just a good thing those kids have me running up and down the football field." Sighing, he thrust a hand through his hair.

"You're disappointed in tonight's game."

"Neal should have been at quarterback. The team fires on all cylinders when he's playing. And frankly, if he doesn't get to play soon, I'm afraid he's going to quit."

"That would be awful."

"Yeah. From what I've seen, his mother is right. Neal needs to be busy. I don't want him to quit."

"Then put him in."

"I'm not the head coach."

"Surely Vance will listen to you."

"He's following Coach Medford's instructions to let Neal sit on the sidelines in punishment for missing so much of the summer practice. He says Neal didn't earn the right to play, that he's only a junior, that he'll have next year. I've talked to Vance, but he's definitely Medford's disciple on this matter."

"But missing practice wasn't Neal's fault. His father—"

"Yeah. Neal's father." Adam's tone was glum.

"So you've met Glenn Scroggins."

"He's a very smooth-talking man. The kind who knows a little bit about everything, but not a whole lot about anything in particular."

She laughed. "I see you've got his number."

"How'd someone as nice as Marnie wind up with him?"

Lainey didn't reply, as reluctant to gossip as always.

But Adam kept on, "Marnie sure believes in Neal. I'll give her that much. Even though she's as impatient to see the kid play as her husband is, she even understands what Coach Medford was trying to get across when he benched Neal. She's not pushing him to quit the way I think his father is." Adam grinned as he caught Lainey's eye. "I know you don't want to gossip, but I'd sure like to know what Marnie was thinking of when she married Glenn."

"I guess there's no harm in just telling you the truth."

"I think Aunt Loretta would say that was all right."

Lainey made a face at him. "It's what you said before. Glenn's a smooth talker. He blew into town, selling something, and met Marnie when she was just out of high school and working at the dime store that used to be on Main Street."

She went on to explain that Marnie's older brother had been killed in Vietnam and she and her father were just barely keeping their farm going when Marnie married Glenn. He tried farming. But after Neal and his younger sister, Jilly, were born, Glenn got restless. Marnie's father died, and Glenn tried to start a restaurant in town. It was a pie-in-the-sky venture, and it cost them half the farm's acreage. Instead of trying to keep the farm going, Marnie went to work at the chair factory in town just to make ends meet. Since then, Glenn had wandered in and out of Marnie and the children's lives.

"She should get rid of him," Adam said. "Put a finish to it."

"The crazy thing is that she loves him. She was the prettiest girl in town and she had her pick of boyfriends. She still could have her pick of men. But she chose Glenn."

"I guess we don't always fall in love with the right people."

"Did you?" The question popped out before Lainey gave it much thought.

Adam eased back in his chair, regarding her warily. "You mean Debbie?"

"Was there someone else?"

He shook his head. "Not since the first minute I saw Debbie." Sadness stole across his features. "I guess you could call it love at first sight."

Thinking of the beautiful blonde in the framed picture Gabe had placed beside his bed, Lainey could understand why Adam had fallen hard and fast. She supposed that was the sort of woman he would look for if he ever considered getting married again. Someone bright and pretty, with perfect makeup and hair. The thought left her feeling hollow.

"What about you?"

She looked up, surprised by the question. "Me?"

Arms crossed on the edge of the table, Adam sat forward. "Did you fall in love with the wrong person, Lainey? Is that why you're not married?"

Not wanting to discuss this with him, she shrugged.

But for some reason Adam was intent on pressing the issue. "There's been someone. A woman like you—"

"What does that mean?" she retorted, stiffening.

"Just that you would make a wonderful wife." He immediately looked as if he regretted the remark, but that didn't stop him from adding, "And a wonderful mother."

Though she told herself not to be ridiculous, she felt her face grow warm with pleasure.

Adam's neck had deepened in color as well. Clearing his throat, he leaned back in his chair. "I'm sorry, Lainey. I shouldn't pry. Your personal business is not my concern."

She should have let it go at that. But there had been few people in her life who had cared enough to chip away at her natural reserve and ask these sorts of questions. And somehow it felt so right to be sitting here talking in low, intimate tones with Adam. Since he had moved in, they had talked like this often, only not so late at night and not about so personal a subject.

But Lainey wanted to answer his questions. "There was someone," she said. "The wrong someone, as you said."

"He hurt you?" Adam asked when she didn't continue.

"It was all my fault."

"Why do you say that?"

"Because I should have seen...should have known that he would never...that I wasn't..." On the table in front of her, she laced her fingers together. She made herself put the words together. "I should have realized he would never really love me."

"And why was that?"

"He was the minister at the church."

"Reverend Hargraves?"

Adam's shocked exclamation made Lainey laugh out loud. "Of course not!"

"Well, he's the only minister I've met at that church."

Lainey couldn't stop laughing because she couldn't get the picture out of her head. She and John Hargraves? She and that very well-married, very meek, very mild and very much older man? The idea was too ludicrous for words. Adam began to chuckle as well, and soon they were both wiping their eyes.

"Good Lord, woman, you gave me quite a shock."

"It would have shocked the Reverend and *Mrs*. Hargraves even more."

"But if it wasn't him, who?"

Still chuckling, Lainey said, "I'm talking about the minister who was here before Reverend Hargraves. About seven years ago."

"I hope he wasn't old and married."

"He was young and a bachelor."

In a move that seemed quite natural to her, Adam reached over and took her hand. "Thank goodness. You've restored my faith in you."

She left her hand in his. "And you've made me laugh about this. That's something I never thought I'd do."

Adam's fingers closed more tightly around hers. Some of the mirth faded from his gaze. "You want to tell me about it?"

What she wanted was for him to go on holding her hand for a long, long time. But she couldn't say that. So she told him about Michael Ames. "He was quite young, maybe only twenty-five or so. This was only his second church. Aunt Loretta used to ask him over for Sunday dinner a lot. I think everyone in the church was hoping he and I would get together."

"So you did?"

"We went for long walks. We talked. We got . . ." She flushed. "We got pretty involved."

"So what happened?"

"One day he called and said there was someone important he wanted me to meet. I thought it might be his parents or the deacon or someone." Lainey sighed, realized anew how gullible she had been. "When I got over to the parsonage, bearing a big coconut cake, of course, I got to meet his fiancée."

Adam frowned. "You're joking."

"I wish I were. They had broken up, he told me, before he took this church. Her father was a minister, too, and wanted to use his influence to get Michael into a more prominent church. Michael didn't want that, and had quarreled with her over it. But I guess after a year in Parrish, Michael had worked through his idealism and was ready to move on to bigger and better things. When he reached that decision, she was willing to take him back."

"What did you do?"

"Bought them a wedding gift."

"Lainey." Her name escaped Adam's lips like a sigh. "You should have rubbed the good minister's face into that cake."

She almost smiled. "Don't think it didn't occur to me."

Adam was shaking his head. "I don't understand. Why would he do that to you? Why call you over there to meet her?"

"Because in his mind we were really just good friends."

"*Very* good friends, I'd say."

Flushing, she glanced away. "But we hadn't...I mean we didn't—"

"But you came close."

Very embarrassed, she tried to release her hand from his.

He held on. "Why do you think this was your fault?"

"Because I read too much into everything that happened."

"A man takes you out. Gets physically intimate. And he's a minister, to boot. What else were you supposed to think?

It all sounded so different when he laid the situation out for her. "I don't know."

"Well, I know," Adam muttered. "I know you escaped from a pretty bad fate. If this guy's still in the ministry, I'll bet he's chasing choir members behind his wife's back."

Lainey had to laugh. "You may be right. But Aunt Loretta thought..." She bit her lip.

"I can imagine what she thought." Adam turned her hand up, and stroked his thumb back and forth along the lifeline in her palm. "I bet Loretta figured that if you got married to a minister, people would stop talking about your mother."

Lainey stared at him, amazed at his perception. "Aunt Loretta was proud, you know. She thought everyone in town knew what my mother had become. Loretta was a lot older than Mother. She practically raised her after their parents died. But Mother was different, I guess. She and Aunt Loretta had a big fight when my father left Mother pregnant with me. And that's when Mother left."

"What happened to your father?"

"Loretta said he was just a man passing through town."

"Like Glenn Scroggins."

"I guess."

"Like me."

This time he didn't resist when she pulled her hand away. But even though they weren't touching, a connection remained as they sat staring at each other. It was a feeling bigger and stronger than any she had felt with any other man. It made her grand passion for Reverend Michael Ames feel quite tame.

"I don't want to hurt you," Adam told her.

"I don't want to be hurt."

"But I do want you. I've been trying to fight it, but it's not working."

She swallowed hard. "You said it had been a long time since—"

"It's not just that. Not anymore." He took hold of her hand again. "Lainey?"

She just looked at him. She didn't know what to do.

But he knew. He pulled her toward him, onto his lap. He kissed her. Deeply. Thoroughly. And when she sighed and shuddered against him, he pushed aside her robe. Through her thin T-shirt, he traced the curves of her breasts. He murmured that she was sweet, that he loved the way her nipples hardened to his touch, loved the way she smelled, the way her hair looked loose around her shoulders.

"I want you naked." His kisses were like whispers feathering up her neck.

At that point, Lainey would have done almost anything he asked. "Okay."

"And I want you to touch me."

She was shaking like a newborn calf. But she wanted to touch him, too. Drawing away, she put her hand to the pulse that was beating at the base of his throat. She let her fingers drift down the line that bisected the lean muscles of his chest. His skin was smooth and warm, but he shivered when she touched him. His eyes were a warm, liquid brown gazing into hers. Obeying some unspoken request, she shifted on his lap and dipped her hand lower, to the hardening ridge of flesh between his legs.

He stopped her before she did more than skim the outline of his erection. "Don't."

Thinking she had done something wrong, she slipped off his lap. He didn't let her get away, however. He drew her back between his spread legs, gazing up at her. "I don't want to hurt you," he said again.

But she wasn't afraid anymore. She just didn't care about the consequences. At this stage of her life, she was more afraid of never knowing what it was like to make love with a man. And she wanted to know. She wanted to know with *this* man.

"We're going to take it slow," he told her. "Real slow."

She didn't know how to tell him that she wanted it fast. Inexperience kept her silent as he pushed her robe to the floor. With slow movements he lifted her T-shirt upward, baring her breasts to his gaze. He kissed them.

Slowly. One and then the other, licking and sucking until she ached for an even more intimate touch.

Hands fastening on his shoulders, she whispered his name, pressing herself to him, shamelessly offering herself for his caress. Adam's mouth moved from her breasts downward, until his tongue dipped into the hollow of her navel, nibbling, teasing, tempting. One arm went around her, his hand settling on the lower curve of her rear, fingers slipping beneath the edges of her panties.

Like a sunburst, pleasure spread through her body. Sharp, bright pleasure like she had never known before. Nothing in her limited experience had prepared her for such overwhelming feelings.

While she struggled to catch her breath, Adam rested his head low on her belly. His ragged-sounding breath was hot against her skin. She touched his hair again, wondering, waiting for what might happen next.

What he did was pull back. He said, "No."

Confusion pushed pleasure aside. Her T-shirt fell to cover her again as he moved away.

"Adam?"

He shook his head. "I want you to think about this, Lainey."

Thinking was the last thing she wanted to do. "I don't understand."

"We need to slow down."

"Slow down? Now?"

"I think so, yes." He reached out, as if to draw her into his arms.

She resisted. "Stop talking to me like I'm a child. I'm a grown woman who knows her own mind. I want to make love with you. Now. Here."

Eyebrow cocked, Adam looked at the table and chuckled low in his throat. "That's a tempting suggestion, but no."

Shame scorched her cheeks. When would she learn? She turned, but Adam caught her.

"Let me go." Her voice shook with fury, and she wouldn't, couldn't look at him.

"I want you to listen to me."

She closed her eyes.

"I want to make love to you. But I want it to be right."

She peeked at him. "Right?"

He touched her cheek. "The way you should be made love to. With all the preliminaries."

"What does that mean?"

"You'll see."

"But Adam—"

"Hush, now." He placed two fingers against her lips. "Let me do this my way, okay?"

She looked confused, and Adam almost reconsidered. But it would be all too easy to take Lainey up to bed. After her story about the insensitive young minister, he was sure she was a virgin. And if Adam took her now, he would be no better than that stupid, unfeeling man. Obviously, no one had ever treated her with the respect and care she deserved. No one had made her feel special or desired. Lainey Bates was an old-fashioned woman. She should be wooed in an old-fashioned way.

He didn't know if he was the man for the job. He probably had more in common with the minister and with Glenn Scroggins than with the sort of person Lainey deserved. Hell, all the reasons he had been trying to resist her for weeks were still as valid as ever. That didn't seem to matter when he considered how much he wanted her, how much he wanted to make this special for her.

What did matter was making sure this wasn't some hasty, hurried coupling that she might regret.

Calling on all his reserves of willpower, he took her hand in his and started toward the front hall. "Come on, Miss Bates. I want to walk you to your door."

She fumed all the way up the stairs. But at her bedroom door, when he kissed her, her exasperation dissolved like sugar in water. When his own resistance was in danger of the same, he ended the kiss. "I'll see you tomorrow," he murmured, and walked to his own room without looking back.

He heard Lainey's door close with an irritated little snap.

Adam went to bed feeling as hard and frustrated as a fifteen-year-old after an interrupted make-out party. He wondered if postponing the inevitable would be worth it.

But the next morning, when Lainey returned from her chores to find the table set with the Parrish family silver and china, a vase of roses cut from her arbor in the center, her smile of wonder told Adam that waiting was, indeed, worth any frustration.

Gabe, who had been camped out on the porch watching for Lainey to appear, giggled as Adam presented her with French toast browned to perfection and sprinkled with powdered sugar and cinnamon.

"For you, madam."

She looked from the plate to Adam, her eyes a brilliant, shining green. "You shouldn't have gone to so much trouble."

"It's no trouble," Gabe piped up. "He's made me French toast lots of times."

"Hey, cut it out," his father told him. "Can't you see I'm trying to impress this lady? Why do you think I risked bleeding to death to pick these roses for her?" He showed her hands with several long thorn-inflicted scratches.

Lainey laughed. "I am really, really impressed." She picked up the vase of full late-summer blooms and inhaled their fragrance. "But you could have worn gloves, you know."

"I wanted you to know I suffered for those roses."

When she laughed again, he leaned down and kissed her. He hadn't meant to, not with Gabe standing right here, taking everything in. Having Lainey as a friend was one thing, but seeing Adam kiss someone other than his mother might be a different matter entirely.

But Gabe seemed to take that kiss as a matter of course. "Hurry up and eat," he told Lainey. "Dad says we're going to have fun today."

"Oh, really?" Lainey replied and looked at Adam before tucking into her breakfast.

"If you have time, I thought we might take a hike up on the ridge." He gestured toward the hill to the west of the farm.

Lainey quickly agreed to the idea, though she had been planning to freeze the tomatoes she had gathered from her fading garden yesterday. A hike with Adam and Gabe was much more appealing. Doing anything with Adam suited her just fine.

The three of them spent the day together. The hike was long and hot, but when they got the top of the ridge Lainey deemed it as worthwhile as ever. Through a break in the trees, Applewood Valley spread lush and green at their feet, a scene of flat pastures and rolling hills.

Lainey wondered if Adam saw what she did, if he would ever see this as home. Last night he had compared himself to her father, a man just passing through. Even knowing that, she wanted to be his lover. But even more, she wanted him to stay. She was setting herself up for a big fall. She knew the risks but couldn't stand the thought of backing away now.

"This *is* a beautiful place," Adam said, turning to draw her to his side.

She rested her cheek against his shoulder. "Uncle Coy told me that when the first Parrishes came to settle here, they came in over this ridge, down the old logging road we walked up."

"I wonder how it looked to them."

"Beautiful, I'm sure. They stayed, didn't they?"

Adam said nothing, though his eyes continued to scan the scenic vista.

Gabe, who had been worrying a lizard instead of looking at the view, came running up with Goldie hot on his heels. "Hey, guys, look at that. We can see home." He was pointing toward the cluster of buildings at the farm.

Home. It was a telling choice of words, Lainey thought. She wasn't sure Adam caught it. He picked Gabe up and pointed out the more distant landmark of Caroline and Reid's farmhouse. If Adam left after the first of the year as he intended to do, Gabe would find another place to call home. To Lainey that seemed so wrong. This farm should be Gabe's home, by birthright and because he loved it here, loved it the way she had as a girl, the way she did now. She wanted to teach Gabe to appreciate and care for this land, just as Uncle Coy had taught her. If Adam and Gabe went away, she might never have the chance.

Perhaps sensing her distress, Adam set Gabe down and asked. "Is something wrong?"

"I was just thinking . . ." She stopped herself before saying what was in her heart. She couldn't hold him here with words. She could only hope that he might grow to love this land. And perhaps love her. That dangerous wish made her shiver.

"Lainey?"

She turned, hoping he couldn't see the emotions swirling inside her. "Coming up here always gets to me." She made a sweeping gesture to include the entire valley. "I see it all like this, and I know I never want to leave."

He stepped close behind her, murmuring, "You couldn't leave. You'd never survive the transplanting."

"You make me sound like a weed."

"A pretty plant, with red-gold blossoms." His arms encircled her waist, and she leaned back, savoring his solid strength. His lips nibbled at her ear. Twisting around, she lifted her mouth to his, but he pulled back, chuckling. "Goodness, Miss Bates, but you are forward."

She thought of last night's intimate, arousing touches and blushed. "You know something about being forward yourself, Mr. Cutler."

"But I've reformed now. We're going to behave properly."

"Aunt Loretta would be so proud."

"Oh, dear, let's not get carried away."

"Let's do," she whispered and lifted her mouth toward his.

Gabe's shout interrupted the kiss before it could happen. He was starving, he said. Grinning, Adam took Lainey's hand and drew her to the big, flat rock where they had deposited the backpacks containing lunch.

They ate in the shade of an ancient oak tree, where Adam fed her grapes and Gabe regaled them both with stories of what monsters might live in the cave they had passed halfway up the ridge. For the rest of the afternoon, Lainey allowed herself to relax, to hold Adam's hand and smile into his dark eyes and accept the light kisses he brushed across her cheek from time to time.

He was flirting with her, teasing her, and she was enjoying every minute. No man had ever looked into her eyes and told her she was lovely. No one had touched a fingertip to the freckles she hated and said they were cute or whispered that he wanted to kiss each and every one of them. If this was what Adam had meant the night before when he had referred to "preliminaries," then she was happy to wait.

Back at the farm there were the ever-present chores. Fred had the day off, so Adam helped Lainey and Neal with the milking. The teenager was in an odd mood, and though Lainey really wanted to spend the evening with Adam, she invited Neal to stay for hamburgers they grilled outdoors. There was a cake to bake and fresh vegetables to prepare for the family dinner planned for the next day. Afterward, she joined the men to watch a tense pennant-race baseball game on television.

Then, once again, Adam walked her to her door and said good-night with a kiss.

But early the next morning there was a note taped to the bathroom mirror that said, "Good morning, beautiful." She held it tight to her chest and then placed it in the bureau drawer that held the dried corsage from her high-school graduation, a handkerchief of her mother's and the cameo brooch Aunt Loretta had worn every Sunday.

Lainey took Gabe to church. She was glad Adam said he needed to stay home and work on some plans for school. She felt profoundly changed, and she worried that everyone would be able to see what was on her mind. For that reason, she sat beside Sammi instead of in her usual place beside Caroline and Reid. Her feelings for Adam were too new, too easily crushed, to share with anyone, even her closest friends.

Everyone came to her house for lunch, however. Lainey tried her best to stay busy and away from Adam. But her gaze kept straying to meet his. He stole a kiss when they were alone in the kitchen. And beneath the dining-room table, he nestled his foot close to Lainey's and grinned wickedly when Caroline said she looked flushed. He laughed as Lainey felt her cheeks deepen to crimson.

Before dessert, she grabbed a moment alone in the kitchen to take a few deep, calming breaths. Unfortunately, when she turned around, Caroline was standing in the doorway watching her with an odd expression on her face.

Lainey picked a chocolate-swirled pound cake up from the counter and nodded toward the stack of dessert plates. "Grab those, will you?" She left before Caroline could detain her.

But she could feel the other woman watching her while the dessert was sliced and served. Thankfully, when they were finished Reid asked for everyone's attention. He stood, grinning like a cat contemplating a bowl of cream and confirmed what Lainey had suspected a week ago. "We're having another baby. Caroline's pregnant."

The room rang with Adam and Lainey's congratulations and Gabe's demands to know if it would be a girl or boy. Sammi, who had known, of course, was beaming with pride. They were all full of excited speculation as they cleared the table.

The males turned on the television, with plans to flip between baseball and football games. Gabe dashed outside to play. Sammi left with her boyfriend. Caroline went to tend to Christopher, while Lainey contemplated the dishes.

Before she began, however, she stood in the middle of the kitchen, just smiling. *Another baby. Another wish come true for Caroline.*

When Lainey was a little girl living in the cottage down the hill, this big house had seemed like a palace and Caroline had been the princess. Lainey had envied her for a long time, until she realized how unhappy this house was. Alcohol had turned Caroline's mother into a vague shadow of a person. Her grandfather was sunk deep in bitterness and failure. Lainey had feared Robert Parrish. She knew he didn't like her, and he certainly didn't want Caroline to play with "that Bates bastard."

But Caroline had defied him when she could. Lainey had grown to worship the older girl, who could spin stories out of thin air. And when the terror Caroline lived with drove her away, there had been an empty spot in Lainey's world. It had meant a lot to Lainey when Caroline came home last year. Her marriage to Reid seemed to complete a circle. The land he farmed had once been part of this farm, and now Caroline's children would grow up here.

It was right, Lainey thought. Just so very, very right.

"That's a beautiful smile."

With a start, she realized Adam had come into the room. She turned her smile on him. "I'm just so happy for Caroline and Reid."

"Yeah. Me, too." He crossed the room and kissed her. She touched his cheek and looked into his eyes. Adam suddenly wished everyone would go home and leave them alone.

She broke the spell by asking if he was going to help her do the dishes.

With a laughing protest that the game was about to start, he spun away from her and headed for the hall, forgetting that he had come into the kitchen for a drink of water. He seemed to forget a lot of things when he looked at Lainey, like how wrong he was for her.

But that troubling truth bubbled to the surface the minute he took a step into the hall and found Caroline standing just beyond the doorway.

"I think we need to talk," she murmured, drawing him toward the front porch.

Chapter Seven

"**D**on't hurt her." Caroline's quiet words came just after she closed the front door behind them.

Adam didn't pretend not to understand. He paused beside one of the front porch's big white pillars and gazed at the lawn through narrowed eyes.

"She's so capable, so independent, people don't realize how easily she can be hurt."

"I realize," Adam muttered.

"Then don't do it."

He finally turned to look at her. "We haven't done anything—"

"Yet," Caroline completed the sentence for him. "I'm not stupid. I've been watching the two of you react to each other ever since you and Gabe moved in here. I watched you at lunch. I saw you kiss her just now. I know what's going to happen."

Her disapproving tone ticked him off. "We're adults, Caroline."

"Lainey will fall in love with you."

Irritation disappearing, Adam hung his head, unable to formulate an answer or a protest, because his sister was right.

"Are you falling in love with her?"

The question jerked his head up. "Love?"

"It's an emotion a lot of people, women especially, require before they get deeply, *sexually* involved with someone. So are you falling in love with Lainey?"

Love wasn't something he considered easily. Most of his adult life had been spent loving Debbie. He had fallen so quickly for her, and she had reciprocated in kind. He hadn't been forced to consider what it was to fall in love with anyone for a long, long time. He didn't know how to consider it now, even with the strong attraction he was feeling for Lainey.

Caroline took a step toward him. "By your silence, I'm assuming you don't know exactly what your feelings for Lainey are."

Giving her a wan smile, Adam said, "I guess it's true what they say about twins being able to read each other's minds."

"Oh, Adam." His sister reached out and took his hand. "Do you know what I would give to see you fall in love with Lainey, to live here with her and Gabe? It would be like all the broken pieces of our lives had finally fallen into place."

He squeezed her fingers. "It's a nice dream, Caroline. It reminds me of the end of one of your books. Happily ever after."

"But unlike the characters in books, real people can seldom be manipulated that way."

"You did a pretty good job manipulating me into this job."

"But I know there's an itch inside you."

"The urge to fly," Adam said, thinking of their father.

Caroline nodded. "If you get involved with Lainey and don't love her, she'll be devastated when you go. I couldn't bear to see her hurting like that. And there's the family to consider. She's a part of it. If you got involved and hurt her, how could you and Gabe come back to see us all? The ramifications of this go pretty deep."

Her reasoning was exactly the same he had used to resist his attraction to Lainey in the first place. All the truths he had chosen to ignore or forget tumbled back into place.

Her eyes dark with misery, Caroline went on, "Regardless of what would happen to the family, it's Lainey I'm most concerned with. If there's something between you, something more than a passing fancy, then no one would be happier than me. But if it's just—"

"Sex," Adam supplied the end of the sentence this time.

"Yes." His sister sighed. "If it's only sex, then I'm not sure Lainey can handle it."

Thinking of the woman who had met his kisses and touches so eagerly, Adam frowned. "Maybe you don't know Lainey as well as you think you do."

Caroline's jaw tightened. "Regardless of what might have already happened between you, I know her better than you. I knew the little girl who was abandoned by her mother, who endured our grandfather's scorn and the county busybodies' gossip. And I've come to know the sweet, trusting woman who wants a husband and a family. She's never told me that, but I know. I can see it in her face. I really don't think casual sex is what Lainey Bates is all about."

"Good Lord, Caroline, you act as if I'm some kind of lecher."

She took hold of his arm. "Of course you're not that. I didn't mean that. But Lainey's like this empty glass, you know. She's waiting to be filled up, and if she's not treated with care, she'll shatter."

Adam managed a soft laugh. "Your writer's mind is showing."

"Just don't hurt her, okay?"

He nodded.

"Promise me."

"Caroline—"

The door opened before he could reply, and Lainey looked out at them. "Did the two of you think you could hide out here and get out of all the kitchen work?"

Caroline's laugh sounded forced to Adam. "I completely forgot about the dishes. I'll come in and help now." She turned back to Adam. "Coming?"

He shook his head, and when his gaze collided with Lainey's, he shifted it away. "I think I'm going for a walk."

"Good idea," she said. "If you'll wait—"

"I need to clear my head," he replied and turned to go before he had to see the hurt come into her eyes.

Lainey frowned after his retreating back while Caroline took her arm and eased her inside. "Let's talk baby names," she said brightly. Too brightly, Lainey thought.

The rest of that day passed in a series of events that were all *too* much. Caroline chattered too much while they finished the dishes. She and Reid and the baby left too abruptly. Adam came back after too long a walk. He worked on schoolwork much too long and ate his dinner much too quietly.

Lainey knew Caroline had said something to him about her, about *them*. Otherwise, why would his demeanor change so radically? All evening, she wanted to ask what had been said, to ask for a chance to talk it over. But it was difficult to begin a discussion she was certain could be painful.

At Gabe's bedtime, after his father had read him a story and Lainey had come in for the good-night that which had become a habit, she found the nerve to ask Adam what was wrong. They were standing at the top of the stairs, just feet from the place where he had kissed her so tenderly two nights in a row.

In that contained space, it was difficult for Adam to avoid her gaze, but he did. "Nothing's wrong."

"Don't lie to me."

He looked at her then and she saw everything she needed to know in his eyes. The regret. The distance. A knot formed in Lainey's stomach. What in the world had Caroline said?

He shoved his hands in his pockets. "I've just been thinking—"

"And talking to Caroline," Lainey cut in. "She's the reason you're acting so strangely."

"No, she's not."

"Then why are you acting this way?"

"Because I've come back to my senses."

Lainey turned and took hold of the intricately carved newel post. The wood was smooth to the touch, the dips and curves familiar because of the many times she had polished them. The crushing sense of failure that closed in around her was just as familiar.

Behind her, Adam continued to speak. "Ever since I came here, I've been on a merry-go-round with you. I was attracted to you from the start, but I told myself I had no business acting on it. Then I lost my head. Then I recovered my senses, again. Then it happened again. And again. Up and down, round and round we go." He drew in a deep breath. "But this time I'm recovering for good, Lainey."

She gripped the wood even harder. "What about what I want?"

"I think in the long run, you're going to be glad I got my head back on straight before we both made some big mistakes."

She didn't trust herself to say anything.

"You're very special," he said when the silence had stretched to the breaking point. "I meant what I said about that. You deserve someone special, too."

Those were words Lainey had heard before. Only this time, she believed them. She thought Adam was special. And she thought she deserved him.

Adam cleared his throat and continued, "You certainly don't deserve a short-term lover. And I'm afraid that's all I would be." He paused, and the old floorboards squeaked beneath his feet.

Lainey could imagine him shifting back and forth, the way he did when he was nervous. But she didn't turn around. She didn't help him out by making it easy.

He finished with, "I'd rather we went back to the beginning and tried to be friends."

She couldn't stand and listen to this. Instead of arguing she started down the stairs, not looking back at him. Asking for what she wanted wasn't easy for a woman who had never been taught how. Her mother and father had taught her about leaving. Aunt Loretta taught her that ladies waited to be asked. Men had taught her she was always second choice. Even Uncle Coy, who had never stood up to his abusive half brother, Robert, had taught her about passivity. There was nothing inside Lainey that enabled her to ask Adam to disregard his instinctive caution, to love her, to make love to her.

Downstairs, she waited, hoping he would come after her. He didn't.

The next day the plumber finished at the cottage, and Adam and Gabe moved back to the bottom of the hill.

Lainey felt numb for days. The house, her perfect family home, was suddenly so empty.

She saw Adam in passing. He didn't go out of his way to see her, and she was glad. Gabe still came to see her every day, still gave her hugs and made her laugh. Daily, she could see how being here, being with her and the rest of the family, was healing the wound that lingered from his mother's untimely death. But Lainey didn't get to kiss him good-night, or share his meals, or help him with his numbers, or pack treats for snack time at school. She wanted all of that. She wanted Gabe and his father in her house. She wanted the sense of family that had made the past few weeks so nice.

Anger took over midweek. Anger such as Lainey had never known. She ripped up the note Adam had left for her on the bathroom mirror. She threw the wilting roses he had picked onto the compost heap. By Thursday afternoon, she was spoiling for a fight.

She tried to work off some energy by grooming her little sorrel mare, the one Uncle Coy had given her nearly fifteen years ago. Almost blind and far too old to ride anymore, Maggie didn't have much time left. The vet had suggested early this summer that Lainey might want to consider having her put down. But Lainey couldn't bring herself to make that decision just yet. The horse spent most of her days in the barn or in the enclosed pasture nearby where she could get some exercise. She was well fed and well loved and not suffering. Several times a week, Lainey made a point of coming down to the barn and brushing her coat and talking to her. Today, she was trying to ease her own pain as well as bring a little happiness to the mare.

Caroline's voice, calling Lainey's name, interrupted the calming ritual. Lainey stiffened. She hadn't seen the other woman since Sunday, though Caroline had left a message on the answering machine and stuck a note on the back door. Lainey didn't want to see her just yet. She leaned against Maggie, hoping Caroline would just go away.

"Hey, Lainey, are you in here?" Footsteps sounded on the concrete floor as Caroline walked down the barn's corridor. She walked right by Maggie's stall and Lainey breathed a sigh of relief. But that made Maggie nicker, and Caroline turned around and saw Lainey.

"Here you are," she said with a puzzled frown. "Didn't you hear me calling?"

"Nope." Lainey passed a brush over Maggie's faded coat, not looking at Caroline.

The other woman hesitated. "Is everything going okay?"

"Just fine."

Another pause. "Adam tells me he's looking for a place to rent."

That news made Lainey's brush falter, but only for a moment. She found she couldn't resist a crisp, "You must be pleased."

"Pleased?"

"He's obviously following the advice you gave him Sunday." Tossing aside the brush, Lainey stooped to examine Maggie's front legs for signs of swelling.

There was a sigh from Caroline. "What did Adam tell you I said?"

"Nothing. I figured it out myself." She moved to the horse's rear legs.

"I was just worried—"

"You shouldn't have been," Lainey retorted, straightening to look at Caroline for the first time.

She stood just inside the stall, her expression troubled as she absentmindedly stroked Maggie's nose. "It just seemed that the two of you were getting involved."

"So what?"

"So, I didn't think it was a good idea."

"I didn't know we needed your permission."

"Lainey—"

"Listen to me." Lainey's hold on her temper snapped. "I love you like a sister, Caroline, and I know you *are* Adam's sister, but I don't appreciate your interference in my personal life."

Caroline had the decency to look ashamed. "I was trying to look out for you."

Lainey's laugh was short. "Oh, yes, please look out for poor, strange Lainey."

"I don't think of you that way."

"But that's how I am. I'm downright odd."

"Don't say that."

"But it's true. If I weren't so odd, then I would... Adam would..." Anger gave way to frustration and Lainey had to swallow a sudden unexpected sob. Damn it, she wasn't going to cry. She turned, steadying herself against the horse.

Behind her, she felt Caroline step closer. "Lainey, I was trying to save you from being hurt."

"I can take care of myself."

"But Adam is...he's..." Caroline cleared her throat. "He's my brother and I love him, but he's not a settled sort of person. Much as we want him to stay here, he probably won't. And then you'd...well, you would—"

"Be left behind," Lainey supplied. "What you're saying is that anything I have to offer wouldn't be enough to hold Adam here."

Caroline's protest was quick and sharp. "Lainey, I didn't say that."

"But it's the truth." Lainey faced her again. "I know it's the truth. I wasn't kidding myself about the future." She had been, of course, but she didn't want Caroline to know that.

Her friend's brown-eyed gaze was steady on hers. "Then what were you doing?"

"Living, for once." The answer felt as if it were torn from her. "Being impulsive. Being something other than plain, old Lainey Bates, Shirley Bates's bastard, a good little replacement for the child Coy and Loretta Parrish couldn't have. My whole life I've minded my p's and q's, and maybe I'm tired of that. Maybe, for once, I wanted to forget what I was *supposed* to do."

"I didn't know you felt like this," Caroline murmured.

"Even if you had known, you would have still told Adam to stay away from me."

Caroline's expression told Lainey she was right. "I'm sorry I've upset you."

Lainey shrugged, the last of the fight going out of her. "It's okay, Caroline. Even if you hadn't said a word, Adam probably would have 'come to his senses,' as he put it." Turning, she reached again for the brush she had discarded.

"I wish—"

"Don't," Lainey muttered, not trusting herself to look at her friend. "Just leave it alone, okay? I don't want to talk about this anymore. What's done is done."

To Caroline's credit, she didn't push. She just went away, promising to call later. And when she was gone, Lainey put her arms around her horse's neck, tears burning in her eyes just as they had when she was fifteen and her heart had been broken by Bobby Maxwell. But she didn't cry. She *refused* to waste a tear on this whole incident.

She was glad she had held on to her control when she walked out of the barn and found Marnie Scroggins's pickup coming down the drive. Marnie wouldn't have asked why she had been crying, but Lainey didn't want her to wonder about it, either.

"Hello, stranger," Lainey said as the truck drew to a stop beside her. She had seen little of her neighbor in the past few weeks.

Marnie wasn't looking too well. She was pale, with dark circles beneath her sky blue eyes. "I just stopped by to make sure you can still help with the chili supper Saturday night."

Lainey had forgotten she had promised Marnie she would supervise the dessert table for the high school's athletic-booster club annual fall fund-raiser. Adam would be there, and Lainey didn't want to go. "Marnie, gosh, I wish—"

"Oh, please don't say you can't," the woman wailed. "I'm about to lose my mind getting this thing organized. I even had to take off the afternoon at work to take care of things. If you back out, I don't know what—"

"I'm not backing out," Lainey assured her quickly. It wasn't like Marnie to act so rattled. "Tell me what I need to do."

Marnie handed over a list of people who were supposed to be preparing desserts. Their phone numbers were listed so that Lainey could call and remind them. Nodding, Lainey put the list in her back pocket, then invited Marnie to come up to the house.

"I can't," she said. "I only stopped because I wanted to give you that list. Glenn's waiting for me at home. His car's on the fritz, so he needs the truck."

"Has he found a job?"

Marnie shook her head, her gaze skipping away from Lainey's. "He's got a good possibility, though."

"Where?"

"I'm . . . I'm not sure." Marnie reached for the gearshift. "I wish I could stay and talk, Lainey, but I've got to go. I've got all kinds of things to do for this chili supper."

She left Lainey standing beside the drive, staring after her with a concerned frown. Lainey figured it was much more than a booster club supper that had Marnie on the run. She imagined Glenn Scroggins was up to his old habits of leaving Marnie and his children home by themselves while he went out looking for something other than a job. From the way Marnie looked and the way Adam had said Neal was acting, Lainey had a feeling all wasn't well in the Scroggins's household.

Her suspicions seemed confirmed Saturday night. While Lainey put slices of cakes and pies on the long dessert table, she watched Marnie and Glenn in a deep discussion over in one corner of the high-school cafeteria. Marnie had arrived late and was distracted all during preparations for the crowd that was now being served on the cafeteria line. Glenn, who was still handsome despite the gray in his blond hair and the slight paunch to his belly, had come in only moments ago. Marnie shoved something into his hand and stalked off.

"Oh, dear," a voice said close to Lainey's ear. "Looks like those two are in trouble again."

Lainey turned to find Karen Hicks, a woman she had attended high school with, nodding toward Marnie.

"I tried to tell Marnie not to take him back," Karen murmured. "That man is just no good."

Pointing to the pair of lemon-meringue pies Karen had just placed on the table behind them, Lainey said, "Would you mind slicing those for me? They look so good. But then, your pies are always just wonderful."

Karen did as she was asked, but she wasn't deterred by Lainey's diversion. "Marnie should divorce Glenn and set her sights on someone else. She's still young. And there is one interesting new man in town."

Lainey followed the woman's nod to where Adam had just stepped through a set of double doors with Caroline, Reid and Gabe. The pretty, young teacher who was taking the money said something that made him laugh. Lainey ground her teeth together.

"I hear he's been staying with you," Karen said, her tone bland, but her interest very clear.

Trying to sound blasé, Lainey said, "He's family."

"But not really your kin." Karen winked. "What would you call it? A kissing cousin?"

Lainey made herself laugh and ignore the innuendo.

Before the other woman could comment again, the first of the diners reached their table. Karen and Lainey were soon adding desserts to trays already loaded with bowls of chili, coleslaw and corn bread muffins. When Adam and the rest of the family came through, Lainey made sure she was too busy slicing cakes to do more than give them all a smile.

For the rest of the evening, she tried to stay similarly occupied. She tried not to pay much attention to Adam. Which was difficult, since every available woman in the county swarmed around him. Even some of the not-so-available ones, like school-board member Cynthia Small. Lainey decided it was a disgusting display, particularly since Adam seemed to be enjoying himself so much. Evidently, he liked the feminine attention. Caroline and Reid left, taking Gabe with them to spend the night at their place. But Adam remained, all wrapped up in something Cynthia was telling him.

Though she wanted to go home, Lainey stepped in to direct the kitchen cleanup after the last of the chili had been served. Marnie was as distracted as could be, and Lainey felt duty bound to help her out. At one end of the cafeteria, a sound system was set up. Lots of people were dancing. The desserts were still out for anyone who wanted a snack. People were eating, talking, laughing. Everyone was in high spirits, even those who were on kitchen detail.

Most of the people helping were friends and neighbors Lainey had known her whole life. Karen's husband, Jeff, and his brother, Rob, had been her best playmates when she was a tomboyish grade-schooler. They were still the same foolish characters they had been back then, delighting in telling silly jokes that made her laugh. When the kitchen was clean, she even allowed Rob to get her out on the dance floor. His pregnant wife, also a lifelong friend, was sitting with her feet up, urging them on.

In the back of her mind, Lainey kept hearing what Karen had said about Adam staying with her. She imagined half of the people here knew they had been living under the same roof. No doubt, they had reached conclusions similar to Karen's. No doubt, they were interested to see him flirting with every woman in sight. And no doubt, they were wondering if Lainey minded.

So it was very important for Lainey to pretend she didn't mind. Aunt Loretta used to say a woman's good name was her most valued possession. For Lainey it was a matter of pride. She was much too proud to let anyone, especially Adam, see that she was the least bit affected by his presence or by the women who were letting him know they were interested. Lainey forced herself to laugh and talk with her friends with more than her usual animation.

Over the shoulder of Cynthia, who was definitely a woman on the prowl, Adam watched Lainey move out on the dance floor with the same pudgy, balding guy she had already danced with twice. She seemed to be having the time of her life. Adam told himself that was wonderful. But there was a tight feeling in his chest as he watched her vivid, happy features.

She looked different tonight. Her hair was in its habitual long braid, with strands that were loose around her face. But she was wearing lipstick and makeup. Her slender denim skirt emphasized the curve of her hips and rear. Her blouse was white, sort of filmy looking, with a neckline lower than her usual style.

When she put back her head and laughed at something the man she was dancing with said, Adam couldn't help but think of how he had kissed the pulse that beat at her throat, how he had pressed his face between her small breasts, taken her pink, pebbling nipples into his mouth.

The tight feeling in his chest deepened and shifted to another part of his anatomy.

"Coach Cutler?"

Blinking, Adam realized he had become so caught up in watching Lainey that he was ignoring the woman beside him. "Yes?"

Cynthia continued, "I just want to say that most of us were thrilled to see you and Coach Trewhitt put Neal Scroggins in the game last night. He's the reason we won, you know."

Adam thought she was right, but he couldn't say that. "It was a team effort."

"Very diplomatic," she said. Cocking her head to the side, she lifted a crimson-nailed hand to stroke her chin and looked up at him. Adam figured she thought this was a seductive pose. Another man might have agreed with her. Adam didn't. Just beyond her Lainey was swaying on the dance floor in someone else's arms. That's what really had his attention. That's what was really getting him steamed.

"Excuse me, Mrs.—"

"Cynthia, please." She had followed his glance to the dance floor, where the song was drawing to a close and Lainey was backing away from her dance partner.

"Excuse me, Cynthia, but I need to talk to someone."

Adam could tell the woman had expected him to ask her to dance, but he didn't care. If he was going to dance with anyone, it would be Lainey.

Murmuring excuses, he made his way through the group of people who separated him from Lainey. She had her back to him, but he put out his hand and took her arm.

She turned, laughing, probably expecting to see someone else. Her smile disappeared for a second, then was set firmly back in place.

"Dance with me," he said.

She shook her head, that unnatural smile frozen on her face. "I need to check on some things in the kitchen."

"No, you don't." He took her hand and pulled her back toward the dance floor. To refuse him, she would have had to make a scene. She didn't. As the music began, she let him take her into his arms.

Adam had no idea what the song was, even though he was certain it was something popular. All he knew was that the beat was slow and that Lainey fit perfectly against him, her head nestled just below his chin, her legs brushing his as they swayed together. Her hair was soft against his cheek. She smelled like crushed flowers, exactly the same scent as the sheets he had slept between at her house. In his hand, her palm was work worn, not soft and pampered like the hands of most women, but he liked the feeling. Tiny as she was, he could feel the strength in her, strength forged by hard physical work.

Thoughts of her muscles tensing, straining beneath his in an even more intimate dance made him groan.

"I'm sorry," she whispered, her voice sounding tense as she pulled away.

"For what?"

"Didn't I step on your foot?"

"No."

"Then—"

"Shh." He pulled her tight against him again. He could feel her tremble. "Just be quiet and let me hold you, okay?"

"But Adam—"

This time he didn't shush her. He kissed her. Hard. Right there in front of everyone. And when she struggled to break free, he stepped back, and pulling her behind him, walked off the dance floor and out the door.

They threaded through the groups of people who stood out in the foyer with Lainey protesting, "I can't leave. The desserts—"

"Can be damned." Ignoring the startled looks of two matrons who stepped out of his way, Adam hauled Lainey outside.

She tried to put the brakes on as they moved down the sidewalk and away from the crowd clustered near the door. "What in the world is the matter with you?"

"Just be quiet."

"I will not," she retorted and refused to budge.

So Adam kissed her again. She resisted, then gave in, then resisted again, finally breaking free.

"Let me go. Right now," she demanded.

From the shadows at the edge of the building, a tall silhouette separated from another. Adam recognized Neal with a girl from his first-period class. Perhaps the boy was thinking of coming to a female's aid, but the moment he recognized Lainey and Adam he stood blinking in the dim light that spread from the nearby parking lot.

"Coach Cutler," he finally croaked.

Instead of pausing to explain, Adam simply swept Lainey off her feet and into his arms. Her protest was an odd, little squeak. "See you kids around" was all Adam said to Neal and his pretty, gaping companion.

As they strode toward his truck, Lainey hid her face against his shoulder. "Oh, God, Adam, what are you doing?"

He set her on her feet beside the passenger door, but kept her bracketed within his arms. "I hope I'm taking you home to bed."

The hands she had clenched in his shirtfront tightened, then loosened while she took a deep breath. It was the same sort of breath Adam had seen major-league batters take when it was bottom of the ninth with two outs and the count was full. At that point, a person either struck out or got on base. He wondered which Lainey thought she was choosing when she said, "All right, let's go home."

Chapter Eight

Lainey rode home beside Adam feeling sure of what she wanted, of what they were about to do. Only in the foyer of her house did she get cold feet. She said nothing, but Adam seemed to sense her hesitation.

He paused with one foot on the bottom step and gave her a long look. Then he pivoted to his right and opened the front door, taking her hand to draw her out onto the porch.

Grateful for his understanding, Lainey drew in a deep breath of the cool September air. A round harvest moon was riding high above the trees. Lainey leaned back against a white column, gazed up at that pale yellow globe and hoped to get her runaway pulse under control.

Adam spoke behind her. "We don't have to do anything you don't want."

She put out her hand and he took it, entwining his fingers with hers as he stepped to her side. "Why did you change your mind?" she asked softly.

He shook his head. "I just . . . knew."

"But there must have been a reason."

"You were dancing with that other guy—"

"Rob?" She laughed. "Don't tell me you were jealous of Rob Hicks?"

"And why shouldn't I be?"

"Because Rob and I went to kindergarten together. And he's married—"

"Since when does that matter?"

"It doesn't to some people. Like Cynthia Small—"

"The woman's a leach," Adam muttered.

Facing him, Lainey took his other hand. "Is this about jealousy, Adam? Do you suddenly want me because you thought someone else did?"

He brought her hands up to his mouth and pressed a kiss to her knuckles. His voice was unsteady as he answered, "There's nothing sudden about my wanting you, Lainey."

"But if that was wrong Sunday night, why is it right now?"

"I don't know. Maybe we're making a huge mistake. All I can tell is that I kept looking at you all night long, kept watching the way you weren't watching me—"

"But I was."

"I didn't see you. What I did see was that you were on one side of the room and I was on the other, and I didn't like it. Not one bit. It felt . . ." He paused. "Wrong. That's the only way I can describe my feelings. You and me not being together felt wrong."

"And now this feels right."

He brought her tight against him. "It feels good."

"And when it's over—"

"Do you always talk about the end before it's really begun?"

"I've never talked about making love before." She swallowed nervously. "I've never made love before."

He feathered a kiss across her forehead. "I know that."

"It's that obvious?"

"You told me you didn't make love with the good Reverend Ames. And if there'd been anyone else, you would have said so."

She leaned against him, absorbing his warmth, listening to the beat of his heart. "I know I'm an oddity."

"Just an old-fashioned woman."

"A woman with few opportunities."

He chuckled. "So you're saying a good-looking traveling salesman might have gotten lucky, if he had pressed his suit around here?"

She had to smile. "Let's just say I'm ready."

Adam's voice deepened. "I'm going to make sure you're ready." He took a step toward the half-open door. "Let's go to your room."

As they walked upstairs, there were a dozen questions tumbling through her. All of them involved the question he had neatly sidestepped a few moments ago. What would happen after tonight? She couldn't ask. If she pressed for an answer, he would probably say that nothing was changed, that making love with her wouldn't alter his plans or his desire to leave. Adam was nothing if not honest. And she didn't want to hear the truth. Putting aside all thoughts of the future, she led him into her darkened bedroom.

It wasn't really dark. Not with the lamp burning in the hall. Not with moonbeams peeping around the ruffled

edges of her curtains and edging the shadows with silver.
It was in a streak of moonlight beside the bed that Adam
kissed her. Slowly, with a just-contained passion she recognized.

"Don't," she murmured against his mouth. He drew
back, looking puzzled, before she added, "Don't hold
back anymore. I'm not so fragile, you know. Not fragile
at all."

He took her at her word. Instead of restraint, he kissed
her with power. She responded in kind. Until Adam set
her away from him. With quick, efficient movements, he
drew back the covers of the bed and sat down on the
edge. Even in the dim light, his eyes were bright as he
looked up at her. His fingers were gentle as they went to
the buttons of her blouse.

Silently, with infinite tenderness, he took off her blouse
and skirt, pausing while she kicked off her shoes, taking
care as he unhooked the front clasp of her bra. It fell
away, and he covered her breasts with hands that were
dark against her pale skin. Lightly, he massaged her
flesh. Her nipples hardened, and lazy spirals of heat began to radiate downward. She almost whimpered when
Adam took his hands away.

But he was only shrugging out of his shirt and shoes.
With those disposed of, he brought her down into his lap.
His hand went to her hair. "Take it loose," he mur-
mured.

She undid the elastic band holding the bottom of the
braid, but Adam was the one who combed the thick
waves free. They fell over her bare shoulders.

With a sound halfway between a groan and sigh, Adam
caught a fistful of hair in his hand. "I like it that no other
man has seen you this way." His laugh was shaky. "Does
that make me a barbarian?"

"I don't care if it does," she whispered, lifting her mouth to his. "I want you to see me this way."

He took the lips she offered. One hand drifted back to her breast, where his thumb encircled the tightened bud of flesh at the center. Lithely, he eased them both back on the bed.

Lainey turned on her side to face him. She touched his mouth with her fingertips, then drew them down his chin to his chest and over to a flat male nipple that tightened the same as hers had done beneath his caress. Drawing in a breath, he took her hand and guided it down to the juncture of his thighs. He was hard beneath the denim. Hard for her. Without thought, she reached for the buckle of his belt.

He brushed her hand away, chuckling. "Wait. All in good time."

When she sighed, he kissed her, and his hand slipped beneath the edge of her panties. Instinctively, she tightened, but his kiss deepened. His hand stroked downward, moving in delicious circles across her mound. So slowly. So easily. She didn't realize she had parted her legs until his finger dipped into the warm, waiting cleft.

She jerked at that first touch. Jerked and sighed and then let herself close around his stroking finger. She fell back against the pillows, drawing away from his kiss, concentrating only on the swirls of pleasure that spread from his delicate manipulation of that tiny kernel of flesh within the most intimate fold of her body. She had been touched here before. Michael Ames had crossed this base. Clumsily. Tentatively. But those touches were never like this. Never had the pleasure been so intense, so purely, perfectly right.

Breathing Adam's name, she let her legs part further. He broke the rhythm of his stroking to draw her panties down her legs and toss them aside. One finger was replaced by two. The rhythm increased, until the pleasure fell around her like shattering glass. Her hips arched off the bed, seeking, needing something more. But only when the tremors of excitement had fallen off to a pulsing ache did Adam get up and take off his jeans.

Lainey turned to watch him, sitting up as he shed pants and white briefs. Outlined by moonlight, his body was sleekly, proudly male. His sex jutted forward, thickened by need, quivering when she reached out to brush the tip with her fingers. He was soft steel beneath her touch. Just looking at him made the lingering traces of her orgasm quicken once again. She felt like a chocolate drop left too long in the sun, melting at the center.

But even as her hand closed around him, Adam brushed her away. He knelt on the bed, kissing her deeply, pressing her back into pillows once more. Easily, he slipped between her legs, but he hesitated, looking down at her.

"Please," she said, touching his cheek.

Then he filled her. There was one burning moment of pain, when her body resisted. But this was Adam, she told herself. Adam, who wouldn't hurt her. Adam, whom she loved. She opened wide to accept him, move with him, to take the hot climax he spilled inside her.

And in the middle of it all, when they fell together, she whispered, "I love you."

Her words were vibrating through Adam's head when he awoke before dawn. He was breathing hard. Perspiration beaded on his skin. Yet beside him Lainey slept with one hand curled under her cheek, looking like the angel she was.

But she wasn't so very innocent. He had taken the sweetest gift she had to offer. She had given him her virginity.

And her love.

He got out of bed and crossed the room as quietly as possible. The window farthest from the bed slid up with well-oiled precision. A glance over his shoulder told him Lainey stirred at the slight noise, but her breathing continued in the steady cadence of sleep.

Bracing his hands on the windowsill, Adam took in a couple of deep gulps of air. Gradually, his heart stopped pounding. The moisture evaporated from his body. But still her words of love echoed inside him.

What had he done?

Even as he asked himself that question, he remembered the way it had felt last night when he took her away from that dance and brought her home. He remembered the *rightness* of it all. He had been seduced by that feeling. He had ignored all consequences and made love to her. And aside from the emotional ramifications, there were other repercussions to think about. What if she was pregnant? He hadn't taken even the crudest of birth-control measures. Having been married so long, and alone since Debbie's death, he hadn't thought about condoms or anything else. And damn it, he should have thought about it. He was the experienced person in this pairing. He should have taken care of Lainey.

Of all the selfish things he had done in his life, this night was the worst.

He straightened and stared out at the landscape which dawn was beginning to touch with light. And he prayed. On his father's soul, he prayed...

His father.

The curious, shivery sense of his father's presence stole through him. The feeling was as sharp as on the first night here on the farm. He closed his eyes, breathing deeply. He smelled pressed flowers. The scent was as strong as it had been his first night under this roof. As surely as Adam knew he was alive, he knew his father, and perhaps someone else, was here, right now, with him.

"Okay, Dad," he murmured. "If you want to do something constructive, tell me what to do."

"What?"

He whipped around so quickly he was thrown off balance. But instead of a spectral glow or shimmering spirit, it was Lainey who stood behind him, wrapping her robe around her.

Sharply, he let out a breath and caught the edge of the bureau beside the window to keep from falling. "You scared me to death."

She switched on the lamp on the bureau. "What are you talking about?"

"I thought you were... never mind."

"You said, 'Dad.'"

He thrust a hand through his hair. She would think he had lost his mind if he told her what had just happened.

But perhaps she guessed, because she said, "You look as if you've seen a ghost."

"Maybe I have."

She stepped closer, one eyebrow lifting in question.

He glanced back outside. "It's nothing I've seen. It's more this feeling. A sense that my father is here."

"Of course he's here."

Her calm statement made Adam look at her again. "What?"

"I feel Uncle Coy's presence all the time. And Aunt Loretta's."

"But you lived here with them. You're reminded of them—"

"Because they're here." She pressed a hand over her heart. "That's why they're with me. I carry them here. And there are times when I know they're standing right beside me."

"I've never felt that way before." Adam glanced around the room. "Not until I came here. Even though Dad told me..."

"Told you what?" Lainey pressed.

He told her his father's dying words, that they would "walk the same path." "I never knew what it meant. If it meant anything, that is."

Lainey's gaze was thoughtful. "Maybe the reason you didn't know what he meant is that you weren't on the same path until now."

"But I have been," he said. "In so many, many ways, I've lived exactly as he did. Debbie..." He sighed, shaking his head. "She used to say I couldn't settle down because I had idealized my childhood and the way my father and I moved from one place to another. She said I thought moving on was the answer to every problem."

There was a moment of silence from Lainey, then a soft, "Maybe Debbie was right."

It wasn't a subject Adam wanted to explore with her right now. There were more important matters to consider, like what had transpired between them last night.

He reached out and touched Lainey's cheek. "Forget about all that. How are you?"

Smiling, she stepped into his arms. "I'm perfect."

He stroked her hair and cuddled her close, but he couldn't avoid facing the problem they might have. "We didn't take any precautions."

She went very still.

"So you could be pregnant. Right?"

After a brief hesitation, she said, "Yes, I suppose I could."

He drew in a breath. "I'm sorry. That's my fault."

Leaning back, she regarded him with a serious expression. "I made a choice last night, Adam. I could have made sure we took precautions. If I'm pregnant, *I* can deal with it."

"*We* can deal with it," he corrected.

"But you..." She paused, biting her lip. Her chin lifted. "You don't owe me anything."

Frowning, he moved away from her. "Owe you? Lainey, what do you take me for? You think I'm that kind of man?"

"I just don't want you to feel obligated to me."

He laughed. "Not obligated to you? Since the first minute I got here, I've been obligated to you in one way or another. For a place to live. For being so kind to Gabe. And now, for last night."

"Last night was—"

"Very special," he completed for her. "And I wish like hell that I had taken care of things a little better. But if we have a problem, then we'll face it together."

"What does that mean?"

"That I won't run from my responsibilities." The look on her face told him she didn't quite believe him. "Damn, Lainey, do you think I'd leave you with a child?"

"But you don't want to stay here."

He couldn't deny that. His refusal to deny it stood like a wall between them. He figured she was thinking of what Debbie had said about his inability to settle down. About the path his father had taken. Just like Debbie and her parents and everyone else who had ever thought to rein him in, Lainey disapproved of the way Adam was living his life. She had made that clear from the start. And as he had done before, he grew angry about the way she was judging him, and by default, judging his father.

He stepped around her and found his jeans on the floor where he had tossed them the night before. Pulling them on, he said, "I know I didn't grow up like you or like Debbie, in one place, with the same friends, the same school, the same everything from year to year. And I'm quite sure my own restlessness is *definitely* a result of the way Dad moved us around after we left here. But I was raised with love and taught to be a good person. My father taught me to take care of myself and what's mine. He was a good man, an honorable man—"

"Then why did he abandon Caroline?"

The quiet question made Adam suck in his breath. He stared at Lainey, who faced him with fists clenched at her side, her jaw squared.

"How can you ask that? My grandfather was a madman—"

"But your father left Caroline here with him, with your mother, who from all reports was pretty unstable, even back then. Why did he leave her?"

"My father didn't have a choice about leaving."

"But surely at some point he could have come back. For Caroline, if for nothing else."

"If he had thought he could, I know he would have."

"And what about his telling you that Caroline and your mother were dead?"

"Maybe that's what he thought. Maybe he tried to contact Mother and Caroline, and Robert Parrish told him they were dead. Maybe he believed that."

Lainey regarded him for a long moment. "Is that what you really believe? Would your father really take Robert Parrish's word without checking it out himself?"

This was the question Adam had been grappling with ever since learning Caroline was really alive, ever since hearing how his mother had believed him dead. Before his mother died, she had found out the truth. Caroline said their mother had been leaving this farm, vowing to find him and their father, on the night their grandfather murdered her. Adam had to wonder what might have happened if his father had come back here before then. If he had just stopped running...

The cowardly picture forming of his father was at odds with the image Adam had of him. John Cutler's heart had been broken by Adam's mother's refusal to defy her father and come away with him. That's why he had never come back to see her or Caroline. It had been easier to tell Adam they were dead, easier for John himself to believe they were dead. Instead of cowardice, that was self-preservation.

As for his never settling down, John was just a free spirit who needed room to fly. That was how he thought of himself, how Adam thought of him as well. Maybe he had been running, but it wasn't away from responsibilities. It was to escape heartbreak. What happened to him here at Applewood Farm had crushed something inside his soul. If he had been willing to risk his heart again, he might have settled down with one of the women who had crossed his and Adam's path through the years. Good women, Adam thought, remembering a pretty young blonde they had lived with in Phoenix and a gentle-voiced artist who lived upstairs from their apartment in Seattle. But John had left them all.

As Adam had been planning to leave Lainey.

The correlation set him back on his heels. He had to wonder if his father had known moments like this, with women who wanted him to stay, but to whom he couldn't make promises. Perhaps John had left a child with one of those women, another brother or sister that Adam never knew existed. But that was wrong. That went against everything Adam himself believed in, everything the man who had raised him had taught him. And if that were true...

"No." He didn't realize he had spoken aloud until he saw the puzzled look on Lainey's face.

"What is it?" she asked.

The conclusions he was reaching about his father had to be shared. He had to say them out loud in order to make sense of them. "It's just... my father... he wasn't a happy man, Lainey. I can see now that he might have made some serious mistakes."

She nodded, not saying anything.

Adam was still grasping for the reasons his father had lived as he had. He had always seen his father as something of a folk hero, someone who had said to hell with the people who didn't approve of him and had gone to live his life the way he wanted. Adam had admired that quality, emulated it to a degree. But at the end, his father had paid a hefty price.

"He was so lonely," Adam murmured. "When he died, there was no one."

"There was you."

"I wasn't enough. No matter what I did, no matter how I tried to make him happy, he needed more. When he died I felt as if I had failed him, somehow."

"What a horrible burden for a boy."

"But it wasn't my fault."

"Of course it wasn't. It was his." With a tired sigh, Lainey sat down on the edge of the bed. "It seems to me that your father ran away from happiness once, and perhaps never thought he deserved it again. If only he had stayed..."

Adam bristled again at her implied criticism of his father. "Are you saying he should have stayed and fought Robert Parrish? That's something even your precious Uncle Coy didn't do." He didn't want to hurt her, but he thought she was forgetting all that Robert Parrish had done to make sure his parents' marriage fell apart.

Her hair fell against her cheek as she looked down at the fingers laced together in her lap. "I suppose I'm romanticizing the whole thing, but I just can't help believing that if your father had tried a little harder—"

"And if my mother had loved a little more," Adam added. "My father told me he asked her to leave with him, and she refused. She chose this house, this farm, her father, over her husband. And over me."

There was a faraway look in Lainey's eyes, a haunted look. "That hurts doesn't it? Knowing your mother would give you away, even if it was your father who took you."

Adam started to say she couldn't know just how much it hurt, until he remembered that she *did* know. Her mother had given her up, as well. "I think that you and I and Caroline have a lot in common, when it comes to parents who made mistakes."

Lainey nodded. "Yes, we do. And you are absolutely right about your mother being as responsible for what happened as your father. It's both their faults, along with your grandfather's, that the marriage ended, that you and Caroline were rippèd apart, and that you..." She hesitated.

Adam supplied what he believed she was thinking. "It's their fault that I turned out to be the sort of man you think would leave you pregnant and alone?"

Her head came up, her eyes blazing. "Stop putting words in my mouth. If I didn't think you were a fine person, Adam Cutler, then last night wouldn't have happened."

He managed a laugh. "So I'm not just a substitute for the traveling salesman?"

She pushed herself to her feet. "You know you're not. If I had truly wanted just any man in my bed, I do think I could have found someone before now. But I chose you. I waited until you came here." She took a deep, trembling breath, but her head was back, her shoulders straight when she added, "I love you."

A knot the size of a grapefruit felt as if it had lodged in his throat.

She took hold of the curved iron railing at the foot of the bed. Her fingers folded around it so tight her knuckles were white. "You don't have to answer me, Adam. I didn't tell you so that you would feel you had to reply."

"I don't know that I deserve something as special as your love."

"But you have it." She looked ready to cry, but she didn't. He admired her for that control, that dignity. He knew he would remember the way she looked right now for the rest of his life.

The rest of his life? Even to himself, he sounded like a man who was leaving. Or running away. Thinking of his father, he wondered if there was a difference.

But could he leave?

The answers seemed to swell inside him. He couldn't leave before he knew if Lainey was pregnant. Not before next Friday's essay test, when he would see if those kids in his class were grasping anything he was teaching them. Not before next month, when the football team would face their toughest challenges and Adam would know if Neal really was the spark that could ignite the whole squad. Not before Halloween, when Gabe was planning to carve one of the pumpkins Lainey had grown at the edge of her cornfield. And surely not before Christmas, when she said they would put a big cedar tree in the front parlor and pack the floor around it with presents.

One by one, he ticked off reasons to stay.

The grapefruit in his throat grew to a boulder and sank to his chest. But he really thought he knew the answer to those questions. More than that, he was beginning to see what his father had meant with his final words.

Facing Lainey, he said, "You know, I'm not much of a person."

"That's not true."

"Debbie always said I was a dreamer."

"But dreams can be good. Dreams are just another word for hopes. I know because I had lost a lot of my dreams before you showed up. I had lost a lot of hope."

"Don't make me sound like a hero. I'll give you my in-laws' phone number. They'll tell you I'm not so heroic, that I dragged my wife and child all over the country, that I kept hoping for the brass ring and fame and fortune long after I was told it wouldn't happen. They'll tell you I should have settled down with a nice, steady job a long time ago."

Lainey gave him one of those looks of hers, the steady kind that made him feel she was seeing straight to his soul. "I don't believe it matters what they wanted you to do. You had to be true to yourself, didn't you. You have to now. You have to do what you want."

"Right now I want to do the right thing."

"And what's that?"

"Stay here with you."

"Adam." She made his name sound like a prayer, but she didn't move. She was still just standing there, gripping the bed rail as if she would fall down if she let go.

He took a step toward her, feeling he should have his hat in hand or should at least go down on bended knee. "My father told me I would follow his path. You said maybe I didn't understand that because I've been on the wrong one. Well, you're right. This is the path my father started down." He gestured to the room around them. "When I think back to the way he talked about this place, I know that beneath the bitterness and the anger there was a yearning inside him. He knew what he lost when he knuckled under to his father-in-law and ran away. Well, maybe what he's been trying to tell me is that I shouldn't lose it, too."

"When I offered you part of the farm, you told me you didn't want what your father couldn't have."

"And wasn't that stupid? I look around here, and I see a home. Here, I have a family like I've never had before. I see my boy laughing, happier than he's been since his mother died...." His voice broke, and he closed his eyes.

Before he opened them, Lainey's arms were around him. Adam wrapped her tightly against him and buried his face in her sweet-scented hair. "I'd be a fool to leave," he murmured. "I'm on the right path. Here. Now. If I left, I'd be making my father's mistakes."

He set her away from him, caught her chin in his hand and looked deep into her dark-lashed emerald eyes. "Marry me, Lainey. Say you'll help me do the right thing."

Shocked, she fell back a step.

"What do you say?" he pressed.

The muscles in her throat worked for a few minutes while she blinked up at him. "I told you," she managed to finally say. "I told you that you didn't owe me anything."

"Owe you? This isn't about owing." He caught her arms to hold her steady when she would have turned away. "This is what I want. This is the *path*. You. Me. Gabe. Here. With maybe a couple more kids. A place for me to put down roots. *Finally*."

Lainey wanted to believe what she was hearing. More than that, she wanted to believe Adam meant what he was saying. But she was afraid he wanted to marry her *only* because it was the right thing to do. She told him so. "The possibility that I might be pregnant isn't a good enough reason for us to get married."

"That isn't the reason." He caught her hands between his. "I've told you the reasons."

Yes, he had told her. He had said everything she wanted to hear, except that he loved her. Without that, could she marry him? Could she even think of marrying him? The cautious soul that lived inside of Lainey just didn't know.

"I need to think," she said, finally, when he just kept standing there, waiting for an answer.

"Of course, you do." He lifted his hand to her face and stroked her jawline with his thumb. Tenderly. Slowly. "You should think."

"There just so much to consider."

"I know." He dipped his head toward hers and allowed his lips to trail along the path his thumb had taken.

"Adam," she said, drawing away. "I can't think when you—"

"Do this?" he completed, just before he kissed her.

She broke the embrace, protesting.

But he kissed her again. Harder, this time. He undid the sash of her robe, as well, and put his hands on her body. Moved his warm, clever fingers across her skin, over her breasts, down to the tender but receptive cleft between her legs.

When he had them both naked and on the bed, she mounted a feeble protest, "We shouldn't."

Breaking off from kissing the sensitive flesh just above her knee, he murmured, "Shouldn't what?"

"Take chances. Be unprotected."

He chuckled, his breath warm against her leg. "We won't take chances."

"But—"

"There's more than one way to make love."

Moments later, when he used his mouth in the most intimate way imaginable, she understood.

Much later, she understood even more, when he showed her how to please him in the same way.

All in all, it was an eventful hour.

The Sunday morning milking and chores were way off schedule. Fred and Neal were never there on Sundays, but even though Adam helped her, Lainey missed church. She supposed that was just as well, since she was now what Aunt Loretta would have called a fallen woman.

Caroline brought Gabe home that afternoon. Lainey thought she and Adam did a good job of acting as if nothing had happened between them. At least Caroline didn't seem to notice any changes. That meant there hadn't been any undue gossip about the way they had left the chili supper.

Of course, Monday morning, Neal gave her a rather sheepish smile. She thought Fred kind of looked at her funny, too. She wondered how they would act if they knew Adam had made a run to the drugstore Sunday

evening, and the two of them had made love in his bed at
the cottage, with Gabe sleeping right in the next room.

What would everyone say if they knew Lainey was really thinking of marrying a man she had known less than
two months, a man who couldn't say he loved her?

Caroline came by with Christopher Monday afternoon. She had been to her obstetrician and was talking
about babies, wondering if the one she was carrying
would be a girl or boy. Lainey held Christopher and
wondered if she was pregnant, and if her and Adam's
baby would look like Christopher and Gabe, with black
hair and shining brown eyes.

She was tempted to tell Caroline what Adam was proposing, to reach across the table, get her friend's hand
and ask her what she should do. But she already knew
that. She knew all of Caroline's reservations. She knew
all of her own.

When Caroline was gone, Lainey stood alone in her
spotless white kitchen. It was so neat, so tidy. Just as or-
derly as her life had been before Adam appeared. That
part of her, the sensible, sane Lainey, said she would be
a fool to marry him. The other part, the wild half he un-
leashed when he touched her, told her to grab what he
was offering with both fists, to revel in the happiness he
was offering. It might not be love. It might not be all she
wished for. But surely it would be enough.

Lainey knew her aunt Loretta would be aghast at this
wild streak, the part she had worked so hard to squelch
in her sister's daughter. She would have some choice
words to say about Lainey's desire to revel. One of Aunt
Loretta's familiar axioms was that those who rolled in the
hay were inevitably pricked with needles long after. She
might have been right.

But Lainey decided she didn't care.

Before she could lose her nerve, she went out to her truck and drove into town. At the high school, her memory led her down the corridors to the classroom where she thought Adam might be.

The door was open, and she could hear his voice. She stood just beyond the doorway and watched, hoping no one would see her just yet. He was sitting on the edge of his desk, talking about the American Revolution. And the students were listening to him, she saw. They were adding their own thoughts about the Boston Tea Party. There was laughter and energy in that room, in Adam's voice. He was, she thought in delighted surprise, a really, really good teacher.

When the bell rang, students spilled quickly into the hall. She recognized many of them, but they were too eager to get to the last class of the day to pay much attention to her. She waited until Adam was alone, his back to the door, stacking papers and books and putting them in a worn leather satchel. In his khakis and knit shirt and tennis shoes, he didn't look like any teacher she had ever had. She supposed that was one of the reasons the kids seemed to like him so much.

"Adam?"

He turned, a smile of surprise and genuine welcome spreading across his face. "What are you doing here?" He frowned slightly. "There's nothing wrong, is there? Not Gabe or—"

"No, there's nothing wrong. There's just..." She took a deep breath. "There's just...yes."

He looked puzzled. "Yes?"

"Yes, I'll marry you."

His smile came back, bigger than ever, as he strode down the row of desks toward her. He kissed her while students for the next class were spilling into the room. They applauded.

And Lainey imagined Aunt Loretta spinning in her grave.

Chapter Nine

They set a wedding date for the second Saturday in October. Adam said he wanted it sooner, but Lainey had to wait. She wanted to make sure she wasn't pregnant, to give him a chance to change his mind, and to give herself the assurance that the possibility of a baby wasn't the real reason for his proposal.

While they waited, she insisted their plans remain a secret. She didn't want to hear what Caroline would say. She didn't want Gabe to be disappointed if no wedding took place. And if she was honest, she also wanted to save face. She didn't want to announce plans that would be canceled and have to deal with the curious questions of friends and neighbors.

But there was no baby. Her period came one morning, on the exact day it should have, about a week and a half before the tentative wedding date. She told Adam that evening after he came home from football practice. They were down in the barn, where Lainey was checking on her aging mare, who had been looking perkier of late. Lainey had chosen their surroundings deliberately. With Maggie to concentrate on, she didn't have to just stand there, holding her breath and waiting for Adam's reaction. He surprised her with his disappointment.

"You mean you're sorry?" She wasn't quite able to believe him.

"Don't you think it would have been neat to have a baby so close in age to Caroline and Reid's?"

"Neat?"

"They could play baseball together, torment Christopher and Gabe together, generally drive us all crazy together."

Lainey ran her fingers through Maggie's mane, not looking at Adam. She still couldn't trust what she was hearing, and she was determined that he have every opportunity to call off the wedding if he wanted. "Since there's no baby, if you want to wait or even—"

"What's this?" He turned her to face him. "Are you backing out on me?"

"No, but if you want to back out . . ."

He encircled her with his arms. "Not a chance."

"I would understand."

He silenced her with a kiss, a very thorough, very passionate kiss. "I've told you what I want, Lainey. I want to settle down here with you and Gabe. I want this to be *our* home. It just feels so right, like the best possible choice we could make. So are you going to marry me?"

She nodded, the reality sinking in. He intended to go through with this wedding, even though their carelessness hadn't resulted in a pregnancy. He wanted to marry her.

Grinning, he patted Maggie on the rump and took Lainey's hand. "Come on, now that this little test of yours has been passed, let's go tell Gabe the news."

She hadn't really thought of it as a test, but she supposed that was an accurate assessment. By not calling off the marriage now, Adam had crossed a hurdle she had set up. If he had gone further and said he loved her, all her doubts and insecurities would have disappeared. But those words didn't come. She told herself not to expect them, that a declaration of love was one test Adam would never pass.

He didn't really love her, not the way Reid loved Caroline, probably not the way he had loved Gabe's mother. She knew that. She accepted it. But even so, she couldn't stop herself from feeling gloriously, perhaps foolishly happy. For Adam desired her with a heat she couldn't deny. He wanted to live here with her, put down roots with her, raise Gabe with her help.

The boy was thrilled by their news. It meant he was going to live on the farm he adored, that he could move permanently into the big corner room at Lainey's house, that Goldie was really and truly his dog. He loved Lainey and loved his father, and the fact that they were getting together fit perfectly into his perspective of the world.

Caroline didn't take such a simple view of the matter. Her objections and observations were as predictable as they were emphatic. They were moving too fast, she said. Only six weeks ago, Adam had been planning to leave. Was he really ready for this marriage? His sister's arguments didn't sway Adam, however, and Lainey took her cues from him. Their plans proceeded.

But on a bright October Saturday afternoon, as she stood in a room just off the chapel of the church, Lainey wished for a word of encouragement from the woman whom she had always looked up to and loved.

Even though she had such reservations about the marriage, Caroline had agreed to stand up with Lainey. She had helped Lainey pick out her tea-length creamy dress, had arranged for the flowers in the church and the food for the small reception after the ceremony. She was taking Gabe home tonight so that Lainey and Adam could be alone. She had done everything that could be expected of a sister or matron of honor. Everything except be happy for the bride and groom.

In the full-length mirror the church provided for brides and their attendants, Lainey watched Caroline arrange the folds of Aunt Loretta's antique-lace wedding veil around her shoulders. Caroline was lovely in a filmy emerald green trifle of a dress that matched the full-skirted style of Lainey's. Only the deadly serious set of her mouth betrayed her true feelings.

"There," she murmured, with one last adjustment to the veil. She stepped back. "You look beautiful."

Lainey found that a slight exaggeration. But another glance in the mirror revealed that she would pass. At Adam's request, her hair was loose around her shoulders. And though her eyes looked almost too large for her face, Caroline's artful use of makeup kept her freckles from glowing copper and her fair skin from washing out against her hair.

"A beautiful bride," Caroline repeated, but she didn't bother to stop her sigh.

Out in the sanctuary, the organist began the music that preceded the bridal march. It was their cue to move to the vestibule, but Lainey remained at the mirror looking at Caroline. "I wish you could be happy for us."

Caroline glanced down at the lace glove she had pulled on. "I would like to be."

"You know he doesn't love me, don't you?"

That brought the brunette's gaze back up to meet Lainey's in the mirror.

Lainey continued, "I'm sure that when you talked to him after we told you our plans, he told you he doesn't love me."

Hesitantly, her brown eyes bright, Caroline replied, "He cares deeply for you, Lainey."

Lifting her chin, Lainey said, "But caring isn't love. I know, because I love him so very, very much. I love him enough for both of us. That's why this is going to work."

Caroline took a deep breath and pulled on her other glove. "I think you know how I feel about all of this. I wanted the two of you to wait, to know one another a lot better before taking this step." Her delicately arched eyebrows drew together in a frown. "Marriage is just so darn difficult, Lainey."

Turning to face her, Lainey said, "You and Reid make it look so easy."

"But it's not. It's hard work. It's day in, day out living together, blending lives, accommodating one another. It's paying bills and doing laundry and changing baby diapers. It's like . . . like a math test."

"Math?" Lainey asked, puzzled.

"You remember those tests, I'm sure." Caroline's smile was fleeting. "In geometry or algebra or one those others that I hated so much—they were the tests with problems that had so many parts. If you got one part wrong, the whole equation was off. One tiny mistake, and you failed."

She looked down again, then plucked Lainey's bouquet and her nosegay from the table beside the mirror.

"Marriage can be like that, Lainey. When one little part of your life goes off balance, the marriage goes off balance, too."

"Then how do you manage to bring it back in balance?"

"With love," Caroline murmured. "A shared love, Lainey. It's the only thing that helps two people past the tests of marriage."

The tests. Caroline's choice of words made Lainey pause. For she had already decided love was the one test Adam couldn't pass.

So what was she doing here?

That question hammered inside her as a knock sounded on the door. Reid, who was going to escort Lainey down the aisle, stuck his head in the room. "Are you guys ready? The organist has played about ten stanzas of this song."

Caroline looked at Lainey. "*Are* you ready?"

Lainey had to reach deep down in herself to find the feelings that had helped her accept Adam's proposal in the first place. If sheer determination could make a marriage work, then she would be okay. So what if Adam wasn't madly in love with her? She was used to making sacrifices, to taking second best. She had replaced the child her aunt and uncle couldn't have. She had inherited the farm by default. She would take what Adam offered—his passion, his affection, his name. As she had told Caroline, it would be enough.

She took her bouquet. "I'm ready."

But as she and Reid paused at the arched opening between the chapel and the vestibule, as friends and neighbors stood and turned toward her, Lainey faltered. It was only when she looked toward the altar and saw the flash of Adam's smile that she was able to square her shoulders and step forward.

She walked down the aisle with Reid, her eyes on Adam, repeating silently to herself, *My love for you will be enough. It will have to be enough.*

Adam thought their marriage got off to a perfect beginning. There was Lainey, looking as lovely as he had ever seen her. There were friends and family around them. There was hope and happiness in his heart. And at the end of the day, there was the fulfillment he found in his bride's arms.

The unseasonably warm afternoon had faded to a rainy October evening. To fight the chill, Adam had started a fire in the shallow, old fireplace in Lainey's room. The glowing logs lit the room as they made love beneath an old patchwork quilt. Every once in a while, when an errant splash of rain made it down the chimney, the embers would sizzle. Adam found that sound a fitting accompaniment to the heat he and Lainey built together. In the afterglow, they cuddled, warm and sated and happy.

Pushing Lainey's hair back from her face, Adam asked, "Was it the wedding you always dreamed of?"

"Um-hmm."

"And how about the wedding night?"

She chuckled. "I'm hoping that's not over."

"You've become quite demanding, Mrs. Cutler."

Turning on her back, she held up a hand so that the fire caught the sparkle of the diamond in her wedding band. That ring had taken a chunk out of Adam's security fund, but it was well worth it to see the happy surprise in Lainey's eyes when he slipped it on her finger this afternoon.

"Mrs. Cutler," she said, sighing. "I like the way that sounds."

"Me, too."

"It was such a nice wedding. So many friends were there."

"I hope you noticed the whole football team."

"How could I not? They all kissed me, and they ate every scrap of food in sight."

"They're still pumped up over winning three in a row."

"Having Neal at quarterback all the time makes a difference."

The mention of Neal made Adam frown. While all the other players had been in high spirits today, goofing off and joking, Neal had seemed down. Adam asked Lainey if she had noticed anything.

"He was kind of quiet. You think something's wrong?"

"I don't know," Adam muttered, thinking about the boy. "Neal's a complex kid. I like to think I'm making a difference with him. I like him. But he's so moody, and God knows he has troubles at home."

Lainey turned on her side, frowning. "Marnie looked like she had been crying."

"And her husband wasn't there at all."

"I wonder what's going on there. Marnie won't talk about it. She was so determined to make it work this time."

Adam shifted so that he faced Lainey again. "I really want to help Neal through this. He's a smart, talented boy."

"You're the man to make a difference with him."

"You sound confident in me."

"I happen to think you're a good teacher and good coach. Everyone says you are. The kids are crazy about you."

"It's funny," he murmured. "I didn't want this job, but now...now I'm so involved. I like my students, even the problem ones. And I think I'm doing something good, something I can be proud of."

With a butterfly's touch, she ran her fingers down his cheek. "I'm proud of you."

He caught her hand and pressed a kiss in the palm, his gaze steady on hers. "Tonight of all nights, why are we talking about my students and players?"

Laughing, she scooted away from him. "You tell me, Coach. I could get insulted by how little attention you're paying me."

He caught her at the edge of the bed and hauled her back against him. They fit together quite well, spoon fashion. But then, he hadn't found a way they didn't fit. His hands drifted from her waist to the curves of her breasts. Sighing, she wiggled her fanny against him with predictable results.

"Again?" she murmured, as he hardened, lengthened against her soft buttocks.

"Are you complaining?"

She shook her head. Her hand moved down to stroke his growing erection, while he continued to draw lazy, arousing circles around her nipples.

"You make me feel so good," she whispered. "Better than I ever thought I could. I used to be so afraid..." Her words drifted off.

He kissed her shoulder. "Afraid of what?"

She hesitated only a moment. "I've told you I never had boyfriends. You know there weren't men in my life.

I used to wonder what this would be like, if I would be able to... if I could respond."

With a soft laugh, he said, "You needn't have worried."

"But I did. I thought that maybe...that perhaps when I was with my mother..."

Adam's hands stilled, dropped away from her breasts. His heart seemed to rise in his throat, so that he had to force his voice out around it. "Lainey are you saying that something *did* happen to you when you were with your mother?"

She shook her head, emphatically. "Oh, no, Adam. I'm certain nothing happened. The only memories I have of the... the men Mother was with are vague shadows. Just impressions of voices and sounds. Later on, when I was old enough to figure out a few things, I knew what those men were, what mother was. But I'm certain nothing happened to me. Despite everything Mother did, I don't think she would have let me come to harm."

"But why your worry about men... about responding sexually?"

"I just felt so out of step with everyone else. I thought there was something buried deep inside me, some trigger that made me so nervous around boys when I was younger, around men later on."

"Wasn't that more your aunt's fault?"

She sighed again. "I suppose. The choices Mother made hurt Aunt Loretta so much that she kept a pretty tight leash on me."

Adam hugged her back against him. "Your mother must have been a desperate woman, Lainey."

"If only she had come home." Sighing, Lainey rubbed a hand along Adam's arm. "On the day we heard Mother was dead, that's what Aunt Loretta said. I remember, she pulled her apron up to her face and she cried, and she said, 'If only Shirley had come home.' ''

Adam felt the sob catch in Lainey's throat, and he held her even tighter, wishing he could take away the pain. She didn't let herself cry. She held it in, and finally released a deep breath.

"I'm sorry," she whispered. "I didn't mean to drag out all of that stuff."

"There's nothing you can't tell me."

She was silent a moment, then said, "Mother died when some man beat her up and left her for dead on the street in New Orleans."

"When was this?"

"I was thirteen."

"And how did you find out?"

"Mother had a picture of Aunt Loretta in her billfold, with an address on the back. The authorities found us. Uncle Coy paid to have the body shipped up here. We buried Mother in a graveyard way outside of town beside a little church she and Aunt Loretta went to when they were young. Just me and Uncle Coy and Aunt Loretta and the minister were there. Aunt Loretta used a mortician from the next county. She was too ashamed to tell folks. She was afraid of the gossip, of what people might say about Mother."

Adam winced at the image of a much younger Lainey laying her mother to rest surrounded by shame and secrecy. That wasn't right. No matter what the woman had done, Lainey shouldn't have been made to feel her mother was a pariah, better off buried where no one who had known her could see her grave. But perhaps more than most people, Adam could understand how Lainey felt. His own father was laid to rest in a northern California town where they had lived only a couple of months. Adam had been surrounded by strangers.

Pushing aside that painful memory, he turned Lainey toward him. "You know what? I think Applewood Farm has seen enough tragedy to last a couple of hundred lifetimes."

"You're right about that."

"From now on, there's going to be happiness in this valley. For me and you and Gabe. For Caroline and Reid and their family. We're all going to live a good life here."

"That sounds like a dream come true."

"It's a promise."

He kissed her then, and touched her again, sliding his hands over her firm, strong body with easy confidence. She responded with a boldness that surprised him, pleased him. With lips and tongue and fingertips, she stroked him to a readiness that came close to pain. He wanted to say to hell with the condom she retrieved from the nightstand. But she put it on, made it a playful game. Then she slipped her body over his, took him deep into her warm, slick folds, and rode him to a completion so intense, so vital, that he felt the two of them were in total sync.

This is the beginning, he told himself. The beginning of the right path.

Before Adam fell asleep, he imagined he could see his father's smile.

Chapter Ten

The weather turned crisp after the rain on their wedding night. The ridges surrounding the valley flamed orange, red and gold. Halloween came. Gabe got his pumpkin to carve, as well as an old-fashioned party to attend at the church. Lainey and Adam were in charge of a "haunted" room, complete with squashed grapes and cold spaghetti that passed for various, gruesomely severed body parts in the dark. Lainey said she wasn't sure who got a bigger kick out of the night—Adam or the kids.

In early November, she and Gabe celebrated birthdays. He was six, and she was to turn thirty a few days later. They had fifteen screaming youngsters at the farm for a party in the afternoon. That night after Gabe had fallen into an exhausted sleep, Adam surprised Lainey with a new watch and a candlelit picnic beside the fire in their room. But she confessed her best present had come that afternoon, when Gabe introduced her as his mom.

"It was just so natural." She smiled as she gazed into the fire. "He brought his little buddy Scott over and said, 'This is my mom.'" Frowning suddenly, she turned to Adam. "That's okay, isn't it? I mean, Debbie is his mother. I'm not trying—"

"Hush," Adam murmured, touching a finger to her lips. "It's perfectly fine with me. I don't want him to forget Debbie. But you are his mom now."

"Do you think Debbie's parents will have a problem with hearing him call me that?" Gabe's grandparents were coming for a visit at Thanksgiving, and Lainey had confessed to being nervous about meeting them.

"They'll take it in stride." Adam sat up and drew her close. "I'm glad Gabe sees you as his mother. What'll make it all just right is when we give him a brother or a sister."

"But Adam—"

He smothered her protests with a kiss. He cajoled her with touches, convinced her with lingering, well-placed caresses. And there, on the pillows and blankets they had placed on the floor by the fire, they began working on a family.

Adam was feeling like a winner. His classes were going exceptionally well. The football team that had faltered so in the beginning was playing with the sort of gumption that made champions out of underdogs. In an extraordinary final burst of luck and teamwork, the Parrish County Cougars won their division playoffs and earned a spot in the state championship game to be played on the first Saturday in December.

The whole team was keyed up, riding high on adrenaline. Adam was worried about Neal, whose mercurial adolescent emotions often interfered with his performance on the field and at school. The boy's father had taken to coming to practice a few times a week. Adam thought Neal was more at ease without that audience, though his gaze eagerly swept the bleachers before practice every day. Obviously, Neal wanted his father there, so Adam kept his mouth shut. He made himself available to Neal to talk, as he did to many of his students. He was gratified by the way many of them responded to his concern. He felt as if he was doing something worthwhile, something that mattered.

Adam's in-laws arrived on Wednesday night before Thanksgiving. By the next morning, he was telling Lainey she shouldn't have been nervous, that she had won them over the minute they saw her love for Gabe. After she served a family holiday meal that was turkey-and-dressing-and-pumpkin-pie perfect, the Larsons congratulated Adam on having settled down at last with a nice, sensible girl.

Lainey, who was clearing the table with Sammi's help, went still when Adam's mother-in-law called her sensible. She wasn't sure why that description caused her such a pang. She *was* sensible, after all. It was a tag that had been applied to her all her life. There were worse adjectives that these people, who were important to Adam and Gabe, might have used to describe her.

But the words echoed in her head, and they were compounded by something Mrs. Larson said to Lainey the day before she left.

The two of them were alone in the kitchen, and Mrs. Larson was clucking over Adam's rattletrap truck, which had become a joke between him and Lainey.

"He just can't seem to wind up with a decent automobile." The woman shook her graying head. "When we first met him, he was driving a horrible old car. I swear it was held together with rubber bands. But he said that if he used any money to buy a new car, he wouldn't be able to afford the gas to come and see Debbie. Every chance he got that summer, he drove that terrible car over the mountains to see her. Quite frankly, I feared for his life. But he was so in love..." She broke off, looking flustered, and darted an apologetic look at Lainey before changing the subject.

So in love. Lainey couldn't get the phrase out of her head.

Once upon a time Adam had been so in love with someone that he had done anything he could to get to her side.

He would never be so in love with Lainey. Not with nice, sensible Lainey Bates. She wasn't the kind of woman anyone braved mountains to reach.

She believed everything Adam said about wanting a home with her. But wanting to settle down wasn't love. It wasn't what he'd had with Debbie. Or what Caroline had with Reid.

All Adam's caring, all his passion, weren't the same as the love Lainey felt for him. And she wanted his love. She wanted to know that Adam would risk anything, give up anything for her, the same as she would for him.

After a lifetime of settling for whatever people gave her, Lainey wanted more than a compromise from Adam. He had told her the night he proposed that marrying her was the right thing to do. Even when it turned out she wasn't pregnant, he had called their marriage the best possible choice. Well, she didn't want to be the just the *right* thing or a *possible* choice. When it came to her, she didn't want him to have a choice. She knew in her heart that real love, deep love didn't leave room for choices.

But if she made demands like that, what reply would Adam make? If she said, "Love me the way I want to be loved or leave me," what could he do? The answer seemed grim to Lainey. Half measures were surely better than none. But she was fed up with half the glass. She wanted it full.

She had never been any good at asking for the love she needed. For all the care and the concern that had existed between her and Aunt Loretta, a wall had always separated them. Uncle Coy, a gentle man bruised and battered by the travails within his own family, had given her an unwavering but awkward tenderness. But there had been so many times over the years when Lainey wondered if either her aunt or her uncle loved her just for *her*, for who she was. The social worker who had brought her to the farm told her they wanted a little girl of their own. They had been good to her, but Lainey was always aware that she wasn't theirs; she was always Shirley's girl, always the leftover, the second choice.

That fate, which Lainey had accepted her whole life, was no good when she applied it to Adam. She wanted his heart, his all.

Unhappiness settled on her shoulders like a cloak. Adam saw it, she knew. He kept asking what was wrong, but she wasn't able to tell him, to risk putting her feelings into words. For days after the Larsons left, she was quiet at the dinner table at night, listening to him and Gabe more than participating. She found work to do upstairs instead of sitting with him while he planned lessons for school. She went to bed before he did, and pretended to be asleep. That week after Thanksgiving, a distance was opened that hadn't existed between them since the first night they had made love.

On Thursday afternoon, the day before Adam was to leave with the football team for the big championship game in Murfreesboro, Lainey's mare fell ill. It was the first really cold day of the year, an end to the crispness of autumn, a hint of the winter that was coming. Lainey went into the barn, and found Maggie lying in the hay in her stall, unable to rise. The other horses in the barn, Neal's Blackie and Lainey's other two, were agitated, whinnying and kicking the sides of their stalls. Lainey let them out into the nearby paddock and ran calling for Fred. He went to phone the vet, while she stayed beside her dying horse.

She was waiting for the vet with Maggie's head cradled in her lap when Adam came at a run down the hill into the barn. Fred had remained at the house to keep Gabe occupied until this was over.

Lainey knew some people, even those who loved animals as she did, would find her reaction to Maggie's collapse pretty foolish. The horse was old and hadn't been well for a while. It was inevitable that she would go. But Lainey saw the beginning of Maggie's end as a sign. The old girl had been hanging in there of late, even perking up a little. It was as if she had responded to the net of happiness that had been thrown around this farm and this family since the wedding. Lainey had begun to hope her dear old friend would last at least another year.

But the net was ripped. Lainey had been ignoring that, just as she had been ignoring the inevitable with the horse. She couldn't ignore the obvious any longer. All the yearnings she hadn't wanted to face were rushing in through that torn fairy-tale net, rushing in like Maggie's life was rushing out.

Even Adam's sympathy upset Lainey. She didn't respond when he tried to comfort her. The vet finally arrived, examined Maggie and said what Lainey already knew, that the kindest thing would be to end her suffering. Adam tried to lead Lainey from the stall. She pushed him away, perhaps a bit more forcefully than was necessary. "I'm not leaving her alone now."

So Adam stood just outside while the vet eased Maggie's last breaths. When the doctor was gone, Adam remained outside, waiting.

Lainey waited, too. For her tears to come. They didn't. She just felt numb. When she finally stepped from the stall, Adam put his arms around her, but she didn't feel him. Everything was so off, so wrong. It wasn't just Maggie, it was Lainey's whole life, the way she'd been fooling herself about this marriage.

"I'm so sorry," Adam was murmuring. "I know you loved her, Lainey. I know Uncle Coy gave her to you and that she was special."

She pulled away, heading blindly toward the barn door. She didn't want Adam to hold her right now. She wanted time to think about the realizations that had come to her while Maggie died. When he held her, she couldn't think.

But Adam caught up to her, took her hand. "I wish you'd say something. I know you're upset about losing your horse right now. But I think it's more than that. There's been something wrong all week. What is it? Did Debbie's parents do something, say something?"

She wondered how she could explain her reaction to Mrs. Larson's unintentionally upsetting remarks.

"Lainey, please," Adam said. "Look at me. Tell me what you're thinking."

She was thinking that marrying him without his complete and total love was the worst mistake of her life. But she couldn't say that—not right now, anyway.

"Lainey?" A thread of impatience vibrated in his tone now.

"Just leave me alone," she said coldly.

"You're upset—"

"Leave me alone!" she repeated, her voice rising.

"Why?" he retorted, bordering on anger now. "Why do I have to leave you alone? I'm your husband, remember?"

Bitter laughter rose to her lips. "Yes, my husband. My *dutiful* husband."

"What does that mean? What in the hell—"

She jerked her arm out of his grasp. She wasn't going to get into this now. Not when her numbness was slipping, giving way to a rising tide of anger and hurt. "Just let me be. For God's sake, just let me be!"

"Dad? Mom?" At the entrance to the barn, Gabe stood, blinking in the light, his gaze moving from Adam to Lainey and back again.

Behind him, Fred appeared, puffing a little, flushed under his grizzled beard. "I'm sorry," he muttered. "He wanted to see what was going on."

Gathering her composure, Lainey told Fred it was okay. Adam went to his son.

Fred started down the corridor to Maggie's silent stall, pausing to give Lainey an awkward pat on the shoulder. He had called his brother, he said. They would take care of getting Maggie out of the barn and on the wagon behind the tractor. Looking away, he said in his gruff but kind way, "Tomorrow morning, you can tell me where she should..." He looked away. "Where she should go."

Only trusting herself to nod, Lainey turned her attention to Gabe, who was asking his father what was wrong.

"Why are you and Mom yelling at each other?"

"We were just upset, son."

"Fred said Maggie was sick."

"Yes, she was." Lainey walked over and knelt beside the boy. "She died, Gabe. Maggie's gone."

He regarded her with his melting-chocolate eyes for a moment. Then he put his arms around her neck. "I'm sorry, Mom."

"So am I." The tears Lainey thought she didn't have flooded her eyes. She held on to Gabe and cried. He couldn't know that her tears were as much for him as for the animal she had just lost. Gabe was an innocent party to this mess she had created by marrying his father. He had known too much pain already in his young life, but the two of them were likely to hurt him again.

Adam stood to the side, feeling helpless, wondering why she hadn't been able to cry with him.

Something was wrong. Something more than the death of a beloved animal. Something that had been building all week.

They all went to the house, where he prepared a simple dinner. He told himself not to push for any explanations from Lainey tonight. But he hated the way she wouldn't look at him. He hated the strain that had been in the air these past few days.

She went upstairs right after dinner. The door to her room, *their* bedroom, was closed when Adam took Gabe up for his bath. But after he read his son a story, Lainey appeared to give Gabe a good-night kiss.

The boy patted her on the cheek. "Don't be so sad, Mom. Maggie's gone to a good place." He looked at his father as if for confirmation.

Adam tousled his hair. "You're right."

"Thanks," Lainey murmured as she pulled the covers up to Gabe's chin. She kissed him on the forehead. "You're a good boy, Gabe Cutler."

In the hall outside their room, Adam took her hand and made her face him. "And you're a good mom, Lainey Cutler. I know how bad you feel tonight. But it meant a lot to Gabe that you came in to say good-night just as usual."

She nodded, but her gaze skittered away from his.

"Please look at me," Adam coaxed. "Tell me what's really wrong."

Before she could reply or avoid him or do whatever she was intending, a knock sounded at the door downstairs.

Adam frowned, glancing at his watch. "Who can that be?"

Lainey trailed him down the stairs and to the kitchen door. Neal Scroggins waited on the porch.

In blue jeans and a light jacket more suitable to early autumn than the bitter cold of this December night, Neal stepped into the kitchen. His cheeks were red and blotchy looking, as if he might have been crying, and instead of taking the seat Lainey offered, he paced back and forth.

"I need to talk to you, Coach Cutler."

What Adam wanted to do was talk to his wife, but he could see something had the young athlete agitated. "All right. Go ahead."

The boy looked at Lainey, one eyebrow cocked. Taking the hint, she left.

Sighing, Adam turned back to Neal. "What's the deal, Scroggins?"

"I'm not playing in that game Saturday night."

Unsure if he had heard correctly, Adam just stood there.

Neal repeated, his voice harsher. "I'm not playing."

Adam regarded the defiant teenager through narrowed eyes, trying to gauge whether this was serious or just nerves or a bid for attention. He pulled a chair out from under the table and pointed to it. "Sit down. Let's talk about this."

Neal shook his head. "There's nothing to say."

"You said you came here to talk."

"I came to tell you. I thought you and Coach Trewhitt and the team ought to be prepared."

"Do you mind telling me why?"

"I don't want to play."

"You did yesterday, last week, last month. Hell, you were as fidgety as a cat in a tuna plant until you got to play."

"I wanted my dad to see me play, to see me win."

"Oh, really?" Adam's hands went to hips as he stared at the kid. "I know that's not the only reason, Scroggins. I think you liked playing for yourself, too. You liked seeing what that golden arm of yours could do."

The boy shrugged. "Maybe. But I know what I can do now, and I'm not doing it anymore."

"You mean you'll let the team down that way? I'm surprised at you."

"I don't care about the team," Neal retorted, almost shouting. He wheeled toward the door.

Comprehension suddenly dawned inside Adam. "Your father's not coming to the game Saturday, is he?"

Neal stopped at the door, one hand on the knob. He looked up, his profile to Adam, and closed his eyes. Then he turned to meet Adam's gaze again. His voice was tight. "Dad's moved on."

"So you're bailing out on the team? Because your father has bailed out on you and your mother and sister, you're following suit."

Tears glittered in the boy's blue eyes. "I hate to let the guys down, Coach, but I just can't play. I've thought about it and thought about it, and I know I can't play."

"Don't do this," Adam said, taking a step toward him. "Don't give up because he did. Play that game for yourself. Show yourself that it doesn't matter what he does."

Neal was shaking his head, crying for real now. "I can't, Coach. Don't make me."

The tough-guy pose was gone completely. Something softened and broke apart inside Adam. He took hold of Neal's arm. "I won't make you do anything you don't want to do, son. But I want you to think about how you're gonna feel about this down the road. You'll regret not following through on an obligation. Do this for yourself."

Flinching away from Adam, the boy scrubbed at his eyes with his fists and took a few deep breaths. When he got himself under control, he looked immeasurably older than the youngster who had spilled out of his mother's truck on Adam's first day here at Applewood. "I'm sorry, Coach. I'm sorry to let you down."

"Don't worry about me—"

"I just can't play, not feeling the way I do." Neal jerked open the door and ran across the porch, disappearing into the cold night.

Adam followed him, calling his name, but he was only in time to see the taillights of the teenager's truck disappear down the driveway. Standing in the cold, with his breath forming a cloud, Adam cursed the boy's selfish father.

Back inside, Lainey was in the kitchen. She had heard the raised voices and the sound of Neal's truck racing away.

Grabbing the telephone, Adam demanded the Scroggins's number. While the phone rang, he filled Lainey in on what Neal had said. Marnie Scroggins answered. She hadn't seen her son since late that afternoon, not since she had broken the news that her husband was gone again. She said Neal had taken her truck and torn out of their place like the devil was in pursuit. She was afraid he was going to do something foolish and destructive. Unfortunately, Adam could do nothing to ease the woman's concerns.

He replaced the receiver, his shoulders slumping. He had been so sure that he was making a difference with Neal. To Lainey he said, "That bastard father of Neal's didn't even bother to say goodbye to his son. He left today, knowing about that game on Saturday, knowing how keyed up Neal is."

"Oh, no." Lainey bowed her head.

"I shouldn't have let Neal leave," Adam muttered.

"How could you have stopped him?"

"I should have seen from the beginning how screwed up he was. But I—" Adam bit off the words. He had been too concerned with Lainey to pay close attention when the boy first got here.

Hands clenched on the back of a chair, Lainey regarded him with stricken eyes, as if she was reading his thoughts.

Adam pivoted toward the door and grabbed his coat from a hook on the wall nearby. "I don't think Neal's going home tonight. His mother is stuck at home without a car. I'm going to see if I can find him."

He drove around until nearly midnight, but there was no sign of Neal or his truck. Stopping at the Scroggins's place as he headed home, he learned Neal hadn't been there. His mother had phoned the sheriff's office. They were going to keep their eyes open for him.

Adam climbed into bed feeling more lost and troubled than he had been since Debbie died. Beside him, Lainey was silent, not reaching out to comfort him, though he knew she was awake. Adam felt as if a chasm separated them, a deep and dark hole he didn't know how to bridge. He was confused and upset. About her and about Neal.

It was a relief to get up early the next morning and go get on a bus full of young athletes bound for Murfreesboro. Even with the shadow of Neal's disappearance hanging over them all, Adam felt some of his troubles slip away with every mile of highway the bus ate up. There was a familiar rhythm to the wheels moving beneath him. It was the rhythm of his childhood, of his life.

In Nashville, however, the illusion of flying away from his problems was shattered. For Neal had been found about the time the bus had left Parrish. On a remote county road, in a ditch, his truck crushed around him. The details of his injuries were sketchy, but one thing was certain—his golden arm was broken.

The Parrish County Cougars pulled off a brilliant upset and won the state championship while Neal lay unconscious. Besides the broken arm, he had a concussion, a fractured leg and a punctured lung. Within days it was clear he would recover, but his future of lobbing touchdown passes or pitching the fastballs he preferred was in doubt.

And Adam blamed himself, of course.

What Lainey had started to say to Adam on the night Neal came to their door remained unsaid during the weeks that followed the championship game. Adam had retreated to a place deep inside himself. He resisted Lainey's clumsy, inadequate efforts to convince him he hadn't caused Neal's accident. She thought her inability to help him only proved how wrong their union was. It proved Caroline had been right about the *tests* of marriage. It proved Lainey's lopsided love wasn't enough to make this marriage work.

And now, as Christmas drew near, there was another problem. Lainey thought she was pregnant.

With the coldness that had settled over their home, it was difficult to remember the long November nights she and Adam had whiled away, trying to get pregnant. But her period was nearly two weeks late, and she feared their attempts had proved fertile.

Feared? What a terrible way to think about a baby.

But Lainey couldn't be happy. She felt as if she was right back where she had started with Adam. They were obviously unhappy, but if she was pregnant he would stay out of duty. She didn't want that. A child deserved a home that was built on love, not obligation.

A child. On the Saturday before Christmas, as Lainey stood in the kitchen, mixing up a batch of sugar cookies, she was assailed by guilt for allowing this to happen. She closed her eyes, praying that her cycle was off, that the stress had gotten to her. If things were as they should be with Adam, she would be thrilled to be having a baby. But this wasn't the right time. It was bad enough that Gabe was caught in this situation.

Glancing across the kitchen, she saw that Gabe, with the faithful Goldie at his side, had his nose pressed to the window. Neal was coming home from the hospital in

Chattanooga today, and Adam had volunteered to make the hours-long drive with Marnie and follow the ambulance home in her car. Afterward, he had promised to help Gabe decorate the big cedar tree that Fred had set up in the front room for them.

Lainey didn't feel much Christmas spirit, but she was trying to hide that from Gabe. He was in a fever pitch of excitement, a bit unsure about the existence of Santa Claus but unwilling to let go of the fantasy just yet.

He gave a shout of excitement as a horn blew outside, but it turned to a groan. "It's only Aunt Caroline. Where is Dad?"

"You know he said it might take a while to get Neal home," Lainey reminded him for at least the fifth time in the past hour.

"But not this long."

"Come help me cut out some cookies. That'll make the time pass faster."

Pouting, he crossed the room. And he soon proved too impatient to do much more than destroy a couple of cut-outs. Caroline came in when he was fretting over a ruined snowman, and Lainey had decided it was safer to send him into the front room to unpack some ornaments.

"You trust him with ornaments?" Caroline asked with an upraised eyebrow.

"It's better than staying in here and driving me nuts."

Caroline set a shopping bag down on the table and clucked in mock disapproval. "Goodness, he must be in a state. You usually have the patience of a saint with him."

Lainey explained why Gabe was so impatient.

"It's nice of Adam to help Marnie," Caroline said. "He's driven over to that hospital an awful lot. I wish he'd stop blaming himself for what happened."

"You and me both." Lainey hadn't intended to sound so frustrated. She had been careful to hide the state of her marriage from Adam's sister. To Caroline's credit, she hadn't been nosy at all. She had given Lainey and Adam some space these past few months, saying she knew that newlyweds needed their privacy. And even though she had been vocal about her reservations prior to the marriage, she hadn't said anything negative since the wedding.

But Lainey's tone drew a sharp look from Caroline now. Frowning, she shrugged out of her red plaid coat. She was wearing a Christmasy green maternity top underneath, and Lainey used that to try to change the subject.

"What are you wearing that for?" she teased. "You're barely showing."

"Says who?" Caroline drew the top tight against her stomach, showing off a distinctly rounded bulge. "I've been popping out all over this month."

"You look cute."

"You'll think cute when it happens to you."

Startled, Lainey dropped the cookie cutters she was holding. They clattered to the floor. She stared at Caroline, unable to hide her dismay.

The other woman had always been able to read her too well. She swooped in with a squeal of delight. "Lainey, are you? Are you really pregnant?"

When Caroline said the words out loud, Lainey had to stop hiding from the truth she knew in her heart. Her body clock wasn't off. Deep in her woman's heart, she knew she was pregnant. On some level, she had known the truth ever since her birthday, when Adam had made love to her in front of the fire. Their baby had been conceived that night.

But the distance between that loving night and the state of her marriage right now was far greater than six and a half weeks.

What were they going to do? Her hand flew to her stomach. What were *all* of them going to do?

Chapter Eleven

Caroline's delight turned to concern as she repeated, "Are you pregnant, Lainey?"

Shushing her, Lainey glanced toward the front of the house. "I don't want Gabe to hear you."

Nodding, Caroline lowered her voice. "What does Adam have to say about this?"

Lainey was gathering up the cookie cutters that had dropped to the floor, so she couldn't see Caroline's expression when she said, "He doesn't know."

She dumped the cutters in the sink and avoided looking at Caroline for as long as possible. When she did, the brunette was regarding her with a troubled frown.

"Don't you think you should tell him?"

"But I don't have proof positive that I'm pregnant yet."

"But still—"

"Things have been crazy, with Neal and everything."

"Then he should welcome some good news."

Busying herself by running water in the sink, Lainey said, "It's just not the right time to tell him."

Caroline took hold of her arm. "Lainey, is this good news? Are you guys okay?"

Taking a deep breath and trying to school her features into an expression of unconcern, Lainey turned to look at her. "We'll be fine."

"You'll *be* fine. That's not the same as you *are* fine."

Suddenly weary, Lainey said, "Don't split hairs with me, please. And don't say anything to Adam."

"About what?" he said behind them.

Both women whirled to face Adam as he came in from the front of the house.

"Where did you come from?" Lainey demanded.

He frowned, pointing over his shoulder. "I used the front door for once. I had a couple of boxes to bring in from the post office. It looks as if Gabe's grandparents have shipped him half a toy store."

"Then we'd better get that tree decorated, so we can put those gifts out for him to rattle." Lainey reached to untie her apron. She knew her movements were jerky and awkward, and she could feel Caroline shooting looks between her and Adam.

"What's the secret?" he asked.

Lainey couldn't look at him.

Caroline was the one who filled the awkward silence with a blithe, "Christmas secrets, dear brother."

A quick look at his face showed Lainey that he didn't quite believe his sister. "Come on," Lainey said, taking Caroline's arm. "Help us get started on this tree."

Getting them started was indeed all the help Caroline provided. With a last, furtive look at Lainey, she left before the lights were strung. Even Gabe bailed out after hanging balls on a few lower branches, preferring to retreat to the den to play the video game his grandparents had brought at Thanksgiving. Lainey and Adam were left to finish the tree trimming alone. In silence.

By the time they were almost done, Lainey couldn't bear the silence another minute. It was Christmas, and for Gabe's sake at least they needed to try for a semblance of civility and normalcy. "Tell me about Neal," she said.

Adam surprised her with the first genuine smile she had seen from him since before the accident. "Believe it or not, the kid's doing pretty good. Now that he's on the road to recovery, I think this whole experience might have shown him there are bigger tragedies than a deadbeat father."

"Do the doctors think there'll be any sports in his future?"

When Adam's smile faded, Lainey wanted to kick herself for pushing her luck. But he replied, "All I know is that it's going to take some strength of character for Neal to do the therapy that'll pull him out of this."

"If all of us encourage him, perhaps he'll find that character. I know it's in him somewhere."

Adam made no reply to that. He just frowned down at the homemade pinecone ornament he was holding.

Lainey tried to revive the conversation. "Marnie told me last night that the team brought the state-championship trophy over and set it up in his room. That was nice of them."

"They're basically all good kids."

"And I'm sure they don't know Neal bailed out on them on purpose."

Adam hung the ornament and stood back to study the placement. "There's no sense telling them something that would just make everyone unhappy and make Neal look so bad. He needs his friends."

"He's got a good one in you."

"Not so good, really."

"But Adam," she protested. "You've been wonderful to Neal, to all those boys. Everyone says you're just a natural coach and teacher—"

"Well, I don't want to be."

His low, furious tone unsettled her, but before she could reply, he went on, "Coach Medford's not coming back after the first of the year. They've offered me a permanent job, but I don't think I'm taking it."

Her mouth went dry. She didn't trust herself to ask him what he intended to do instead.

Standing there, looking at her set features and bowed head, Adam was gripped by a good fury. Ever since Thanksgiving she had been so different, so remote. She had tried to help him through this tough time with Neal, but he had sensed the distance in her. He didn't know what had happened, but he was damned sick of worrying about it. Clearly, she was unhappy. And he had only one solution to the problem.

Trying to keep the anger from his voice, he said, "We've made a mistake, haven't we, Lainey?"

She looked at him then, and her green eyes, usually so expressive, were curiously blank. "Have we?"

"I know there's a knot in my gut every time I walk into this house."

Her lips trembled. "I'm sorry, Adam."

"Don't be sorry." He was hoarse from trying to restrain his emotions. He wanted to put his arms around her so much that it hurt, but he knew that would be his undoing, so he didn't. "I thought we could make this work, you know. But obviously..."

She just kept looking at him, and the muscles in her throat worked as she swallowed. Finally, she said, "Let's get through Christmas, okay? For Gabe's sake. After the holidays, we'll talk. We'll decide what we want to do."

Her suggestion made a lot of sense. He nodded, and turned back to the lighted, colorful tree, unable to continue looking at her. He felt, rather than saw her leave the room. Then he let out a long breath and sank down on the couch that faced the tree.

He was so tired. For weeks, he had felt like a man who had fallen from a great height. On the pinnacle, his life had been going so well. Gabe had been so happy. The job Adam hadn't expected to like had turned into a pleasant surprise. He had felt so productive. He had believed he was doing important work.

And then there had been Lainey, offering him passion and warmth. She had made him believe he could settle here, that they could build a home and family together. She had said she loved him.

What had happened to that love? He knew Lainey wanted something more from him than what he had given her. But what he had offered was his best. Maybe they might have worked all this out weeks ago if everything hadn't happened as it did. But Neal's accident had made Adam realize that he was living in a fool's paradise about his job, too. He wasn't making a difference. All the frustrations and stresses that had driven him from teaching several years earlier had come back to haunt him. He had forgotten that teaching was a world of small successes and big failures. He didn't think he had what it took to make it work. There was a part of him that would like to try, but...

That didn't matter now. Any thought of hanging in with this job was pointless, with Lainey so unhappy. Just as Caroline had cautioned, they had rushed headlong into this marriage without adequate preparation. Hell, he knew he was the first man to treat Lainey with the sort of respect she deserved. He was the first man to touch the deep vein of passion she hid beneath her serene, sensible exterior. Inexperienced, she had mistaken passion for love. In the day-to-day life of a marriage, she had obviously realized her mistake. That's what her distance was about, that's what she had tried to tell him weeks ago.

He wouldn't hold her to a commitment that didn't work. And he . . . he would fly.

As he said the words to himself, he paused, half expecting a clap of thunder or the voice of his father to speak from the walls of this old house. But nothing supernatural happened. That eerie sense of his father's presence was gone, if, indeed, it had existed in the first place. Like this whole interlude at Applewood Farm, it was a mistake.

If his father had really left a legacy for Adam, then it was the path he already knew. He was going to pack up, take Gabe and move on.

But not without regrets.

Adam spent the holiday memorizing every detail of the life he had discovered here in this valley. The ice that crusted the wavy glass of the upstairs windows on Christmas morning. Gabe's face when he came down the big, old staircase and found a new red bicycle waiting beside the tree. The scent of Lainey's Christmas ham baking in the oven. The feel of Caroline's hand slipping into his as they stood together during holiday services at church, the knowledge that his sister was here, real, alive. The burst of emotion that caught at his throat when he came in the den and found Lainey and his son snuggled together under one of Aunt Loretta's crocheted afghans.

Their two heads, a flame and a shadow, were tucked close, as close as these two had become.

How could he take Gabe away from her? After promising that they would stay here and be a family, how could he explain to his son that it had all just been a mistake? But what was the alternative? To continue a marriage that wasn't working?

By New Year's Day, Adam felt he was strung tight enough to snap. Lainey didn't broach the subject of their marriage. He found he couldn't. He wanted a way out to open up, a decision to be made. But his life had taught him not to wait for fate to intervene. Departures were easiest when you knew where you were going. So he got on the phone, called friends, put the wheels of his departure in motion.

Two days later, his contacts called him at school, where he was continuing to teach until a permanent replacement for Coach Medford could be found. He had the promise of the job he had envisioned for himself at the end of the previous summer. If he wanted, he could join the last baseball organization he had worked for as a pitching coach at one of their farm teams. They wanted him in spring camp by February.

Lainey was wrapped in a blanket in the chair by the fire in her room when she heard Adam come in with Gabe from school. Without football practice, they got home earlier. It wasn't like her to be idle this time of the afternoon. But she had felt nauseous and tired all day. A by-product of early pregnancy, her doctor had told her just this morning, after confirming what she already knew. Her baby was due in late July.

Somehow, she had to tell Adam.

Every day she told herself they had to talk. And every day she put it off. She avoided being alone with him as much as possible. That wasn't so difficult since he had moved out of this room before Christmas. But she couldn't avoid it any longer. For all she knew, someone who worked at the doctor's office had seen her test results and would congratulate him on the expected baby.

From downstairs, Gabe yelled for her. She called for him to come up. He flew in, waving a picture over his head.

"Look what I drew," he said, launching himself into her lap.

He was still cold from outdoors, and Lainey hugged him close as she studied his picture. There were four stick figures, one of them distinctly canine, with a lopsided Christmas tree in the middle and the outline of a house in the background.

Gabe turned a beatific smile up to her. "It's our family Christmas. Mrs. Lee said I was 'quite a little artist.'" His dead-on imitation of his teacher's nasal voice made Lainey laugh. But the laughter stopped when she looked over Gabe's head and saw Adam standing in the doorway.

Frowning, he advanced a few steps into the room. He looked ill at ease, his gaze flickering to the bed and then back to Lainey. "You feeling okay?" he asked. "You look kind of pale."

"I'm fine."

"You want me to bring you some cookies?" Gabe asked. "Dad stopped at the grocery store on the way home."

Lainey gave him a hug, but shook her head.

Adam said, "Go down and have your snack, son. And feed Goldie, too."

Grumbling good-naturedly, Gabe started for the door. Halfway there, however, he made a U-turn back to Lainey and handed her his picture. "I forgot. I made this for you." Then he was gone.

Adam closed the door after him. And Lainey's heart began to pound.

In quiet, measured tones, he explained what he was planning to do, that he had a job he wanted waiting for him. She was silent as he said that he would tell Gabe, that they would go soon.

"I think we've made each other miserable long enough, don't you?" he said, his voice sounding raw. "For the past couple of weeks I've been trying to think of how I can explain this to Gabe. There's no good way, though, is there?"

Lainey closed her eyes, and shook her head.

"Well..." She could hear Adam shuffling his feet, exactly as he always did when he was nervous. "Lainey?"

She looked at him, struggling to hold onto her control, but she couldn't bring herself to say what was in her heart.

His eyes had narrowed, his hands gone to his hips as he regarded her. "Isn't there something you want to say?"

"Just that I...I..."

He stepped forward, a light in his eyes that hadn't been there moments ago.

She wanted so badly to tell him about the baby, to say that she loved him and needed him and didn't want him to go. But she was paralyzed by the thought of watching his face go cold and set, of hearing him say that he would stay, knowing it wasn't what he really wanted.

The light went out of his eyes. He looked like a man who had taken a punch to the gut. And without another word, he turned and was gone. She heard his footsteps clattering down the stairs, heard the front door slam.

She turned back to the fire, already feeling as lost and alone as she would be when he left for good. Looking down, she realized she was still holding the picture Gabe had drawn. Only she had crumpled it in her hands. Trembling, she smoothed out the folds and stared long and hard at the stick figures.

She saw it through Gabe's eyes. Through the eyes of a child not yet aware of undercurrents, of lost hopes and fallen dreams. It was a home and a family. *Her family*. The one she had wanted for as long as she could remember. The family she had dreamed of having in this house.

As a little girl, she had dreamed of moving into a big house with her mother and the father she never knew. She came to Applewood Farm and dreamed of moving up the hill to this big house. That happened, but her family, her aunt and uncle and herself, were no different here than they were in the little cottage down the hill. They had lived together, cared for each other. But this house had never rung with bright voices, eager to see one another, to be together. They hadn't exactly been unhappy, but they hadn't really been a family, either. Because Lainey had always been just on the outside. She didn't really belong.

Good, docile little Lainey had accepted what they could give without making demands.

Just as she was accepting that Adam was leaving her. Taking Gabe away from her. Leaving her and their child.

What was wrong with her? Why was she just sitting here? She had lost sight of the woman who had decided to stop letting life pass her by. She was out of touch with the person who had so eagerly seized the passion and warmth Adam had offered with his proposal. That woman wouldn't let him leave without fighting. That woman would fight to hold on to her children's family.

But what could she do? Adam was intent on leaving here. His desire to go was more than just her. He didn't want to teach. He wanted that job in baseball, the one he'd been bound for when he came here last August.

So...

There was only one thing to do.

Throwing off the quilt that had been wrapped around her, Lainey got up and headed for the cedar closet where she had stored all their summer clothes.

Adam remained on the front porch for as long as he could stand the cold. He looked out over the bare trees of the farm's apple orchard and kept thinking Lainey would come out here, would say something to him. If she did, if she gave one little indication that she wanted to try...

He shook his head. It was no good. She didn't really love him. The only solution was to go and go now, before this mess got any deeper.

He went inside, checked on Gabe, who was blithely watching television. He would wait and tell the boy their plans when everything was set. Going upstairs, Adam found Lainey's door open. He paused, seeing that she was sorting through clothes on her bed.

Their bed, Adam thought with a sudden burst of anger. He put his head down and started to walk on when Lainey called for him.

Taking a deep breath, he turned around and went back to the doorway.

"What do think?" she said, facing him with a pair of shorts held up in front of her. "Will it be warm enough in Florida for these?"

He stared at her, not sure what to say.

When he didn't answer, she gave a disgusted sigh. "You're going to have to tell me what to pack, Adam. I've never been to Florida, you know." She gave a rueful smile. "As you said once, I've never been much of anywhere."

He was beginning to feel as if he had stepped into "The Twilight Zone."

Lainey was still babbling. "I'm sure Fred and his brother will be happy to take over most of the work around here, if I give them a share of the profits. Caroline and Reid will watch the house, of course—"

"Lainey," Adam cut in when he could find his voice. "What are you talking about?"

"If we're going to spring camp in Florida, we're going to have to make some plans."

"If *we're* going?" A tingle had started to spread outward from his chest.

"Yes, *we* are going." The determined set of Lainey's shoulders was one he recognized. "You're not leaving here without me."

He couldn't believe what he was hearing. "Lainey you said . . . you acted—"

"I know. Aunt Loretta would say I've been acting like a person with more brains than sense."

"Come again?"

Her green eyes were very clear and very bright as she crossed the room and took his hand. "I love you, Adam Cutler. I want you to love me just as much. But if you don't, then . . ." She took a deep breath. "Well, if you don't, that's your loss. But regardless, we're married. We have a son. And . . ." She closed her eyes for a moment, then added, "We're going to have a baby."

Joy hit him harder than any pitch he had ever taken. It was that physical, that sharp. His hands went to Lainey's trim waist. "A baby?"

A gentle smile was teasing the corners of her lips. "It didn't take much trying, did it?"

He shook his head, astounded and thrilled. But a sobering thought brought him down to earth. "You're not going to stay married to me just because of a baby, are you?"

Lainey put back her head and laughed. Full-throated, room-filling laughter. She continued until Adam thought she was growing hysterical. He was urging her toward the chair by the fire when she finally managed to catch her breath and wipe the tears from her face.

She put her arms around him. "The reason I haven't told you about the baby was that I didn't want *you* to stay out of duty." She shook her head when he started to protest. "Don't say you wouldn't do that, because I know you would."

"But Lainey—"

"Just hush." She hugged him closer, laying her head against his chest. "Just hold me, Adam. I don't care why you hold me. Right this minute, I don't even care why you stay with me. Just promise that you will. Promise that you'll let me try and make you happy. Let me try and make you love me."

"But you already did that."

She went still in his arms. "What?"

"Of course I love you." Adam wasn't sure when those words had become a reality. On the night he proposed? Perhaps on their wedding day. Or maybe on just an ordinary Tuesday when he came home and found her romping on the floor with Gabe and Goldie, her red hair in a tangle and her vivid features bright with laughter.

This love, so different from the sharp, immediate feelings he had known with Debbie, had come to him gradually. Perhaps that's why he hadn't said the words to Lainey before now. Because it had taken all this time to work itself into his psyche. This love was as easy and rolling as the Tennessee hills surrounding this valley. It hadn't reached out and grabbed him with any sudden impact. But it was deep and rich. Like this land, it was a love in which a man could anchor his life.

Lainey had drawn away from him and stood looking up, her face filled with wonder. "I didn't believe you could really love me, Adam. I know you were so in love with Debbie—"

"A part of me will always love her," he cut in.

He saw Lainey swallow and hastened to reassure her. "Debbie's a beautiful part of my past, Lainey. But she's gone, and if there's one thing I know about her, it's that she wouldn't want me or Gabe to be alone."

"But I'm different from her."

"So? You're Lainey. And you're exactly what I want."

It was her wish come true, Lainey realized. To be loved for just being herself. But if Adam loved her, what about his plans to leave. "If I'm what you want, why are you going?"

"I thought you wanted me gone, that we had made a mistake. You said—"

"I didn't say anything about a mistake. You said it. You said you didn't want to teach or coach anymore. You were so cold and distant to me."

"And you weren't cold to me?" Adam challenged.

"I was afraid," she said. "Afraid that I couldn't live without you really loving me. I was afraid if I ever started telling you how I felt, I'd make a fool of myself, I'd make you feel miserable and guilty—"

Adam cut off her explanation with a kiss. Until that moment, Lainey hadn't realized how much she had missed his kisses. She hadn't allowed herself to think about them. But now, as his lips moved over hers, she sighed, settling into the kiss with a distinct feeling of homecoming.

When he broke away, he murmured, "I love you. Don't ever doubt that. I'm going to spend plenty of time reminding you."

Feeling warmed through and through, she smiled. "You can spend *all* your spare time in Florida convincing me. We can have a real honeymoon."

"But we're not going to Florida."

She stepped back, sputtering, "But the job you wanted, the team, the—"

"I know I can have a job right here if I ask for it. They haven't found a replacement."

"But you'd be miserable. You said—"

"I was miserable because of you. When I'm being honest with myself, I know I love teaching. I know I love working with those kids. I'm better at that than I ever was at throwing a pitch or swinging a bat."

Lainey had taken hold of his hands again, her gaze intent on his. "I want you to be happy, Adam. I'll follow you anywhere."

His smile was gentle. "Like I told you before, you'd die if you tried to transplant somewhere else."

"Not if you're there."

But he shook his head. "We're not going anywhere, Lainey. Why should we go, when we've got everything here? This house. This land. This is solid, real." He gestured toward the front of the house. "My father walked away from this place and always regretted it. He and Mother couldn't hold on to their love. And all my life, every time I flew off in some new direction, I was running the same as he was. I was looking for something. For roots, I think. And they're here.''

He touched her face. "This is where I belong. This is where our children belong."

Believing him, loving him with all her heart, Lainey stepped once more into his embrace.

But before they could kiss, Gabe interrupted. Standing in the open door of the bedroom, he demanded, "Are we ever going to have dinner tonight?"

Laughing, Lainey pulled away from her husband. "Come on, family, let's see what we can rustle up in the kitchen."

Gabe clambered from the room, making as much noise as a small tribe of little boys. Adam grumbled something about demanding, mouthy children. Lainey just leaned close and promised him the time of his life that night.

But before they could follow Gabe, Adam felt a touch, lighter than air, on his shoulder. He turned and a draft moved through the room. The smell of pressed flowers drifted over him.

He heard Lainey catch her breath, and he saw in her eyes that she felt the same thing.

Then the sensation, the scent was gone. But something remained, Adam realized. There was a fullness in his heart that had never been there before.

Taking Lainey's hand, he grinned. "Don't try to understand it."

But at the doorway, he gave a salute to whomever or whatever remained unseen, and said, "Thanks."

Epilogue

"Come on, Dad, pitch me a good one."

The batter had a braided ponytail. A red one. A lot like the one her mother had worn when her father first met her. Suzie Cutler was ten, and she loved baseball.

"Sure you can handle it?" Tugging his cap a little lower on his forehead, Adam fingered the ball.

From behind the plate, Suzie's twin brother, Coy, slapped a fist into the mitt on his other hand. "Give her some heat, Dad. She'll never hit it."

Behind Adam, a chorus of voices gave their agreement. Sixteen-year-old Gabe. The McClure brothers, Christopher and Barrett. They all jeered at Suzie's chances of connecting with the ball.

From the spectators, Lainey, Caroline and Reid, who were keeping a row of lawn chairs occupied, there were shouts of encouragement. And seven-year-old John Cutler, who proclaimed to hate baseball and was sitting on his glove somewhere near first base, called out, "Make 'em eat it, Suzie!"

Ignoring the call for heat, Adam let loose with his best slider, at least the best slider a graying high-school coach could have.

And Suzie whacked it. Up, up and up the ball sailed. Down the right-field side of the baseball diamond Adam had carved out of the apple orchard several years back. The boys gave chase, but that ball was gone, hooking foul as it soared up the slope toward the house, landing with a shattering *plump* on the windshield of Reid and Caroline's car, which was parked in the front drive.

Jerking off his catcher's mask, Coy muttered, "Damn...I mean, darn, Suzie, that's the third window this summer."

Lainey buried her face in her hands. "Adam, tell me it didn't happen again!"

"She's your daughter," he said, winking at Suzie.

From behind him, there was another shout. Gabe called out, "You guys, it's three o'clock. The game's on the tube, and Neal's supposed to pitch."

That cleared every young male, including the disinterested John, from the field. Neal had made the majors at last, and they weren't going to miss his debut. Caroline and Reid went to check out the damage to their windshield. Only Suzie, Adam and Lainey remained in place.

"Don't you want to go watch Neal?" Adam asked his daughter.

She shook her head, the determined set of her shoulders reminding him of her mother. "I want you to stop throwing trash and give me a good one."

"Oh, really?" Laughing, Adam snagged a new ball from the bag nearby. "Lainey? You up for catching duty. Or are you just going to sit there looking beautiful?"

Lainey left her comfortable seat and picked up the mask and mitt her son had left behind. But before she took her position, she pulled on the brim of her daughter's cap. "Keep it in the park, this time, all right? This is getting expensive."

From the pitcher's mound, Adam grinned. The same grin that had made Lainey's toes curl in delight a decade ago could still make her pause. Still make her hot. Smiling back at him, she said to Suzie, "Your father is so cute. It's a pity he can't pitch."

Suzie made a disgusted sound and took her batter's stance. "If you two are finished making eyes at each other, I want some batting practice."

After trading one last smile, Lainey put on her mask and Adam threw a pitch. Suzie splintered wood. Sunlight sparkled on the many windows of the house on the hill to their right.

It was just an average summer Sunday at the Cutler family home. And Lainey Bates Cutler thought it was just perfect.

* * * * *

Get Ready to be Swept Away by
Silhouette's Spring Collection

Abduction
& Seduction

These passion-filled stories explore both the dangerous
desires of men and the seductive powers of women.
Written by three of our most celebrated authors, they are
sure to capture your hearts.

Diana Palmer
Brings us a spin-off of her Long, Tall Texans series

Joan Johnston
Crafts a beguiling Western romance

Rebecca Brandewyne
New York Times bestselling author
makes a smashing contemporary debut

Available in March at your favorite retail outlet.

A ROSE AND A WEDDING VOW (SE #944)
by Andrea Edwards

Matt Michaelson returned home to face Liz—his brother's widow...a woman he'd never forgotten. Could falling in love with *this* Michaelson man heal the wounds of Liz's lonely past?

A ROSE AND A WEDDING VOW, SE #944 (3/95), is the next story in this stirring trilogy by Andrea Edwards. THIS TIME, FOREVER—sometimes a love is so strong, nothing can stand in its way, not even time. Look for the last installment, A SECRET AND A BRIDAL PLEDGE, in May 1995.

AEMINI-2

Silhouette

SPECIAL ✦ EDITION™

A RANCHING FAMILY

Though scattered by years and tears, the Heller clan share mile-deep roots in one Wyoming ranch—and a single talent for lassoing hearts!

Meet another member of the Heller clan in Victoria Pade's
BABY MY BABY
(SE #946, March)

The ranching spirit coursed through Beth Heller's veins—as did the passion she felt for her proud Sioux husband, Ash Blackwolf. Yet their marriage was in ashes. Only the unexpected new life growing within Beth could bring them together again....

Don't miss **BABY MY BABY,** the next installment of Victoria Pade's series,
A RANCHING FAMILY, available in March!
And watch for Jackson Heller's story,
COWBOY'S KISS, coming in July...only from Silhouette Special Edition!

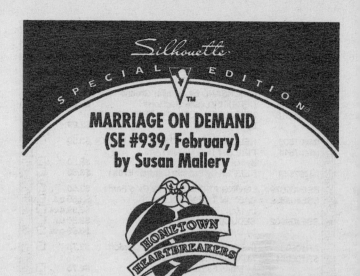

Silhouette

SPECIAL EDITION™

MARRIAGE ON DEMAND
(SE #939, February)
by Susan Mallery

HOMETOWN HEARTBREAKERS

Hometown Heartbreakers: Those heart-stoppin' hunks are rugged, ready and able to steal your heart....

Austin Lucas was as delicious as forbidden sin—that's what the Glenwood womenfolk were saying. And Rebecca Chambers couldn't deny how sexy he looked in worn, tight jeans. But when their impulsive encounter obliged them to get married, could their passion lead to everlasting love?

Find out in *MARRIAGE ON DEMAND*, the next story in Susan Mallery's *Hometown Heartbreakers* series, coming to you in February...only from Silhouette Special Edition.

SILHOUETTE... Where Passion Lives

Don't miss these Silhouette favorites by some of our most
distinguished authors! And now you can receive a discount by
ordering two or more titles!

SD#05786	QUICKSAND by Jennifer Greene	$2.89	☐
SD#05795	DEREK by Leslie Guccione	$2.99	☐
SD#05818	NOT JUST ANOTHER PERFECT WIFE by Robin Elliott	$2.99	☐
IM#07505	HELL ON WHEELS by Naomi Horton	$3.50	☐
IM#07514	FIRE ON THE MOUNTAIN by Marion Smith Collins	$3.50	☐
IM#07559	KEEPER by Patricia Gardner Evans	$3.50	☐
SSE#09879	LOVING AND GIVING by Gina Ferris	$3.50	☐
SSE#09892	BABY IN THE MIDDLE by Marie Ferrarella	$3.50 U.S. $3.99 CAN.	☐ ☐
SSE#09902	SEDUCED BY INNOCENCE by Lucy Gordon	$3.50 U.S. $3.99 CAN.	☐ ☐
SR#08952	INSTANT FATHER by Lucy Gordon	$2.75	☐
SR#08984	AUNT CONNIE'S WEDDING by Marie Ferrarella	$2.75	☐
SR#08990	JILTED by Joleen Daniels	$2.75	☐

(limited quantities available on certain titles)

AMOUNT	$_____
DEDUCT: 10% DISCOUNT FOR 2+ BOOKS	$_____
POSTAGE & HANDLING ($1.00 for one book, 50¢ for each additional)	$_____
APPLICABLE TAXES*	$_____
TOTAL PAYABLE (check or money order—please do not send cash)	$_____

To order, complete this form and send it, along with a check or money order
for the total above, payable to Silhouette Books, to: **In the U.S.:** 3010 Walden
Avenue, P.O. Box 9077, Buffalo, NY 14269-9077; **In Canada:** P.O. Box 636,
Fort Erie, Ontario, L2A 5X3.

Name:_____

Address:_____City:_____

State/Prov.:_____ Zip/Postal Code:_____

*New York residents remit applicable sales taxes.
Canadian residents remit applicable GST and provincial taxes. SBACK-DF

Silhouette®
™